Returning Home:
A Freedom Lake Novel

Toni Shiloh

Scripture taken from the New King James Version®. Copyright © 1982 by Thomas Nelson. Used by permission. All rights reserved.

Edited by Peri Bever. Proofread by Carrie Schmidt.

Cover design by Toni Shiloh.

Cover art photos © iStock.com/PeopleImages used by permission.

Published in the United States of America by Toni Shiloh. www.ToniShiloh.wordpress.com

Returning Home is a work of fiction. Names, characters, places, and incidents are either products of the author's imagination or used fictitiously. All characters are fictional, and any similarity to people living or dead is purely coincidental.

ISBN: 1973710749
ISBN-13: 978-1973710745

DEDICATION

To the Author and Finisher of my faith.

Prologue

$\mathcal{E}$ van Carter stared at his girlfriend, admiring her beauty. Brenda's pixie haircut framed her pretty face and a soft smile graced her lips. She wore charm and gentleness like a cloak as she gracefully changed lanes. She drove his new Altima like it was made for her.

He loved that Brenda suited every aspect of his life. She was a slam dunk in the girlfriend department. He ran his fingers over the velvet box in his pocket. Tonight was the night. The restaurant staff had been informed of his plans. With their help, his proposal would be flawless.

"Should I adjust the temp?" he asked.

"I'm good, sweetie," she smiled at him, then quickly faced forward again.

Brenda would make the best high-school coach's wife. His students loved her and she loved basketball as much as he did. It was so easy to be with her.

"Evan, you made the perfect choice. This car is so quiet. I can't believe we can't hear the outside noise."

"I know. That's what sold me." He pointed up ahead. "Make a right at the light." He hadn't revealed their dinner location. If he didn't pay close attention, they'd miss a turn.

"Are you sure you don't want to tell me where we're going?"

"I'm sure. I still think you should have let me drive. Then it would really be a surprise."

She laughed. "Of course, it would have been better, but I've been itching to get behind the wheel ever since you bought it."

"Well now—"

A black truck swerved in and out of their lane.

"Baby, slow down. Watch out for that truck!"

There was nowhere to pull over, no way to avoid the impending collision. The two-lane road had no shoulder and the truck was picking up speed.

The black truck righted itself. But before Evan could even sigh in relief, the truck corrected, ending up in their lane, headed straight for them.

They were going to collide.

Evan held his breath, clenched his eyes, and braced for impact. Brenda's scream pierced the air, but it seemed far away. His seat belt locked tight as the car came to an abrupt stop.

A weight dropped onto his leg. Pain exploded, smoke filled his nose. His body struggled to make sense of what happened. Finally, he closed his eyes and gave in to the darkness.

～～

The pain was unbearable. Was his left leg on fire? A cry of agony tore from his throat.

"Hold on, Mr. Carter, we're almost to the hospital."

The voice barely penetrated through the pain. How could there be so much pain? Evan groaned, wishing it would stop.

Brenda. He tried to form her name, but the pain proved too much. Darkness closed in, as panic choked him. Overcome, he faded into oblivion.

～～

Evan struggled to open his eyes. The burning sensation in his leg was still there but not as intensely.

He let out a slow steady breath, afraid that any movement would increase the pain once more. *What was that noise?*

A steady beep played in the background. He turned his head slowly and stopped as a man in blue scrubs stepped forward.

"Mr. Carter, I'm Dr. Johnson. You've been in a car accident and suffered a severe trauma to your left leg."

An accident?

The truck. It had careened toward them. He inhaled sharply. The beeping noise began to increase.

"Brenda," he rasped as the beeping noise filled his ears.

"Take a deep breath and try to stay calm. You're in good hands, Mr. Carter. We need to take you into the OR to repair your leg, okay?"

But what about Brenda? He tried to nod, but his body felt too heavy to accomplish the movement. His mind was a jumbled mess. Why couldn't he focus? Why did his leg burn?

Dear Lord, please make it stop.

～

The blinding light made his eyes water. Evan closed them and conducted a quick mental assessment of his body. The burning was gone. Relief poured out in a sigh. He tried to move the leg in question and frowned. His body wouldn't cooperate. He lay there, trying to get his bearings, and noticed hushed whispers for the first time.

"I'm afraid we couldn't save his left leg. We had to amputate it right above the knee."

He frowned. *Who were they talking about? Who lost a leg?*

"Oh, my God, no!" a woman's voice cried out.

The voice was eerily familiar, but he couldn't place it. He tried to think but he just couldn't. His head and limbs were heavy with fatigue. Or maybe it was the medicine they gave him. That had to be the reason the burning sensation left.

"He'll have a long road of recovery ahead of him, but Chicago has the best rehab unit in the state."

That voice. Wasn't that the surgeon? Were they talking about him? He gasped as the implications took hold.

The beeping noise became frenetic.

Voices began shouting.

Amidst all the noise, he made out the woman's voice, "God, please save my baby."

Chapter One

Two months later

J o Ellen Baker slammed the tailgate of her pickup shut. Another successful job completed. She grinned as she rounded the truck to hop in. For the past year, she'd poured every last ounce of energy into her father's construction business. The one he left solely to her.

"I hope you're proud of me," she whispered.

Sometimes, she felt guilty that her father's death had landed her a dream job, owner and sole proprietor of Baker's Renos & Repairs. Then again, she couldn't imagine doing anything else. She'd always been the one to work with her father, not her older brother nor her little sister.

Pulling out of her latest client's driveway, she headed back home. The crisp fall air filled her lungs as a gentle breeze blew in from the open window. She glanced outside, catching a view of Freedom Lake, the town's namesake. The view looked like a scene right out of one of Bob Ross' paintings. The trees wore their autumn foliage proudly. Their beautiful array of colors reflected across the lake's surface. If fate was kind, she'd take her last breath in this town.

Her cell phone rang, startling her. She frowned, noting the caller ID. Why would Mrs. Carter be calling her? Mr. and Mrs. Carter ran the only Bed and Breakfast in Freedom Lake. Perhaps they needed something repaired. She answered the phone.

"Jo, I have a huge favor to ask of you."

"How can I help you, Mrs. Carter?"

"Well, see, Evan is back in town. You remember Evan, right?"

Jo nodded, too numb to speak. *Evan's back?*

He'd left town twelve years ago, shortly after their high school graduation. A fact she'd celebrated with her best friends, Chloe and Michelle. Once upon a time, Evan had been a friend. Then high school happened. If she never saw him again, it would be too soon.

"I remember."

"Well, of course you do. I mean Freedom Lake isn't that big and you two did go to high school together. Anyway, the reason I called was because I need a place for him to stay. You know the B&B stays busy. Besides, he can't live in the butler's pantry forever. Just because it can fit a twin-sized bed, doesn't mean the space will work for him. Anyway, can you renovate the carriage house into an apartment? I would just love for him to be able to have his own privacy, yet still really close in case he needs anything."

Jo blinked. How did Mrs. Carter not run out of steam? Yet, there seemed to be an underlying layer of nerves behind the forced cheer. Perhaps she knew Jo was tempted to say no.

"Jo?" Mrs. Carter asked softly.

I don't want to do it! "Hold on a sec. I need to look at my calendar."

She pulled over on the side of the road and grabbed her clipboard. But she didn't have to look at her calendar to know the rest of her Friday afternoon was wide open. "How about today at one thirty. I can look it over and come up with a plan. Is that doable?"

"That sounds wonderful, Jo. Can I fix you a late lunch or anything?"

"No thank you, Mrs. Carter. See you then."

"You sure will."

"Another job," she whispered. On the one hand, a potential job was always a good thing. But the thought of running into Evan again chilled her down to the bone.

But don't you want to see what he looks like now?

She shook her head at the thought. Knowing her luck, he'd still be good looking. Not that she ever admitted to noticing. But maybe, just maybe, he'd have a pot belly and premature balding. With a smirk she turned, navigating the truck up the street known as Prosperity Ridge, where the descendants of the founding members of Freedom Lake resided. The homes on Prosperity Ridge showcased the Victorian and Queen Anne era architectural style. Of course, the Baker place happened to be Jo's favorite. Then again, she was biased.

She pulled into the driveway and stared at the closed garage. Was her mother home? The garage door opener stared at her, begging her to check, but that wouldn't work too well. If she was home, the garage door would alert her to Jo's presence. No, it would be best to walk quietly into the house. She closed her eyes, willing a calm to come over her.

Slow deep breaths. Calm from the center in and out.

Slowly, Jo laid a hand on the front doorknob. *Please don't be home, please don't be home.* The door opened without a sound, thanks to her great home maintenance. Silence greeted her ears as she entered the front door. She turned her head to the side, trying to pick up any hint of noise. If the situation wasn't so dire, she'd laugh at herself. It's not like she was a canine.

Her stomach grumbled, reminding her of her need for lunch. Jo took care to tread carefully in her heavy work boots, tiptoeing across the hardwood floors through the living room and into the kitchen...where her mother stood.

No!

"Where have you been, Jo Ellen?"

"At a client's." She headed for the fridge.

"Jo Ellen, you need to put this ridiculous notion aside. You are *not* some...some carpenter." Her mother's tone reverberated in her head like a clanging cowbell.

Same argument, different day. You'd think a year would have given her mother enough time to get used to the idea.

"Mother, Dad left me the business. Plus, I *love* my job." If she could honor her dad by being who she truly was, then she would. Her mother would have to get over it.

"But walking around in those hideous overalls isn't going to get you any dates." Her mother sighed, a long tragic sound. "You're not getting any younger, Jo Ellen. When will you find a nice man and marry? You need to settle down like your sister."

Just what she wanted to be: a gold digger. Fortunately, Vanessa's husband didn't seem to mind shelling out money on a woman fifteen years his junior. Guess that was a perk of being a doctor.

"If a guy can't accept my job or how I dress, why would I want to be with him?"

She opened the plastic container that housed her leftovers and popped it into the microwave.

Her mother's heel tapped against the wood floor. "Do you know I'm the only one in the bridge club who doesn't have a lot of grandchildren? I have just two, that's all your brother has given me. At least he has a sense of what's right. Time is ticking for you, young lady."

Not fast enough.

Could she head for the Carter's B&B now? The thought of listening to her mother's complaints any longer set her teeth on edge.

"I asked you a question."

"Mother…" she sighed, trying to remember to be respectful. "I haven't had lunch. I'm tired and I have another appointment soon. Could we have this conversation another time?" *Like never?*

"I can't believe how you always neglect me. You know I'm a widow now. I just want the house filled with the laughter of my grandchildren. Is that so much to ask for?"

Jo chewed her food, thankful for the excuse not to answer her mother.

"Fine, whatever, Jo Ellen. Eat your food. Run around in your masculine overalls. Good luck getting a man to look at you twice and see if I care."

Her mother stalked out of the kitchen, her heels echoing in her wake.

Indigestion reared its ugly head. She set her food aside and grabbed her keys. In a few minutes, she could be at the Carter B&B and far away from her mother.

And that's just what she did. Jo made it to Summit Drive, which had the second best view overlooking the lake, in record time. As she pulled into the Carter's driveway, she took in the features of the 1900s-era home. Painted a tan color, its white trim gleamed in the autumn sunlight. Walking around the side of the house to the front, she exhaled at the sight of the porch.

Ever since she could remember, she'd had an obsession with wraparound porches. The B&B's was only a three-quarter wraparound, since the three-car garage took up one side, but it didn't take away from its appeal at all. The porch practically begged for someone to sit and take in the majestic view of Freedom Lake. To top it off, the second floor had a balcony, complete with bistro seating. The view was why the place was so popular with tourists.

She rang the doorbell and winced as the jangling sound pierced her ears and jarred her nerves. She shoved her hands in her pockets, trying not to fidget as she waited for someone to answer the door. *Would Evan be here?* Would she have to 'make nice,' as her mother was so fond of saying?

I hope not. Please, let Mrs. Carter answer the door.

A crack in the doorframe drew her eye. It seemed out of place. She trailed the path it made, noticing the gaping hole at the end. She would have to advise Mrs. Carter to patch it up. The sound of the door opening drew her attention away from the hole. *And oil the hinges.*

The problems with the door evaporated from her mind once she realized something was severely wrong, because Jo had to look down in order to see Evan. Evan who had to be at least six feet tall. Her eyes momentarily widened in shock.

She straightened to her full height, intent on ignoring his deep scowl and glaring black eyes. Drawing on the years of debutante training her mother had insisted on, she schooled her facial features into an expressionless mask. She *would not* show her real feelings, which took considerable effort, because Evan Carter sat in a wheelchair...missing a leg.

～

Evan let out a whoosh of air. Jo Baker stood illuminated in the doorway by the sun's light. He knew returning home raised the potential of running into his former classmates, but he never thought he'd see Jo again. He figured she'd be long gone by now. The last time he'd seen her, she'd had braces, frizzy hair, and big-framed eyeglasses and was walking across the graduation stage.

The woman standing before him now was a far cry from the awkward teenager he used to tease. It was obvious she fell into the late bloomer camp. Sure, she had dressed in a long-sleeve shirt and overalls, but her curves couldn't be ignored. Her black hair had been swept into a ponytail. Was that the reason her cat-shaped eyes seemed more pronounced? Gone were the glasses and braces. Her copper-colored skin glowed and her cheeks held a rosy hue.

Was she wearing makeup?

He hid his surprise. He never pegged her as the type to wear the stuff. Despite her shockingly good looks, the venom in her facial expression couldn't be ignored. Her rich brown eyes seemed to drill a hole right through to his soul. He froze at the shock of her anger. No one had ever glared at him like that. *Especially,* since he had landed in a wheelchair.

"Good afternoon, I'm here to see Mrs. Carter."

There was no mistaking the frost in the air. Jo's voice had traveled into winter territory. It took every effort not to gape. He couldn't believe it. She acted like she didn't remember him. Acted like she didn't see him in the stupid chair. *Everyone stared at the chair.* Everyone.

He puffed up his chest, trying to appear taller. If she wanted to cop an attitude, he could definitely oblige her. "And hello to you, Four Eyes. Although, I suppose I'll have to find a new name for you." He gestured to her face, referencing the lack of glasses. Hopefully the snide look on his face came across as strongly as he intended it to.

"Ah, still up to your old ways, I see. Why did I ever imagine you could have grown up?" She walked right past him as he struggled to move out of the way. He rolled backward and let go of the door, hoping the weight would close it.

He turned and found her waiting impatiently. So, she did remember him. How dare she act as if seeing him in a wheelchair was an everyday occurrence. "High and Mighty." The words slipped loose.

"What?"

"Your new nickname."

She crossed her arms in front of her. "That's absurd."

He felt a tinge of pleasure at bringing her down a peg. "So is the way you waltz in here like you own the place. What are you even doing here? Did you buy a non-refundable ticket to the one-legged freak show?" He felt the anger rise and encouraged it. He refused to be treated like a sideshow.

Jo raised an eyebrow and looked down at him.

Evan bristled.

"If I had known you'd be home, this would have been the last place I'd come. However, your mother requested a meeting with me."

Evan wanted to protest her presence. If he kicked her out, would his mother find out? He glared at her with indecision. "Whatever," he said with a bite. Making a choice, he wheeled ahead of Jo. "She's in the kitchen."

Could this day get any worse? He'd never thought he loathed the *chair* more than he did now. Of all the people to see him in it, it had to be her? The girl who'd once been his friend. The girl who always had it together, no matter how many barbs he threw at her.

Should he be thankful she didn't mention his leg? No one had ever ignored the glaring space where his left leg used to be. *No one.*

He continued down the hall and entered the kitchen, heaving a sigh of gratitude that there were no doors to prevent his entry. The tantalizing mixture of nutmeg and cinnamon did little to cool his anger. He watched as his mother pulled an apple pie from the double oven. *Traitor.* Why would she have any business with Jo?

As if his thoughts burned her ears, she looked up. A genuine smile spread across her face upon seeing Jo. Although gray strands were becoming more prevalent in his mother's tiny braids, the headband she wore pulled them away from her face, giving her a youthful look.

"Good afternoon, Jo. Why don't you have a seat at the bar?" His mother gestured to the barstools, and then turned to Evan. "I can cut you a slice of pie if you want to eat while I take Jo to the carriage house."

"Why do you need to show her the carriage house?" The disrespectful tone of his voice was unintentional, but he needed to mask the dread pooling in his stomach.

"Jo's going to give me an estimate on renovations." His mom looked at him as if he should have known that tidbit of information.

"Wait, *she's* the Jo who's going to do the renovations?" Evan looked back and forth between his mom and Jo. When his mom said Jo was coming over, he had assumed it was some guy. Not his Jo.

Whoa, he didn't mean it like that. He shook his head to dislodge the thought. How did she even know the difference between a hammer and a wrench?

"Who were you expecting?"

He managed to hide the wince as Jo's voice dipped into icicle range. He stared at her, wondering if she knew how regal she looked. It should have appeared ridiculous on her, but she obviously didn't get the memo that overalls weren't high-and-mighty material.

"I just assumed Jo was a man's name," Evan said cautiously.

"Well as you can tell, I'm *not* a man. And I'm fully capable of handling a renovation."

"I'm sure you are," Evan murmured. He couldn't believe it. Not only did he run into her again, but he'd have the possibility of seeing her every day while she renovated.

13

God this is torture!

He quickly stifled the thought. He and God weren't on speaking terms. Not since the loss of his leg and Brenda.

Jo turned away from Evan and smiled at his mom. "Mrs. Carter, why don't you show me the carriage house and tell me what your vision is?"

"Oh, I'd love to."

They walked out of the room without a backward glance. In a matter of minutes, he'd been ignored twice.

Chapter Two

$\mathcal{M}$ rs. Carter led the way to the carriage house, talking the whole time. How anyone could talk that much fascinated Jo. Did she ever run out of steam? Her friend Michelle could also chat the night away. No matter the subject, the girl had something to contribute. And Jo's mind wandered away in a heartbeat.

Like now.

She ran her finger back and forth along the chain of her necklace. *How did Evan lose his left leg?* The fact that this piece of information had remained absent from the Freedom Lake grapevine was somewhat of a miracle. There'd been no word of his return or his injury. Had there been a split in the fabled telephone game?

What would it be like to lose a leg? What did that do to one's psyche? Sure, Evan appeared more brusque than normal, but she chalked it up to his bitterness finally catching up to him. Yet, when they were in the foyer of the B&B, his features had vacillated between angry and sad.

Now, her earlier conversation with Mrs. Carter made sense. There was no way his wheelchair could fit through the doors of the butler pantry. It wasn't even a decent-sized space for an able-bodied person. This wasn't New York. How did he get in to go to sleep? If she took this job, she'd need to bone up on her wheelchair accessibility information.

"I'm so happy to have Evan back home."

Mrs. Carter's words refocused her wandering thoughts.

"Is he home for good?" She hoped she sounded nonchalant.

"He's taking it one day at a time. He still needs help, but once he becomes independent I have no idea if he'll move away again. His father and I are praying he stays in Freedom Lake. However, we want the property renovated regardless if he'll stay or not. Besides, maybe it'll entice him to stay or at least visit more often." Hope shined in Mrs. Carter's round face.

If Evan hadn't graced his parents with a visit in all these years, it seemed unlikely he'd be tempted to visit if he moved away again.

They stopped in front of the carriage house and Mrs. Carter entered a code on the side of the building. As the garage door screamed its way up, Jo cringed. *Does no one use WD-40 around here?*

Mrs. Carter gestured inside the carriage house when the garage door came to a stop. "As you can see, we no longer store the cars in here. But it's big enough to hold three of them." She gestured to the right. "Those stairs lead to a loft."

Jo took everything in. "Do you plan on having Evan stay downstairs or do you want him to be able to access the loft?"

"Honestly, I don't know." She wrung her hands as she spoke. "The loft is a little outdated, but it has a small kitchen space and room to have a bed and living area. My prayer is that Evan will decide to be fitted for a prosthesis, but even if he does, I'm still not sure how easy it will be for him to navigate stairs."

Jo noted Mrs. Carter's furrowed brow and the lines drawn down around her mouth. She'd been so focused on how this was affecting Evan that she hadn't even considered how his parents were dealing. *Way to go, Jo.* She stepped closer to Mrs. Carter. "How are you handling this?"

Evan's mother smiled, but it didn't quite reach her eyes. "One day at a time. The Lord's carried us through and I know He'll see us through to the other side. It's just hard to watch him suffer."

At the mention of God, Jo froze. Although she wanted to cover her ears like a child, she didn't. Mrs. Carter had always been kind, despite claiming to be a Christian. She would just pretend God hadn't entered the conversation.

"When you have children, Jo, you'll understand."

Children. Not something she wanted to rush toward. If her mother had her way, she'd already be married with 2.5 kids, a home, and a white picket fence—which was utterly ridiculous, considering how long it had been since she'd been in a serious relationship.

She offered a smile as she glanced around the loft. It was definitely outdated, and the thought of renovating the property left her unsettled. Seeking calm, she ran her finger back and forth on her necklace. A gift from her dad, it provided more comfort than the deep breathing exercise.

Could she manage this?

There weren't too many people in Freedom Lake needing wheelchair access. Most of the seniors in town lived in one-story homes or at the senior community center, which was already wheelchair accessible.

Before she could voice her doubts, Mrs. Carter began speaking. "If you think it's best to renovate the garage area into an apartment space versus the loft, I'm all for it. Just tell me how much money you'll need to make it easy for Evan to live independently."

"Mrs. Carter, I have to be honest. I've never renovated a space to be wheelchair accessible. Have you considered someone else?" She couldn't believe she was giving her an out. The income would be nice, but would the loss of her peace of mind be worth it?

"I understand that, but I'm not sure I want to put my trust in someone I've never met."

Jo smiled. "Well then, if you don't mind, I'd like to contact an architect I use for big jobs and get her opinion on the space. By any chance do you have the original blueprints for the carriage house?" She held her breath, hoping for a 'yes.'

"I sure do. Evan, Senior I mean, has all that stored away. He's an organizational freak," she answered with a twinkle in her eye.

"Great. If I can take those with me, that will help. Meanwhile, I'll take a look at the county's laws and regulations on this type of renovation. Once I gather all the information I need, I can come back out here with a proposed budget and show you the plans. What do you think?"

"I think that sounds wonderful and I thank you for being honest. I saw the work you did on the Deans' home and I just knew you'd be the person for this."

Jo warmed at the praise. The Deans' kitchen had been a fun remodel. She shook Mrs. Carter's hand and made plans to meet up in a week.

～～

The next day, Jo called Michelle. Since her friend lived in Kodiak City, an hour north of Freedom Lake, a phone call sufficed for catching up.

"Hey girl, you on your lunch break?"

Michelle snorted. "Please, I'm eating at my desk. Why? What's up?"

"So," Jo said, in a drawn out note. "I have a potential renovation project."

"Okay," Michelle replied, matching her tone. "Judging by the way you said that, you don't want the project."

"It's Mrs. Carter."

"Really? Why? Didn't the B&B just get a remodel a couple of years ago? What could she possibly want to change?"

Jo took in a deep breath before she began. "She wants the carriage house renovated into an apartment for Evan."

"You've *got* to be kidding."

Jo pulled the phone away from her ear at Michelle's loud exclamation.

Michelle continue on, "She wants *you* to renovate a place for Evan? *You*, the girl he mercilessly teased all throughout high school?"

Jo could practically see the look on Michelle's face. Her friend's hazel eyes were probably flashing with indignation.

"I know. I was shocked as well. But once I saw that Evan was missing a leg and in a wheelchair—"

"What?" Michelle yelled, cutting Jo off in the middle of her sentence. "How on earth did he end up with a missing leg?"

"Chelle," she said, reverting to her friend's nickname. "I have no idea what happened." Jo started to reach for her necklace and stopped. "He looked so angry when I saw him, but I refused to give him the satisfaction of seeing how much I cared. I gave him the cold shoulder instead."

"Glad to hear it. That man deserves none of your kindness." A slight pause filled the air. "Are you going to do it?"

Jo was glad this conversation was taking place over the phone; otherwise, Michelle might try and treat her to "the look."

"The look," as they referred to it, served Michelle well at her job. Since she was the only female attorney in her firm, she needed to show she couldn't be messed with and it worked.

Jo wanted to remain silent, but she knew the silence was probably killing her chatterbox friend. "Okay, okay. Yes, I'm going to take the job. I was on my laptop all last night reading up on accessibility standards."

A sigh filled the air. "Well, knowing you, I can't change your mind. Plus, I like Mrs. Carter. It's not her fault her son didn't get her kindness gene."

She laughed. "So true. I'll be coming up to the city Friday to meet with Skyler to go over blueprints."

"Fantastic! How about you stay the night? We can watch chick flicks and go shopping Saturday before you head back."

Jo rolled her eyes. She hated shopping, but knew Michelle wasn't complete without making a visit to the mall at least once a week. "Sounds like a plan."

After hanging up, she left the comfort of her porch chair and leaned over the rail. As the sun made its descent, a burst of color filled the sky. The sunset colors were amazing over the reds and yellows of the trees. An image of Evan popped into her mind.

It wasn't fair that he had all his hair and a trim waistline. He looked just like she remembered, except the boyish look of youth had faded. His oblong face still held the same full lips and thick eyebrows and his hair had been closely shaven, the hairline meticulously straight. His jaw had become quite chiseled, and his warm brown skin had the same gorgeous earth tones. Evan's thick, wide nose added character and spoke to his ethnicity. And his eyes...she sighed thinking about the anger in the depths of his dark brown eyes.

Despite the hurt he'd caused, she hated to see him hurting. But that didn't mean she wanted to be near him. Taking the Carter job would increase her chances of seeing him more than she'd like. If her luck would just hold, maybe the job wouldn't be so bad.

And maybe her luck just ran out.

~~

Silence filled the car as Evan's dad drove into the city. His occupational therapy appointment loomed over him like a dark shadow. He hated that he couldn't drive himself. How much longer did he have to depend on his parents?

Forever.

The corners of his mouth sank downward in resentment. If it weren't for his missing leg, he'd still be on his own. Living with his parents again at thirty years old, after tasting the sweet life of adulthood was like a slap to the face. Failure greeted him in the mirror daily. He leaned back against the headrest, stifling a sigh.

"Chin up, son. Life won't always look as bleak as it does now." His father, affectionately known as 'Senior,' spoke in a calm tone. Nothing shook his dad.

Instead of feeling comforted, he bit back a retort. The platitudes and patronizing comments were driving him insane. The bitterness inside spread through him like a vine overcoming a trellis. Life was bleak and there was no mystical light at the end of the tunnel. All his mom and dad wanted him to do was to trust in God. Well, the last time he had trusted God, the doctor cut off his leg.

"Whatever," he huffed.

"Look, boy, I know you're grown, but I'm still your father. You're not the only one who's been dealt a bad hand. But you can't forget that the Lord will always be with you."

"Yeah, I don't seem to remember Him hanging around when my leg was being cut off."

"You watch your mouth, boy. You might not see it now, but He was there. He was in just as much agony as you."

Evan grabbed his iPod and put his headphones on. He had no desire to hear Senior drone on and on about a

God who would let something like this happen. Everyone wanted to talk about his leg and how he was 'feeling' but he refused. Talking wasn't going to bring his leg back. And expressing his feelings just alienated what little friends he had left.

While in the hospital, his parents had asked him to see a counselor. He conceded just to get them to stop hounding him. And after one session, he never went again. How could he bare his soul to a person perpetuating the myth that they had it all together?

He wasn't truly mad at the counselor. The guy was only doing his job. Yet, it had quickly become apparent that the man had no real experience with Evan's type of loss, so he stopped talking and sat in silence for the remaining thirty minutes. Unburdening himself to someone who truly didn't understand wasn't going to help any.

His dad touched his arm, but he ignored him. The sweet sound of Miles Davis poured forth from his headphones. He closed his eyes and let the sounds of the trumpet transport him to another world.

When they arrived in the city, he removed his headphones. Still, he made sure the don't-talk-to-me-because-you-don't-know-how-I-feel sign remained posted on his forehead. As he and his father sat in the waiting room, the noise from the TV filled the space.

"Evan Carter," a woman's voice called out.

"We're coming." Senior pushed his wheelchair toward the nurse.

Why did the man insist on pushing his chair? It's not like Evan had lost his arms. He clamped his mouth shut. He wasn't going to argue in front of witnesses.

His dad lifted him out of his wheelchair at the nurse's prodding. Evan could feel his face heat with shame. He stared at his cargo pants, refusing to meet anyone's eyes.

Senior was treating him like a baby, instead of the grown man he was. Injustice burned up his throat like bile.

The nurse weighed his chair on the wheelchair-accessible scale. Once she was done, his dad put him back in the chair to get the added weight.

"Never seen one of these before," his dad said.

"We have a lot of patients in wheelchairs. It's easier for them." The nurse faced him. "Now that we know how much the wheelchair weighs, you won't have to get out of it the next time."

Great. He could avoid the humiliation next time. Evan ignored her, but the brightness never left her voice.

"Follow me, guys. You'll be meeting Dr. Benson in room eight." She pointed to an open room down the hall.

Once again, his father pushed him down the hall. When they entered the room, Evan glanced around. It didn't look any different from any other exam room. The only change was the various pictures of athletes covering the walls. A picture of a man crossing the finish line, arms raised in victory, caught his attention. The man's silver prosthetic leg didn't seem to take away from his win.

He looked away as a lump grew in his throat. *Don't show any emotion.* If he did, his father would open his mouth and offer unwanted advice.

A little while later, a knock sounded. In walked a short, stocky white man with Harry Potter-esque glasses.

"Ah, good afternoon, Mr. Carter. I'm Dr. Benson," he said in a deep voice.

It sounded odd coming out of such a short man, but the doctor had a presence about him that suggested his height wasn't a limitation.

"Afternoon. This is my dad, Evan Senior or you can call him Senior." He jerked a thumb toward his dad, still not ready to engage in a conversation with him.

"The Senior, huh?" The doctor shook his father's hand.

"Yeah, his high school friends took to calling me that and it stuck." His father responded.

"Alrighty, then." The doctor sat down on a black swivel stool and turned to face Evan.

"I've read the files that Dr. Johnson sent over. You'll be able to pick right up with your therapy here at our office. You'll need to come in weekly to see Drew, your therapist."

"Understood." His gut tightened at the thought of more therapy. *Would it never end?*

"Hop on up here, and let's get you checked out." Dr. Benson patted the examination table.

His father jumped from his seat and lifted him onto the table. Dr. Benson raised his eyebrows, but Evan ignored him as heat flooded his face again. The doctor washed his hands and then bent over him, examining the remainder of his left leg. Evan gulped, trying to swallow the sorrow that hit every time he saw it. His mind couldn't seem to accept the fact that his lower leg was gone. At night, he often sat in bed looking down at his legs imagining them both there. On a really bad night, the phantom pain woke him.

"Well, it looks like they did a great job shaping the leg for a prosthetic. Did they fit you for one?"

"No," he answered sharply. He had refused, but the doctor should know that if he had read his chart.

The doctor looked at him, his disconcerting gaze never wavering. Whatever he saw made him take a step back. "Have you seen a counselor regarding the loss of your leg, Evan?"

"Yes, I have and no, I don't want to try a new one." Evan glared at Dr. Benson, who simply nodded.

"Any phantom pain?"

Evan nodded curtly. He wanted this visit over with.

"Well, your leg is healing fine. If you ever change your mind, I see no problem fitting you for a prosthetic. It will give you more independence than you have now." Doctor Benson paused, his hawk-like eyes assessing him. "It's really easy to set up an appointment with our prosthetist, Julie."

He remained mute.

The doctor sighed. "For now, you'll continue your occupational therapy. I'll make sure Drew gets you to practice moving in and out of your chair *unaided*. Cassie will come in to direct you to where the therapy room is located."

Dr. Benson shook their hands and left the room. Evan glared at the offending member of his body. If he couldn't have his real leg, he saw no reason to replace it with a weak imitation. There was no way he wanted to depend on a prosthetic. It would only be a crutch, just like trusting God.

Yet the whispered words, "more independence," beckoned to him like a siren's song.

Chapter Three

*T*he sun shined brightly as the wind continued to blow the leaves off the trees. Today was colder than yesterday but the steady flow of heat pumped from Jo's truck, keeping her warm. It seemed winter might be knocking on her door sooner than later. Fortunately, she didn't have to work outside today. She'd just left the meeting with Skyler, who recommended two blueprint options for the Carter's renovations. Now, she was headed to Michelle's.

After her father died, she moved back in with her mother. Her mother had been shocked by the sudden loss, and Jo had been the only Baker sibling willing to move back in. Since then, visits with her friends had been relegated to phone calls or coffee dates. This would be her first night out in a year.

Thank God.

She shook her head at the idiotic statement. She knew she wasn't really talking to Him. Jo wasn't sure if He was real, but if her mother was an example of who He was, then she would choose to put her faith elsewhere. She'd let fate and luck fuel her onward.

A guard shack sat at the entrance to Michelle's community. Jo slowed, coming to a stop in front of the gate, and rolled the window down to speak to the guard. He checked her name on his trusty clipboard and waved her on with a 'Have a nice visit' and a friendly smile.

The gate lifted and she proceeded, driving straight to Michelle's condo, memories of the past leading the way. Back to when life had been more carefree and her father had been alive. Funny what could happen in a year. Never would she have imagined she'd be back home, living with her mother…or rather, hiding from her.

Just that morning, they'd had another altercation.

"Jo Ellen, where on earth are you going dressed like that?" Her mother folded her arms and tapped a high heel-encased foot.

"I have an appointment with Skyler."

"You're going to the city dressed like that?" Her mother pointed to her overalls as if she found them morally repulsive.

"They keep me warm. Plus, I like them." But she did try and switch it up every now and then. Today just wasn't the day.

"You're going to a business meeting, Jo Ellen. Change before you go."

Jo had snorted and that had been the beginning of the argument. She smiled, remembering how she walked out the door, still clothed in her overalls. The argument may have contributed to a headache, but the satisfaction of walking out in the clothes she picked was worth it.

Shifting into park, she grabbed her duffle bag from the floorboard. Michelle would cringe when she saw it, and that's exactly why she brought it with her. The bag had seen better days, but that's what made it so great. Sure, it had a couple of holes, and the handle hung on by a thread, but it didn't need to be fancy just to hold her clothes. However, her friend saw things differently. If it didn't have a respectable brand name, Michelle wouldn't touch it.

Before Jo made it all the way up the stairs, the door to Michelle's condo flew open. Her friend came out squealing and enveloped her in a hug. Jo sighed; she'd missed her friend and her exuberant personality.

After a moment, Jo pulled back and looked at Michelle. How did she manage to look classy wearing jeans and a t-shirt? Michelle's five-foot-ten-inch frame stretched the jeans forever. Her black hair had been styled into a sleek bob, angled in at the chin. The elegant look seemed to add even more height to her lithe stature. Her skin was a flawless caramel color and her hazel eyes sparkled with delight.

"Girl, it's been way too long." Michelle looked down and raised an eyebrow at her duffle bag. "I knew you'd bring that nasty thing along. I still love you though."

Jo chuckled. "I can't believe you're wearing jeans and a shirt. But knowing you, it's not an ordinary pair of jeans."

Her friend smiled and sat down on the love seat with her leg folded underneath her. "Duh! They're made by Gucci."

Jo shrugged. She knew there had to be a catch. She dropped the duffle bag next to the black-and-white chevron patterned wingback chair, the only acceptable piece of furniture to sit on. Michelle's couches were too white for her taste. She sat down and raised her feet to prop them on the black coffee table.

Before Jo's boots hit the table, Michelle snapped out, "Jo Ellen Baker, now I *know* you're not about to put your dirty ol' combat boots on my coffee table. You're lucky you even made it this far with those horrendous things still on."

Jo stopped, her feet hovering in the air, and felt her face warm. How could she have forgotten how particular Michelle was with her things? "My bad." She put her feet down and removed her shoes.

Born and raised in Boston, Michelle had moved to Freedom Lake their freshman year of high school. Even though, she was no longer a Boston debutante, she never shed her affluent upbringing.

"How's work going?"

"Girl, I just got a OWI case." Michelle used the Indianan acronym for Operating While Intoxicated. Her friend got up, moving her hands as she spoke. "You know of course, this isn't the man's first offense. I made sure to get Judge Hatchett. He hates drunk drivers more than I do."

Jo grimaced inwardly, realizing Michelle's operating-while-intoxicated campaign remained as strong as ever. Her crusade started at eighteen and the girl wasn't happy until the OWI offenders received maximum time for their penalty.

She watched Michelle pace back and forth, as she ranted and raved about the injustice and horrors of drunk driving. Finally, she stopped walking, as if realizing Jo was still in the living room.

"Sorry, girl, you know how I can get."

"No worries."

Michelle waved a hand in the air. "Anyway, I've got Chinese food on the way and DVDs ready to be watched."

"Which ones?"

Michelle pointed to the coffee table, which held a slew of movies featuring Taye Diggs. Her friend's crush on Taye Diggs went as far back as she could remember. She took one look at Michelle before the two high-fived and wiggled their fingers at one another.

Jo fell back against the chair, laughing. She'd missed the easy camaraderie that came with having a life-long friend. Sure, they met at fourteen, but their friendship was such that it felt like it had already been a lifetime. She sighed. This weekend would be the perfect thing to revive her.

～

As she pulled into the Carter B&B driveway, Jo took a deep, cleansing breath. *Please, don't let Evan be here.*

She needed to go over the plans with Mrs. Carter, but didn't want to have to deal with him. If he was there, her Monday would continue to go downhill. Too bad her weekend with Michelle had to end and reality begin.

Jo knocked on the door. Her eyes immediately gravitated to the hole in the frame. She slapped her forehead. How could she have forgotten to talk to Mrs. Carter about it? Her eyes narrowed. It was all Evan's fault. Seeing him had completely erased all thoughts from her mind. She hadn't been prepared to see him. She'd been all too happy leaving every memory of high school behind.

Then maybe you should prepare now.

She swallowed as the pounding in her ears picked up speed at the twist of the knob.

"Hey there, Jo. Come on in." Mrs. Carter motioned her into the foyer.

"Hi, Mrs. Carter." Jo's shoulders dropped, as the tension in them deflated like a pricked balloon. "I have the plans and pricing to discuss with you."

"Fantastic! And you can call me Marilyn. Come on, let's head to the library."

Jo followed her down the hall, conspicuously checking the other rooms to make sure he was nowhere to be found.

"Evan's not here today, dear." She smiled at her. "He had an appointment."

"Oh, I wasn't looking for him. I just realized I've never taken a tour of the B&B, so I was trying to peek into the rooms." Her insides squeezed at the white lie.

Mrs. Carter—no, Marilyn--stopped and looked at her, mouth gaping wide. "You sure haven't, have you?" She placed her hands on her hips. "We'll have to remedy that right now." She pointed to the floors in the foyer. "Your daddy refurbished the original floors when we decided to make this a B&B."

Marilyn led the way, pointing out the parlor, library, and formal dining room. Each room was filled with crown molding and natural colors to preserve the historic nature of the Victorian home. As they made their way upstairs, Jo took in the white-painted rails. Thankfully, the hand railing remained the original cherry wood color. She watched, rapt, as Evan's mother pointed out the four bedrooms. Another set of stairs led to the attic, which had been refurbished into a bedroom suite as well.

"It's gorgeous."

"Thank you," Marilyn beamed.

Once the tour was over, they settled down at the table in the library. The rich green wainscoting warmed the room. Of course, the beautiful fireplace helped. She couldn't believe it was one of eight. Jo looked down at the table, refocusing her thoughts. "I consulted with an architect and I've come up with two options. This is option one." Jo placed the blueprint in front of Mrs. Carter. *Remember to call her Marilyn.*

"Okay," she said slowly. "I know I'm looking at a blueprint, but that's about all I can make out."

Jo let out a chuckle. "Of course, these are the blueprints for the carriage house. I informed the architect how you wanted it to be accessible for Evan."

"Okay, I'm tracking so far."

"We added a wheelchair lift for the loft, so that Evan can access it with no problem. The bathroom has been changed to add a roll-in shower space. All of the doorways will be widened to accommodate his wheelchair. The counters will also be torn out and lowered for ease of use. All outlets will also be changed to be put within his reach."

Jo reached for her laptop. "Here, I'll show you what the renovations will look like once they're complete."

Marilyn gasped at the model Jo had created with her renovation software. "Wow, that's amazing. You can have that all changed?"

"Yes. It should take about a month."

"Okay, now you said there is a second option available? What's that entail?"

Jo took a deep breath. She had no idea how the older woman would feel about option two. She thought it was the better of the two, but it was the costliest. She put the second set of blueprints in front of Marilyn and then got the files ready on her laptop.

Marilyn stared at the prints in front of her. "Again, I'm not an architect, but I do realize these look nothing like the last ones. Why?"

"Because this is a completely different structure."

"Explain, please."

Jo told her that if they built another home on the Carter property, it would be designed to Evan's specifications from the ground up. She showed her the pictures of the one-story structure and all the wheelchair-accessible features that it could include.

"How much would these two options cost?"

Jo held her breath. This was the part that had her chewing antacids before coming over. Freedom Lake residents weren't rich. Sure, they had the Prosperity Ridge residents, but they were from old money and weren't wealthy by today's standards. Her estimate was not an outstanding amount of money by renovation and home building standards, but it might be too much for the Carters. After all, they had just done some renovations. She told her the sum.

Marilyn gave a tiny nod of her head.

What was she thinking? "If these prices are too much, I can change some of the materials to a less costly version, but they won't hold as long as the ones I priced here in the proposal."

"It's a good thing my mother won't be providing the funds then. She has nothing to worry about."

At the sound of Evan's voice, her stomach immediately tensed. It felt like she swallowed a hard rock. Cautiously, Jo turned and saw Evan just outside the doorway. Apparently, his chair couldn't fit through the door. She didn't know whether to feel relief or pity. Jo chose neither. "I thought Mrs. Carter would be funding this project." Why did her mouth feel like cotton?

"No," Evan said, shaking his head. "I received compensation for my injuries and duress," he replied sarcastically. "Which will be used to fund this project. So, *I'm* the one who will have to approve the price."

"Evan dear, I thought you wanted me to handle everything?" Her gaze darted between him and Jo.

Did he change his mind because she was a woman? No, that didn't make sense. If that was the case, why wasn't his father handling everything?

"I did until I heard her trying to rip you off. I don't understand why a simple renovation would cost so much." His lips twisted in derision.

"That's because the price you just heard is for a brand-new structure on the property. It isn't just a simple renovation." *How dare he question my integrity.* She met his stare head-on, refusing to blink. She would not back down. His gaze traveled over her face, making her flush. She told herself it was from anger and nothing else.

Evan cleared his throat, "So you aren't going to do the renovations?"

"Evan, dear," Mrs. Carter stated. "Why don't you come in here and hear everything from the beginning."

He threw a look of irritation at his mother. "I would if I could, but you seemed to forget the chair doesn't fit."

"Right, sorry." Marilyn's voice sounded soft and flustered.

PS_BX07601362

CreateSpace
222 Old Wire Rd
Columbia, SC 29172

Question About Your Order?
Log in to your account at www.createspace.com and "Contact
Support."

11/01/2017 08:56:21 PM
Order ID: 191850698

Qty.	Item
	IN THIS SHIPMENT
1	Returning Home 1973710749

Jo's heart when out to her. Just because Evan lost a leg, that wasn't an excuse to treat his mother with a lack of respect. "We can have this conversation in the dining room or the kitchen. Whichever is better for you," she replied in an icy tone.

"Fine," he said through his teeth. He whirled around and headed down the hallway.

After settling into the dining room, Jo repeated the information for the two options. Thankfully, Marilyn had stayed to act as a mediator.

"I see now why there is a difference in price. Thank you for being fair."

Jo sat back, trying to hide her surprise. He was okay with the amount?

"I really like option two and I can swing the amount with no problem." He turned toward his mother. "How are you and dad going to feel about having another building on your property?"

"Well, I'd be okay with it, but I'm not sure how your father will feel. We can ask him when he comes home from work."

Marilyn was her hero. She didn't need a husband to run a successful business. Maybe she should bring that up for the next argument with her mother.

Jo watched Evan while he thought. Despite being relegated to a wheelchair, he still had a commanding presence about him. He looked the same as he did in high school except now his mouth had lines pulling it downward.

Probably from frowning so much.

Would the grooves appear around his mouth if he smiled? Were his teeth still pearly white? For a moment, she had the insane urge to make him smile. To wipe away the severity that clung to him like an albatross.

"That's what I was thinking as well. So, here's another idea." He looked at Jo, raising an eyebrow quizzically.

Had he noticed her staring? She felt her cheeks heat up under his direct gaze and wanted to scream at herself for blushing. He wasn't that good looking.

Liar.

"I really like the idea of having my own home and not having to live with my parents. No offense, Mom."

"None taken, Son."

"Do you have any idea if there are any lots for sale around here? Then, I could go with option two and be more independent. It's hard to maneuver around this place, but I've always viewed it as temporary. If I could have my own place..." he stopped, his voice faltering.

Jo tried to restrain the sigh that was welling up inside. She had no idea how he handled the loss. If she could bring back some independence for him, she would. No matter how much she disliked him, she hated to see another person in pain. "I don't know off the top of my head, but I'll check on it first thing tomorrow."

"Thank you," he answered stiffly. He turned around and wheeled out of the room.

Well, good-bye to you too.

She huffed, fighting the urge to let a scream loose. Instead, she made her good-byes with his mother. Jo's voice was extra syrupy, but she couldn't help but feel the need to make up for Evan's bad manners. The woman was a saint to put up with his foul mood.

As she walked to her truck, the meeting replayed in her mind. The simple renovation was turning out to be anything but. If Evan wanted his own land, then she guessed he wasn't leaving Freedom Lake anytime soon.

Bye-bye, luck.

～

The glossy sheen of the ceiling in the butler's pantry held Evan's gaze. His parents had removed the storage items to the carriage house and put in a twin bed. How mortifying to know his father had to "tuck him in," since his chair couldn't fit. If he had to use the restroom in the middle of the night, he had to text his father.

Evan swallowed at the injustice of it all. He stared at the rivets in the ceiling that used to be bumpy from the popcorn look. The room wasn't big enough for him to do anything but lie down and think. But it was his thoughts he wanted to escape from the most. A memory of Brenda's tear-stained face materialized in his mind.

"Knock, knock," Brenda murmured.

Evan smiled and motioned her inside. A visit from Brenda always brightened his day in the hospital. "Hey, Babe." He patted the hospital bed, hoping she would sit by him. She hadn't come near him since the accident.

Today would be no different. She shook her head, her bangs shifting against her forehead. "I don't want to sit." She pulled the strap of her purse through her fingers. "Evan, I need to talk to you."

He gulped, wiping his hands down the hospital sheets. No man wanted to hear those words. "What's up?"

She took a step forward, the sound of her heels clicking. "I...I...well, I think..."

He inhaled, trying to catch a breath. The moisture gathering in her eyes wasn't a good sign. "What's wrong?" Trepidation filled his voice.

"We need some time apart," she blurted.

Somehow, he had known this conversation was coming. Since she'd been discharged, the distance between them had expanded daily. At first, she'd stand near the hospital bed, then slowly but surely her footsteps landed closer to the door and farther from his side.

Yet, knowing all of that, he still felt the shock of her words, the piercing stab that ached in his chest.

"We've been apart. I've been confined to this bed for weeks. How much more time apart do you need?" He huffed, the force of his words echoing in the room. The unsteady beep of the monitors echoed his frustrations.

"I'm not ready for a commitment, Evan. I know it's not fair to you, but I have to be true to myself. If I stayed by your side, it would be because of guilt. I…I can't help but feel I landed you here."

"Brenda, babe, it's not your fault. That guy was drunk."

She held up her hands, as if to stop the flow of his words. "He was drunk, but I was still the one driving."

"Listen, if you feel guilty, don't. I'm not mad at you. If the roles were reversed, would you blame me?" How he wished he could get up and hug her.

"Of course not!"

"Then believe me when I say it's not your fault."

"But staying with you just because you lost a leg would be a mistake. Then it would truly be my fault. I'm sorry, Evan. I just can't be with you."

Nausea rolled through him as the memories played out. He felt like he was in an IMAX theatre, the images up close and personal. Sweat beads dotted his forehead. His arm pits dampened.

Why couldn't he forget that day? He'd called out to her as she hurried away from his room, but it was no use. She never returned. Never answered a phone call. A text. How could it truly be over?

He flung an arm across his face as another recollection surfaced.

"How are you feeling Mr. Carter?"

Even stared at the clock. A minute had passed.

"Are you still in pain?"

The seconds ticked by quietly, but he felt them echo in his pulse.

"Sometimes, the best way to heal is to talk about what hurts."

Two minutes down. Twenty-eight minutes left.

"Mr. Carter, I can't help you if you won't talk."

"Will it make the time pass faster?"

"Of course it will. Do you want to talk about how it feels to lose your leg?"

"Do you want to talk about how it feels to lose your hair? No? Thought so."

Somehow, the man's sigh lasted five seconds. When would the minute be over?

"Mr. Carter, we all suffer from loss. But it's how we deal with it that matters."

"Oh, spare me. Other than your hair, what have you lost? Please, enlighten me." How dare he. "I don't hear you speaking. So, let me get this straight. I lost my leg, my girlfriend, my job, and my car, if you care about that, and you've lost nothing. Absolutely nothing. How can you help me heal?"

As the silence remained, he shook his head in derision.

Evan had refused to talk the rest of the meeting. He never went back to see the counselor. That man couldn't help him. No one could. He hated that he couldn't escape the memories. The sound of the crash. The antiseptic smell of the hospital. The tears in Brenda's eyes as she rushed out of the room.

He rolled over to his side, imagining his leg was still there. Was he being foolish to think he could live on his own? Sure, he could wheel himself around, but could he really do everything else on his own?

Freedom.

Evan wanted it so badly, he could taste it. It would be like an ice-cold glass of sweet tea. Or better yet, the frozen goodness of a Popsicle that he *stood* to grab out of the freezer.

It seemed so close, yet so far away. Could he gain his independence back? The counselor had tried to tell him that his life wasn't over, but he had been too hurt to believe it. He wasn't going to listen to a person that hadn't suffered any deformities of his own.

Now, all he could picture were the floor plans Jo had shown him. She assured him she could make things accessible for him. He closed his eyes, stifling the longing. He wanted to go back to the day before the accident. When he still had two legs and an almost fiancée.

Had he been too hasty in rejecting a prosthetic?

Dr. Benson said his leg could still be fitted for one. The image of a steel pole flitted through his brain. It could never replace his leg. Never. His breathing picked up speed at the unfairness of it all. Of losing his leg. Losing the girl. Losing his freedom.

He'd never be whole again and he'd never be free.

Never.

Chapter Four

$\mathcal{T}$he shops of Main Street were a mixture of old and new businesses. The older generation owners refused to update their look. However, the younger generation of business owners preferred a more modern appearance. It was only a matter of time before the town would call for a more cohesive exterior. Despite the hodge-podge of businesses, Jo loved Main Street because of the continuity it represented. Old or young, Freedom Lake residents would thrive.

The smell of cinnamon and spice beckoned from LeeAnn's Bakery. Although the urge for a scone called to her, she didn't have time to indulge. She needed to talk to Chloe. Jo paused in front of her friend's business, the bright yellow storefront greeting her with its cheer.

The Space, Freedom Lake's only interior design store, enticed patrons to enter. There was something so warm and inviting about the place. Inside, the colors of gray and yellow melded perfectly. Jo immediately became full of peace whenever she walked in. Then again, it could be Chloe's presence. She didn't know what it was about her friend, but the woman exuded a Zen-like calm.

At the tinkle of the chime, Chloe looked up from her design board and smiled broadly. "Hey, JoJo. What brings you by?" She came around the desk to give her a hug.

"Hey, Chlo," Jo squeezed her back, using her old childhood nickname. "Needed to pick your brain and then realized I hadn't talked to you in a few days so…"

She trailed off with a shrug. Jo never felt the need to be overly articulate around Chloe. Somehow her friend always knew what she was thinking.

"I meant to call you the other night, but then a client called with a theme change and I spent all night redoing the plans I had." Chloe spoke with her hands, punctuating each word with movement. It practically became its own art form.

"Not a problem. I was in the city hanging with Michelle. Part business. Part pleasure. The business part is the reason I'm here."

"Okay. Do you mind if I draw while you talk?" Chloe pointed to her board.

"Not at all."

Jo sat down on the yellow love seat, propping her boots on the coffee table. She launched into her monologue, telling Chloe everything from Evan's loss of his leg, his need for an accessible home and ending with his want of his own place. When she was done, she looked up and saw Chloe studying her with steady patience.

She knew those eyes saw more than most. Most people would overlook her friend, thinking her personality matched her petite stature. Yet Chloe radiated a strength that couldn't be denied. She reminded Jo of a black Tinker Bell, small and willowy with honey-kissed skin. Her chin-length black hair had been braided into twists. A mole above the left side of her lip and a sprinkle of brown freckles across her nose completed the fairy-like appearance.

They were complete opposites, but Chloe's fierce loyalty made her the perfect friend.

"So what do you think, Chlo?"

Her expression gave nothing away. "How are you handling Evan coming back to town?"

"His return has no impact on me."

"So, you don't care that Evan is back?"

"No," Jo replied nonchalantly, though her friend's close scrutiny had her wanting to sink into the cushions.

"You don't care that he's missing a leg?"

"You knew, didn't you?"

At Chloe's small nod, Jo lost it. "Why didn't you tell me? Do you know how I felt when I first saw him? In a *wheelchair*? For a moment I saw my friend, the one before high school reared its ugly head." She took a deep breath, letting all her emotions out. "I may hate the way he treated me and I thought of a million torture devices he deserved, but seeing him in that chair..." Her voice broke off. She sat forward, resting her elbows on her knees. *Breathe in. Breathe out.*

"So, you do care." Chloe's words were more statement than question.

Jo looked up, about to protest, and saw Chloe's ah-ha smile.

"*No!*" The fist squeezing her heart made it difficult to breathe. *Why should I even care?* He treated her like dirt all throughout high school. She tried to block out the memories of his teasing.

"*Hey Four-Eyes, did you forget to take a shower or have you been hanging with the cows?*"

She squeezed her eyes shut. "I'm angry. He hurt me Chloe. Really badly." The unshed tears began to clog her throat. It ached from the pressure but she was in no hurry to unleash them. She pictured Evan in the wheelchair, angry at the world, and the pressure erupted.

"Oh, Chloe, when I saw him...all the emotions I thought had faded away came rushing back. Seeing him in that chair, all I could imagine was the year he broke his collarbone. You remember?" Jo didn't wait for her answer. If Chloe made any gesture Jo would have missed it, so caught up in her thoughts.

"He broke it in seventh grade. We were still friends, and I carried his books from class to class. And now, I want to help him again. Despite the hurt he's caused. Does that make me a glutton for punishment?"

Chloe shook her head as she studied Jo. "You're kind, Jo, always have been. You could have reported him to the principal a million times, but you never did."

Because I'm dumb.

What good had ever come from liking him? She'd never forget the feeling of betrayal the first day of high school. She'd waved to him in the freshman hall of Freedom Lake High, excited about the last phase of school. He'd taken one look at her and ripped her to pieces. He said she looked like an electrocuted poodle, complete with glasses and braces. The laughter from the guys around him seemed to add fuel to his comments.

How could she sympathize with him? She smoothed a hand over her straight ponytail, reminding herself she was no longer that awkward teenager.

"Do you still have a crush on him, Jo?"

The sound of her heartbeat filled her ears. How could she? The boy had filled her locker with manure their sophomore year.

"No way," she shook her head adamantly. "I refuse to be with someone who would treat me like a pile of...."

"Don't you think he's grown up by now?"

A bitter laugh escaped before Jo could rein it in. Hadn't he called her high and mighty just a few days ago? "Chloe, you see good in everything. If you talked to Evan, you'd see nothing has changed."

"I'll continue praying for him. I have been since I heard about the leg."

"You do that." The acrimonious tone made her cringe inwardly, but she didn't apologize.

"Sometimes that's all we can do, Jo Ellen."

Jo threw herself against the sofa. She might have known Chloe would find a way to bring God up in their conversation. It infuriated her to no end. But the rawness of the memories was too close for her to consider leaving The Space.

"Okay, Chloe. I get your point."

A change in conversation was needed. She stood up, wiping her hands down the side of her jeans, stopping as her thumbs hooked onto the belt loops. "I actually wanted to ask if you have any idea who's selling land around here."

"Does Evan want to live in town or around the lake?"

"Honestly, I forgot to ask." She frowned in concentration. "If the core of him hasn't changed since middle school, then the lake." *Why did she still know that?*

"I'm not sure if there is a lot of land for sale, JoJo. But maybe someone would be willing to sell their home?

She had a point. Freedom Lake was no longer in the land selling business. Land had been a hot commodity in the 1940s but now all the lots were filled. "Like who?"

"Hmmm...why don't you ask the Nelsons? Ms. Myrtle is moving into the senior community home on First Street. She has no children to leave the house to, so maybe she'd be willing to sell it."

Myrtle. Nelson.

As the idea took root, Jo hoped she'd be willing to sell her home to Evan. It had a great view of the lake and the Carter's B&B. It seemed like a win-win to her. Hopefully, Evan wasn't too set on an open plot of land.

~~

Evan breathed in the lake air. The leaves' reflection danced across the lake. He stared at the running path from his spot on the front porch. If only he could run out his frustrations. He thought back to Dr. Benson's office and the picture of the one-legged athlete. He'd been able to run. What would it feel like to have the pavement under his feet again? He snorted. If he could just walk down the hall to the bathroom, that would be good enough.

He sighed. Was he being stubborn refusing a prosthetic? He ran a hand down his face, wishing for calm. Right now the lake was so still, the only movement came from the reflections. Why couldn't he find that peace?

Jo said she could build him a place. One that would enable him to get around freely. Freedom was just a few nails and a hammer away. He could own his own place. It seemed so close, yet so far away. Could he gain his independence back?

If he had a prosthetic, would Brenda come back? He shook his head, quickly closing that line of thinking. She didn't give him a chance when he needed it the most. She'd been so consumed by her pain that she'd never bothered to look at his. Something told him Jo wouldn't be like that. Sure, she ignored him and was caustic at every turn, but that was because of high school. She didn't let a missing leg turn her wrath into pity. Oddly, he admired that.

Would people ever look at him as a man again and not just a burden? Sometimes he despised the wheeled contraption. Nonetheless, it was here to stay. *Unless, you get a prosthetic.*

He groaned. He was half-tempted, but the thought of looking down and seeing metal where flesh and bone used to be nauseated him.

His cell phone rang, startling him from his pity party. A Freedom Lake area code flashed on the caller id. He answered the phone, wondering who was calling him.

"Hello, Evan."

He shook his head. Jo's frosted tone carried across the wires. "Hello."

"I talked to my friend who said Mrs. Nelson might be willing to sell her place. Do you want me to talk to her or do you want to talk to her? Or better yet, do you want to get a realtor involved?"

Evan paused. Mrs. Nelson had a huge place, but it was already built. Wouldn't he run into the same problems as he did here? Or would it take less time than an open lot? He didn't know what to think.

"Hello? You still there?"

"Yes, I'm here. Sorry, you threw a lot at me and I was digesting it all."

"Oh, well, do you want to call me back and let me know your next steps?"

Evan winced. He was sure she didn't even notice what she said. Then again, not being able to walk was his hang-up not hers. "Give me a minute, Jo." He sighed, rubbing a hand over his face. "I was kind of hoping for a plot of land to buy. If I have to deal with renovations, shouldn't I just stick to my parent's place?"

"Do you want to be that close to home?"

Did he? Wasn't freedom the whole point of having his own place? As long as it wasn't on the B&B's plot of land, wasn't that a plus? "Not really."

"I didn't think so. But the main reason I'm suggesting her place is because land is scarce. You'll have to renovate a place or ask your parents for space on their plot."

Great.

Jo continued talking, "If Mrs. Nelson's home isn't structurally sound, you could always have it torn down and have another structure built in its place. Or, if you like it you can renovate it."

Evan nodded, then realized Jo couldn't see him. "Makes sense. Let me think about it and I'll call you when I've made some decisions."

He hung up and resumed gazing at the lake. What was he going to do?

The front door creaked and his mother leaned out. "Hey sweetie, are you hungry? I just made some chocolate chip cookies. I could bring you some."

His mother stared at him expectantly. He wanted to tell her to stop feeding him, it wouldn't grow his leg back, but he knew she meant well. After all she'd done for him, he should figure out some way to bridge the gap. How could he stop the constant ache and bitterness from seeping into every aspect of his life?

"Actually, Mom, I need your advice." He took a deep breath, ready to extend an olive branch. "Jo just told me that Mrs. Nelson is selling her place, but I still want my own land. Should I lean toward renovation or a brand-new home?" Why did the idea of land pull at him so?

"That's a tough choice. Have you considered praying about it?"

He scowled. As far as he was concerned, praying was a waste of time.

"Now don't make that face at me, Evan Carter. You seem to think that God put you in this chair, and I'm here to tell you that you're wrong. He wasn't behind the wheel of that truck and He certainly didn't cut off your leg. He has been here every step of the way, watching over you. How can you explain away the fact the doctor said you should have died from the impact?"

He stared at his mother stoically. He didn't want to answer her, but he felt a prick penetrate his conscience. At the last minute, the truck driver had tried to right himself at the same time Brenda had swerved left to get out of his way. The result, his side had been pulverized.

She continued, as if he hadn't given her the shut-up

stare. "What about the fact that the driver willingly paid the settlement instead of hashing it out in court?"

"What about the fact that now I'm girlfriendless?"

"Oh please, Evan. Brenda was not the girl for you. Now, don't get me wrong, she's a sweet woman, but she never challenged you. I've certainly never seen you go out of the way to become a better person because of her. You were happy being the same old Evan."

Evan turned away, hoping the gesture would end his mother's preaching. He didn't want to hear that. He belonged with Brenda but, thanks to a missing leg, she didn't want anything to do with him. *Then doesn't that mean she's not the woman for you?*

Evan shook away the thought. Who would want to deal with a man with a missing leg? No, he certainly didn't blame her for that.

"Evan, until you turn back to God, you'll have no peace, and this bitterness will continue to take root and choke out every truth you know about God until you're godless."

The closing door echoed his emotion. He felt shut off from the rest of the world. Shut off from all that mattered. All because he was missing a leg. A leg that God could have saved, but didn't. A leg that caused the woman he loved to hit the road without a backward glance.

Godless.

He sighed. Had he become godless? Was life better without God? He struggled for breath as the enormity of his thoughts pressed against him.

He needed an escape, but where could he go that would give him freedom? He rolled closer to the railing, deciding not to confront his feelings. Gazing at the lake, he tried to bring back the calm but the quiet had dissipated. Boaters had come out, and the noise of their engines canceled any thought of solitude.

Chapter Five

*H*umming to herself, Jo hammered the last nail into the deck. Her grandmother had called her a couple of nights ago to ask if Jo could fix her deck. It seemed some of the boards were rotted. Unfortunately the term rotten was an understatement. So Jo had torn up the old wood and created a new, more functional, deck. The sounds of Coltrane had kept her company via her iPhone. Sitting back, Jo perused her work and nodded with approval.

Movement caught in her peripheral, drawing her gaze toward the sliding door. Her grandmother stood in the doorway with a plate of cookies. Although her Nana was petite and short, there was no mistaking the steel spine and quiet dignity emanating from her. Her salt-and-pepper pixie cut only accentuated her short frame. Some people made the mistake of thinking she was a pushover, but Nana Baker was a force to be reckoned with.

Jo removed the headphones from her ears. "What do you think?" She gestured to the new deck.

"Oh, JoJo, it's even better than before. Thank you so much for taking the time out to do this for me. Plus, it gave me more time to see your smiling face." Her grandmother reached up to pat her cheek.

She grinned at her grandmother. "Nana, I think it's all these cookies you keep feeding me that put the smile there." The last plateful had quickly disappeared. She stood up and reached for an oatmeal cookie. "Mmm, these are fantastic. When are you going to give me the recipe?"

"Humph. When are you going to give me great-grandchildren?"

"Kind of have to get married to do that, Nana. Plus, Darius has already given you two." Her brother was the only Baker sibling with kids. She figured her sister's husband was too old to give Vanessa children.

"Yes he has, and I already gave Darius' wife the recipe. You and Vanessa seem to be in cahoots on making me wait."

Jo snorted. The thought of her and Vanessa sneaking off and conspiring with one another was laughable. They may be sisters but that's as close as they got. Vanessa couldn't stand Jo, and she returned the sentiment.

"Now, Jo Ellen Baker, is that any way to think of your sister?"

"What?" She gave her Nana a wide-eyed stare. "I didn't say anything."

"No, but I saw that look on your face." Nana shook a finger at her. "I know you don't much care for one another, but eventually you'll come to realize that she's the only sister you have. Don't let resentment and bitterness take hold of you. That's just what the devil wants."

Jo slowly nodded. For some reason, when Nana Baker talked about the battles of heaven and hell, she could almost believe it. Her Nana was like the Carters' in that regard; she practiced what she preached. She never forced her beliefs on Jo, but she didn't hide them either. If only Chloe would take a page from her book.

"I wouldn't mind burying the hatchet, but Vanessa is too happy wielding a sword. She constantly approaches me like an enemy. I don't get it. It's not like I ever stole a boyfriend or treated her unkindly."

She shrugged. Vanessa's hatred eclipsed her understanding. You would think being married to a wealthy doctor would make her sister happy, but it had only increased her bitterness.

"Well you can't help how Vanessa behaves, just how you respond." Nana patted her on the shoulder. "Now, you come inside and tell me how the business is doing."

Jo sat down on the barstool in front of the kitchen counter while her Nana began cleaning. She told her Nana about the job with Evan and how he was looking for land or another place to renovate. The other day, he called to inform her of his interest in Mrs. Nelson's place. He was waiting for a call back to let him know if she wanted to sell. He was ready to get the process started and had even talked to their town realtor.

"Oh, Mrs. Nelson's place is kind of big. What's a single man going to do with all that space? You should have told him about old man Joseph's place. That seems more up his alley."

Jo looked at her in surprise. She didn't know what caught her attention more: the fact that Nana called someone old or that Mr. Joseph was selling his property.

"Mr. Joseph is moving? Why?"

"He's moving into the senior community home on First Street like Myrtle. Once you hit a certain age, not only is it lonely living on your own, but for some it's not safe. I'm half-tempted to move there myself."

"Nana! You're not that old."

Her grandmother gave her a no-nonsense look. "JoJo, I'm almost eighty. Sure, I get around just fine and have all my faculties, but it's also quiet as a church mouse out here. I don't have a house crawling with visitors every day. Most of my friends have died or moved to the home already. It only makes sense to consider the move as well."

All of a sudden, the atmosphere shifted. Jo could feel the gloom hovering in the air like a dying person's last breath. She shuddered. A move to the old folks' home was just a step away from . . . she didn't want to think about that. What would she do without Nana Baker? She was the only family member who loved Jo the way she was. "I'll do my best to come out and visit more often. Not sure why I don't."

"Oh, hush now." Nana said, waving off Jo's comment. "I know you have your business to run and your own life. I don't expect you to cater to my every mood. However, if you would visit because you love me and miss me, then I'll welcome the company."

"Of course I love you." Jo came around the counter and gave her a hug. "You love me and accept me just like daddy did, and for that I will always be grateful."

As Jo lingered in the embrace, she realized just how frail her grandmother had become. Age had taken its toll, though you wouldn't know it by the strength of her voice. Jo hoped her Nana had a lot more years left. She wouldn't mind having a child and sharing that moment with Nana, who was more of a mother to Jo than her own.

A short while later, Jo drove away. Spending time with her grandmother reminded her how much she missed her dad. She was thankful for the time they'd had together. He had been the best parent she could ever hope for. He never tried to change her, but embraced all of her.

If only mother could love me for who I am.

She shook her head at the futility of the thought. Her mother would never change, that she was sure of.

Jo left the forested section of Freedom Lake to make her way back to Prosperity Ridge. Her grandmother didn't live around the lake, but in the wooded section of the town where the one-story cottages were located.

The cottages had once belonged to African-Americans who had made Freedom Lake their vacation spot in the summer. It had been the only area opened to them. A place where they could relax and have fun like their white counterparts.

She couldn't imagine what it had been like to be segregated. Freedom Lake was now home to all races.

She sat unmoving at the stop sign and looked around at the aging homes. *Wasn't Mr. Joseph's place near here?*

Mr. Joseph lived on the east side of Freedom Lake and had a view of the lake. If she remembered correctly, the south side of his house should face the beginning of the wooded area of Freedom Lake. Evan would have the best of both worlds. He might even enjoy the country-style home.

Making a right at the stop sign, Jo headed toward Mr. Joseph's home. She didn't know if Mrs. Nelson was going to sell to Evan, but it didn't hurt to have more options.

〜

Fighting back disappointment, Evan hung up the phone. After much consideration, Evan had contacted a realtor. His father had pointed out that he may need one to pave the way for the buying process and recommend a lawyer for when he entered a contract. His new realtor Mike had just called to inform him that he was too late.

Mrs. Nelson was indeed in the market to sell her home; unfortunately, she had just entered into a contract to sell her home to another buyer. He didn't know what he was going to do, but hopefully Mike would search for another place. Mike had informed him there was no land for sale in Freedom Lake, and buying a house was his only option.

Guess I have no choice but to renovate.

Evan leaned back against the wall. He really hated the butler's pantry. The walls literally felt like they were closing in on him. Fortunately he had an appointment with his occupational therapist that afternoon. He'd be able to get out and feel the air.

And have everyone stare at you too.

He frowned. He hated how much attention he received. You'd think no one ever saw a man with a missing leg before.

They haven't.

Evan shook his head. Deep down, he knew a man with one leg was an oddity, but it didn't help with his coping skills. *Or lack of.* He hated the wide-eyed stares, the pity in people's eyes and the remorse in their tone as they stammered to find some line of sympathy. It was pathetic. *I'm pathetic.*

So get a prosthetic.

His left eye twitched.

Was he really considering it? It seemed traitorous, as if he was considering joining the dark side. After all, shouldn't he just stand on the principle of not having a crutch? *You can't even stand for crying out loud. Lord, please, guide me. I need to—*

Evan stopped in the midst of his prayer. He was praying. Honest to goodness praying. He inhaled sharply, surprised by the ease in which he had slipped into it.

Slipped. Why had he treated God and prayer as a place where he had to be cautious? His heart picked up speed and his chest began to burn with emotion. He'd been so tense and stressed because he'd been consciously trying to avoid prayer. A thing he used to love more than anything.

More than your leg?

Tears welled in his eyes. Had he valued his leg more than a relationship with God? He stared down at the limb in question. He wanted his leg back more than anything. It kept him awake at night. It caused an ache so wide he knew he'd never overcome it. Had the longing closed him off to God?

But God did this to me.

"For God cannot be tempted by evil, nor does He Himself tempt anyone." The words of James flooded his soul. Hadn't his mother told him? *He wasn't behind the wheel of that truck.*

Her words echoed along with the Bible verse. God had tried to show Evan that he wasn't alone, but he had been too stubborn to listen. He hung his head. Had he wrongly placed the blame at the feet of the only One who could comfort him?

When was the last time he prayed unabashedly?

Evan thought he was done with a God who would let bad things happen, but apparently not. Suddenly he felt ashamed of the many nights and days he had blatantly ignored Him. Was it really worth it to ignore the only One who had always been there for him? The One who could give him the sweet peace he desired? As shame overtook him like a summer storm, Evan knew what he had to do to fix it. He bowed his head and clasped his hands before him.

Lord, please forgive my silence. I was angry, and I knew I could take it out on You. I knew You would still love me. You're the only one who loves me regardless of what I do or what I look like.

Evan closed his eyes in wonderment. He didn't know where the words came from, but they were there and flowing freely. Somehow his soul had known God could handle his anger.

That shouldn't be an excuse though, Lord. I am truly sorry for my behavior. Please take this hurt and anger from me. Please heal me, not just the pain of missing my leg but also the pain that Brenda caused. She hurt me deeply, Lord, and I'm not sure I can ever trust another woman again.

Trust Me.

Peace began to flood his soul at the still small voice. The words appeared in his mind as clear as day. Could he trust Him?

How do I do that?

"Therefore do not worry about tomorrow, for tomorrow will worry about its own things. Sufficient for the day is its own trouble."

Matthew 6:34 was his mother's favorite Scripture. She would recite it and then say, "One day at a time, Evan, one day at a time."

He would have to take this new change one day at a time. And, deep down, he knew God was the only One he could trust. God would make all things work together for his good.

Okay, Lord. I trust You.

Chapter Six

*G*lancing at her watch for the fourth time, Jo wondered what was taking Evan so long. He said he'd be here at four, and fifteen minutes had already passed. Jo drummed her fingertips against the steering wheel. She hated waiting for people, especially when she had something worth sharing. She just knew he would love Mr. Joseph's house.

Mr. Joseph said he'd leave the house key under the plant on the front porch. Now if only Evan would show up, they could get this show on the road. The sound of a vehicle broke into her thoughts. Jo glanced to her left as Mr. Carter's van came to a stop.

"Oh," she whispered to herself. How could she have forgotten Evan couldn't drive? Of course he needed a ride.

I should have offered.

She shook her head. As much as she wanted to help him, being stuck in the car with him was a whole different matter. No one would ever accuse her of being reckless and she wasn't about to start just because he tugged at some nurturing instinct in her.

Evan's dad grabbed the wheelchair from the back of his van.

She got out of her truck. "Good afternoon, Mr. Carter."

"Hello there, Jo. Evan's excited to see the house. Apparently someone bought Mrs. Nelson's place. Do you think his chair is going to fit?"

"I guess we'll see."

She leaned against her truck as she waited. What must it be like to have every single thing altered by a wheelchair? She really hoped she could give him the type of home he needed. The ADA requirements were pretty straight forward. He just needed everything within reach...from a wheelchair.

She watched as Senior helped Evan into his chair. Funny, even though the chair made him appear shorter than her, Jo still saw him as he used to be. The varsity basketball star who had made the high school girls swoon and the boys puff out their chests with pride that he was their friend. Only she seemed to have experienced his darker side.

Her eyes squeezed shut at the memories. *He can't affect you anymore. You're not the same girl.* Jo looked up as Senior pushed Evan toward her.

"How did you hear about this place?" Evan stared at her expectantly.

Shaking off the uneasy feeling developing in the pit of her stomach, Jo marched forward.

"Nana told me that Mr. Joseph was moving to the senior community. He said I could show you the place. I think you'll love it. The driveway can be widened if necessary to give you more room if you ever get a wheelchair-accessible vehicle. It will also allow for visitor parking. I can level the staggered sidewalk for you as well."

Jo pointed to the front porch with the steps leading up to it. "I can also change those steps to a ramp."

"Fantastic, but how is that going to help me today?"

She fought the urge to roll her eyes at his snarkiness. It was a good thing Senior was there. His presence would remind her to keep her manners in check. "Go through the garage."

She pointed to the garage doors. "His garage floor is level with the inside, so you don't have to worry about navigating a step. That's probably the only thing I won't have to change."

Jo retrieved the key from under the plant and unlocked the front door. As she made her way to the garage, Jo slowly realized she had been silently repeating *please like it, please like it, please like it.*

∽

Evan waited patiently as the garage door slowly made its way up. It was in obvious need of updating. It was slower than a sloth reaching for a noonday snack. He stiffened in irritation when Jo entered the garage from the house.

He could tell he had angered her earlier, but he didn't care. *Maybe you should apologize for being rude.* He snorted. *Not likely.*

Ignoring his conscience, he rolled into the garage, finally taking control of the chair from his dad. If he was going to live on his own he needed to show he could be independent despite his missing leg.

Surprisingly, the two-car garage had plenty of room even with the workbench that took up the whole right side.

"Can that come out?"

Jo walked over to the bench and examined it. "It's a beauty, but yes it can come out. Is the space adequate for your current or future needs, do you think?"

He wanted to smirk at her business tone but refrained. Like it or not, he needed her expertise. "It looks fine. But I know I'll never need the work bench." He watched as she ran a hand over it one more time. She looked at him and then turned toward a door.

"This leads to the utility closet and that one to the house."

He followed her as she walked through the last door. "It opens right into the laundry room."

It was a tight squeeze but Evan managed to maneuver into the room.

"Of course, I'd widen the door from the garage into here. Also, we can enlarge the laundry room if necessary. On the other side is the dining area. We could probably take a couple of feet from it to make this space more functional."

"That sounds great, don't you think?" his dad asked him.

At his nod Jo proceeded to show them the rest of the house. Evan was amazed that the place was a one-story. It seemed like most of the homes that had a view of Freedom Lake were two stories. He asked Jo about that.

"Well, you're right, those homes are two stories, but Mr. Joseph's place actually falls into the woodlands category."

"Learn something new every day," Evan replied.

"So what do you think of the place?"

His brow wrinkled as he thought. He took a calming breath to smooth it out and to help him concentrate. "Well there seems to be quite a few things you'll need to alter. Wouldn't it be better to just build a new place?" *Why couldn't he let the thought of land go?*

"Sure, building a home from scratch would be easy as far as it having every specification you'd desire. However it also takes the longest and you would have to find land. You know as well as I do that Freedom Lake is not an up-and-coming town. This place has a history and with that comes older homes and a lack of land."

Evan watched as she folded her arms across her chest. He raised an eyebrow and smirked. Jo was always so defensive. "There's got to be some unoccupied land left."

"How? This place was prime real estate in the forties. Every black person who could afford a vacation home bought one. Now you have nothing but their descendants, and people looking for a small town to live in, taking up residence. There is *no* land, so get over it."

Her gaze flashed to his father. "Sorry, Senior."

"No problem. I agree with your advice." Evan felt his dad's hand on his shoulder. "Son, this is probably your best option."

Fine. Intellectually, he knew that but he had enjoyed needling Jo. She became passionate when she fought. Her cat-eyes flashed and her cheeks flushed pink. Watching her eyes spit fire and her lips purse with indignation was the most fun he'd had in a while.

She's stunning when she's angry.

He gave a shake of his head. What was wrong with him? Considering their history, he should steer clear of her and keep his mouth shut.

Or open it and apologize. He grimaced inwardly.

She continued on, "Look, I get your desire for something brand-new, but I can take this house and turn it into your dream home. The doors can be widened; kitchen counters can be torn down and replaced with customized counters. You name it, I can do it. The catch is working with the original framework of the home. This home is 1,800 square feet. It's not huge, but it's not so small you'll be bumping into the walls in your chair. I've also done an in-depth walkthrough. Mr. Joseph was good to his home and has done a lot of upkeep. I don't suspect any unknown water damage, or structural damage. This is a good, *sound* home."

"I'd like to think it over before making a commitment."

A flash of irritation lit her eyes so fast he thought he was mistaken.

"Understandable. I'm sure if you have any questions, Mike can help you. Plus, Mr. Joseph could give you the history of his home."

He nodded. "I appreciate you taking the time to show us the place."

Her eyebrows lifted in surprise, and he hid a smile. It seemed his kindness had unnerved her.

"No problem. If you make an offer and it gets accepted, let me know and I'll start working on plans."

"Thanks, Jo."

She tossed a nod in acknowledgment and walked away. He had no clue what she was thinking but, for a brief moment, he thought he imagined her shiver at his kindness.

Maybe I should do that more often.

Chapter Seven

B are.

Jo studied the contents of the fridge and bit back a sigh. At least there was a carton of eggs and some vegetables. Hopefully, it would sate the beast.

"Guess it's time to hit the store," she muttered aloud as she pulled out eggs, green onions, and mushrooms.

An omelet would have to do until she hit the market. Her mother acted like it was beneath her to shop for groceries. As she whipped the eggs, the woman in question walked into the kitchen. Jo quickly looked down, watching the omelet set in the skillet.

Please, don't say anything. Please, don't say anything.

"Good morning, Jo Ellen." The high-cultured tone laced with ice made her wince. That tone meant her mother was itching for a fight.

"Good morning, Mother." She gave her a smile hoping to keep the storm at bay. "I made an omelet. Would you like one?"

Please say no, please say no...please!

"No, thank you. I'm meeting the bridge club for brunch. Besides, I think it's time for a run to the market. There's nothing edible in that fridge."

Thank goodness she was leaving the house. "If you make a list, I'll make a run." *That should make her happy.*

Jo's mother slapped down a piece of paper on the marble countertops.

"I wrote the brand names down so you don't bring home some inferior product." Her mother gave a delicate shudder. "I detest the store brands."

Can't have Victoria Baker seen eating inferior products. She stifled the eye roll begging to make its entrance.

Jo took a good look at her mother. She looked perfect in her linen pantsuit. The top half of her hair had turned gray, with the bottom clinging to the black strands of her youth. Her perfectly coiffed hair accentuated her square face, softening the edges. Of course her makeup was flawless, emphasizing her brown eyes and covering the few wrinkles that had begun to make an appearance. Her mother was aging gracefully...no surprise there. Did her mother ever tire of looking perfect? "Yes, Mother. I'll make sure I get only what's written."

Once, Jo had made the mistake of getting store brand items, thinking she would save her money. The fit her mother had thrown could rival a toddler's. She had walked on eggshells the rest of the week.

Move out!

"See that you do. I put some items on there that I'll need for a dinner party. Please make sure to get everything *exactly* as written. If you have a question, call my cell." Her mother stared at her, perfectly shaped eyebrows arched in expectation.

"All right." She picked up the list and scanned it, inhaling sharply. There was enough food on there to feed an army. "Can you write me a check to cover this?"

"Really, Jo Ellen? You can't take care of this for your mother?"

She closed her eyes. If this line of questioning continued, heads would roll. But despite the fact that her mother was warning her by speaking in third person, there was no way she could afford all these groceries on her budget.

The money she had in her account was going to cover a job. She had already dipped into her savings to fix Nana's deck.

"I'm more than happy to assist you by picking up the groceries, but Mother, I can't afford to pay for all of this."

Her mother waved the comment away. "Please, Jo Ellen, just take it from your business account."

"This isn't a business transaction."

"If your father was here, *he'd* take care of it."

I'm not Dad! "Mother, you can't simply ask me to dip into my business funds for your food. Your food, *you* buy it." She slapped the list on the counter and began washing her dishes.

"Don't you take that tone of voice with me, young lady. I am your mother, and this is my house. You *will* respect me."

"I understand. I really do." She rubbed the back of her neck. "But you need to understand this is my business and my funds go toward business transactions, not a market run for my mother."

"You ungrateful…"

"Don't lose your cool, Mother. What would your friends think?"

Her mother squinted her eyes. Victoria Baker hated to be unladylike and Jo would remind her of that fact whenever necessary. Besides, she didn't want to fight; she just didn't want to have to pay for the groceries.

"Get out of my house."

"Fine. How about I move out permanently?" She folded her arms and stared her down. For once, she was thankful for the height her dad had blessed her with.

"Ex-cuse me?"

Jo tensed at the hostility laced through her mother's tone. She widened her stance, bracing herself for whatever tantrum her mother would kick up. Truth was,

Jo had finally reached her limit. There was no need to continue living here. Her mother no longer suffered from intense grief. She was barely ever home.

But the look on her mother's face showed she was taken aback at Jo's suggestion. Her perfectly arched eyebrow disappeared under her bangs. The look would seem haggard on anyone else, but they wouldn't dare appear unseemly on Victoria Baker.

"What did you say?"

"How about I move out?" Each word was spoken slowly, clearly.

"I see. Well, if you no longer feel the need to take care of your dear mother in her time of need, I suppose moving out is what you must do. I do wonder what my friends will think knowing my daughter will no longer fulfill her family obligations."

Her teeth clamped down, causing a shooting pain to go up her jaw, but she refused to give voice to the thoughts raging in her mind. Her mother had a PhD in the art of guilt trips.

"Mom, it's been a year."

"Do you think there's a time limit on grief?" The shrill tone of her voice rang in Jo's ears. "Besides, how do you think you'll manage on that measly salary, Jo Ellen?" Her mother stared at her expectantly, a French manicured nail tapping on the counter.

"Maybe I'll share a place with someone."

"Who?" her mother scoffed. "I pray it's not Chloe, that child is too…" Her mother gestured as if searching for the perfect word. "…too bohemian. Michelle would be a much better choice. Now there's good breeding. She'd improve your status in Freedom Lake as well as your style of dress."

Her mother ended the last comment with a slow perusal of Jo's clothing. Suddenly, her white shirt and jeans seemed lacking. A jolt of anger, mixed with hurt, stiffened her spine.

"You do realize I cannot wear Dolce & Gabbana while working on people's homes. You'd die if a stain ended up on something so expensive."

"Well, if you got a real job instead of playing carpenter," she said venomously, "then perhaps you would have the opportunity to wear Dolce, Gucci, or even Versace."

"How can you say that? This was Dad's business. No, more than that, it was his heart and soul. The least I can do is give it my best in tribute."

"Oh Jo Ellen, spare me the hysterics." Her mother's eyes darkened, making them appear lifeless. "Your father's business was barely surviving. It's a wonder he had anything to leave you. The only reason you're hired for any job is out of pity and lack of competition."

"Glad to know I have your support." What did she expect? Her mother would never approve of anything that meant something to Jo.

"Oh my dear, you do. Anytime you decide you want to find a suitable husband and quit this ridiculous hobby of yours, then yes you have my full support. In the meantime, don't look to me to applaud your miniscule efforts."

"Well, thank God I won't be living here anymore."

"Do not take His name in vain. He has nothing to do with it."

"Oh, I didn't mean it as a curse. I'm genuinely thankful I don't have to live here with you anymore."

She passed her mother, thankful that tears were nonexistent. It never paid to show weakness in front of Victoria Baker.

～～

Evan looked out the kitchen window. His father stood outside, unloading groceries from the van. He looked down at the empty pants leg. He was utterly useless around here. *God, I don't want to be useless anymore. What do I do?*

His phone rang, interrupting his plea. The caller id showed the picture of his high school friend, Guy. He hadn't talked to him since the accident. The phone rang again. He had made it a point to avoid his old friends, but he knew Guy had it worse.

His wife had died three years ago, leaving him to raise their newborn twins by himself.

Evan answered the call, holding it to his ear.

"Evan?"

The sound of his friend's slight Haitian accent brought back memories. "Hey, G, long time no talk."

"I know man," his friend said on a sigh. "Sorry about that.

"No worries. What have you been up to?"

"I'm moving back to town next month."

"What?" Would his friend gawk at his leg? "That's great, man. I moved back home as well. What made you decide to move back?" He prayed his friend couldn't hear the false cheer. Silence greeted him. "Guy, you still there, man?"

"Yeah, sorry. I was just wondering how to answer that. To put it simply, I can't raise the girls alone anymore, man. I need help."

Evan sighed. He had no idea how Guy had managed this long. He knew his mother had moved to Virginia to help Guy raise Rachel and Rebekah, but she had returned to Freedom Lake a few months ago. Without Guy or the girls.

"How are the girls?"

"They're trouble," he responded with a chuckle. "My mom is no longer willing to help out with them, and preschool is too expensive here in Virginia.

So, I accepted the sheriff's position in Freedom Lake and bought a house."

"Wow. Judging from our last phone call, I thought you were going to make the FBI a career."

"I wanted to, but plans change. I can't be gone all hours and raise the girls by myself. The Sherriff's position should enable me to do what I love to do, but not take any time away from the girls."

"I feel you. I'm trying to buy a house myself. I assume you heard what happened?"

"Yeah, your mom told me. How are you dealing, man?"

"Hanging in there, G, hanging in there. First step, trying to find a place that will accommodate my new set of wheels." He couldn't believe he was talking about it so calmly.

"That's great, whose house are you looking to buy?"

"Well, I wanted Mrs. Nelson's, but now I'm trying to get Mr. Joseph's."

Guy laughed. "Man, I bought Mrs. Nelson's home."

"You're the one who bought it?"

"Yep. You snooze you lose."

"Obviously." A chuckle escaped. It felt good to laugh instead of being angry. "I'm glad it was you who bought it. Are you going to need any help moving in?" Evan faltered, almost forgetting, and cleared his throat. "I can ask my dad to help you. I'm not walking yet, but time will tell."

Did that mean he was finally ready to try the prosthetic? He didn't know, but he couldn't keep living like this.

"I appreciate the offer. I'll let you know."

"How are you handling the girls without Charlene?"

"Not too well. It seems God has abandoned me just like he abandoned her and left her to die."

Silence penetrated the air.

"You know what," Guy said. "I'll talk to you later."

Evan stared at his cell, looking at the tiny image of a cheerful Guy. The irony struck him hard. Something told him his friend was battling hardships worse than he could imagine.

Chapter Eight

 o knocked on Michelle's door. She'd made it to the city in record time thanks to the voice of her mother chasing her down the highway. Hopefully her friend would provide the much-needed girl time. Maybe she'd stop by Skyler's office and talk to her about Mr. Joseph's place. She had a good feeling Evan would be a homeowner soon.

The glimmer of hope in his eyes when they toured the place had touched her. He had to be excited about having his own place and gaining back his freedom. Considering her current situation, she could sympathize. Living with your parents after years of adulthood was a hard pill to swallow.

Sharing a place with her mother had slowly driven her insane. Maybe she should ask Chloe for space on her couch. But was that alternative any better? She had the option of getting insulted twenty-four seven or hearing about the sovereignty of God all day long. The thought drew her mouth down. They were both distasteful.

What was taking Michelle so long to answer?

She glanced down at her watch and let out a long sigh. *Of course.* It was only three o'clock. Michelle was probably still at work. Jo turned her back to the door. What was she going to do until her friend got home? Wait, what time did she get out of work?

Jo called her to find out.

"Hello?" her friend answered groggily.

"Michelle? You sound terrible."

"I know. Thanks for pointing that out."

She shook her head. Not even a cold could keep the girl from spouting sarcasm. "You sick?"

"No, I'm unemployed."

"What?! Wait, where are you?"

"I'm at home."

"Then can you let me inside?"

"You're outside?"

"I take it you didn't hear me knock."

She turned toward the door, waiting for it to open. How was it possible Michelle got fired?

When the door opened, she could barely muffle her gasp. Her friend's eyes were puffy and red. *That must have been one horrible crying jag.*

"Ah, Chelle, what happened?" Jo enveloped her in a hug.

"Come on in and I'll tell you."

Jo stopped to take her shoes off in the foyer and then followed Michelle to the couch. Her friend sighed, as if the weight of the world pressed upon her shoulders.

"Girl, you know I was up for partner, right?"

At her nod, Michelle continued.

"Well, yesterday they brought all the associates into the conference room to announce the new partner."

Jo leaned forward, resting her elbows on her knees.

"They gave the job to Marvin."

Jo frowned in confusion. "Who's Marvin? I don't know if I've heard you mention his name before."

"That's because he was just hired six months ago. And get this, he hasn't even passed the bar yet."

"Okay," the sound came out low and long. Jo tried to make sense of her thoughts but they resembled a jumbled-up Rubik's cube. "Why would they promote a person who hasn't even passed the bar? *And* who hasn't even been at your company that long? You've been there since you've graduated law school, right?"

"Exactly! JoJo, I was so mad. I was fuming. I pulled Bruce aside and asked if could I meet with him later. I tried and tried to calm myself down, but by the time I met with him, I was seeing red."

Her friend began pacing, punctuating each emotion with a fist hitting her palm. "Turns out Marvin is Bruce's *godson*. I just lost it. I've been busting my butt to show them I was a shoo-in for partner and turns out I never even had a chance because the man has a freaking godson?"

Jo leaned back as Michelle's voice went up an octave. How could she help her friend? There had to be some silver lining. "Chelle, what angers you more? That someone else was picked for partner or that you worked hard for nothing?

Michelle stopped pacing and stared at her in bewilderment. "That I worked hard for nothing. I put six years into that company for a position I will never get. I can handle being passed over, especially if someone is better than I am. But Marvin wasn't and it wouldn't matter if he was. Bruce was going to give him that position all along."

She sniffed and sat back down on the cream loveseat. "I have to find another job but I have no idea where. To tell you the truth, after the whole fiasco yesterday, I have no desire to work for another firm anyway. I don't want to play politics."

"So don't," Jo offered.

Michelle looked at her in confusion.

"What? You can be your own boss and won't have to worry about someone being promoted who doesn't deserve it."

She saw the light click on for her friend.

"You know, that's actually a great idea. I had thought about doing it a few years ago, but that was the same time Bruce announced the race for partner."

Michelle shrugged. "So, I ditched the idea."

"Really? You were thinking about it? Did you have a business plan and all your i's dotted and t's crossed?" Jo smirked. Michelle had the tendency to be obsessive and compulsive.

Her friend laughed. "Girl, you know I did. Let me go get it. I know exactly where it is."

Crisis averted. She breathed a sigh of relief. *Thank God.*

She frowned. That was twice in one day she'd used that phrase. She always made sure to avoid it, because it's not like she believed in Him or anything. *Did she?*

Of course not.

She was merely talking to herself. It's not like she entertained the idea that God was really real. Then again, she had once acknowledged the possibility of a God. She just couldn't believe He was as good as people claimed.

How could He be, when she lost the only parent who loved her and was left with a mother who could barely disguise her disdain? However, if she was instinctively calling out to Him, then maybe deep down she believed the truth of what Chloe and Nana Baker had always preached to her. That He was real and maybe even good. She chuckled. *You're losing it, Jo Ellen.* This business with her mother was messing with her psyche.

Michelle made her way back into the living room, interrupting her thoughts.

"So I found the business plan." She flipped through the pages of a purple, plastic folder with brads. "Believe it or not, I was looking at a place on Main Street to lease for an office."

"Main Street? Freedom Lake's Main Street?" Jo asked.

Michelle nodded.

"Wow, I never imagined you returning home to Freedom Lake, but I would love it if you did." She held her hand out. "Let me see this plan." Flipping through the pages, she searched for the mentioned location. Jo gasped. "That's right next to The Space."

"I know. Do you think Chloe would like being office neighbors?"

"Chloe would love it. I know how much she misses you" She looked at Michelle, noting the dark brown lines in her hazel eyes. "How come you two don't talk anymore? She won't tell me. Just changes the subject whenever I try and poke and prod."

Jo held her breath, hoping Michelle wouldn't lash out. She didn't know what caused her two best friends to stop speaking; she just knew she missed being part of a trio.

Michelle looked pensive. "It happened after the accident."

Jo stilled. Michelle never talked about that.

"I'm sure you remember it."

She nodded wordlessly, hoping her friend would continue.

"My parents were driving back home from the city." She smiled softly. "They were celebrating getting me through school. I was with you and Chloe."

Jo nodded, remembering that awful night. Michelle's eyes welled up with tears and Jo felt corresponding ones fill up her own.

"When the police told me they didn't make it…I couldn't think straight. Both of them dead was incomprehensible. It wasn't until a few days later that I found out they'd been hit by a drunk driver." She cleared her throat. "Anyway, Chloe came over after work one day and I was going on and on about how unfair it was…" She sniffled.

Jo hated to see her friend in so much pain. Being an only child, Chelle had no family members to lean on when her parents passed away, so Jo and Chloe made sure they were always there for her. She knew her best friends had argued with one another, but never knew about what.

"I told her they were too young." Michelle's face twisted with bitterness and she looked straight into Jo's eyes.

She shivered at the darkness swirling in them.

"Chloe told me...that God could work all things for good. I asked her how on earth my parents' death could be good." A detached look entered her eyes. "Actually I yelled at her, called her every insult I could think of and then kicked her out. I told her I never wanted to see her again. We haven't spoken since then."

"Oh, Chelle. You know how Chloe is about God. She probably meant to be comforting, not pretentious. She can't help how she is."

"I know, Jo. I know. Believe me; I regret how I reacted, but...I was just so...hurt." Michelle shrugged. "I just never knew how to talk to her after that. I didn't want to apologize but then again I did. I didn't know how, so I didn't. And now it's been twelve years of silence."

"Then it's time to speak. Call her, and do it before you show up next door to her as an office neighbor."

Michelle leaned her head against Jo's. "Okay, Mama Jo."

She laughed, glad that the mood had lightened. Jo couldn't believe that was the root of their strife all these years. Hopefully the two could mend fences. "Apologize, Chelle. She'll forgive you."

"Okay, I'll apologize if you'll consider moving in with me."

Michelle lifted her head and Jo turned to look at her. *She looks serious.*

"Really?" Jo asked. "You want to share a place together?"

"Yes, it'd be great. Then again, if you want to continue living with your mom, by all means have at it."

She burst out laughing. "You're funny. I just told her I was going to move out. Of course, I threaten to after every argument."

"Well then it's settled. We'll find a place for the both of us. Guess that means I'm returning to Freedom Lake."

Jo gave her a high five. Life was finally looking up.

~~

Evan wheeled out of Mike's office with a huge grin. Things were beginning to look up. Mr. Joseph had accepted Evan's offer, and he was now a soon-to-be homeowner. He couldn't wait until Jo came up with renovation plans. The quicker he could move in, the more independent he would feel.

He sighed as he rolled toward the parking lot where his father waited. Maybe he should find out about getting his driver's license. Being able to drive would be a dream come true. But could it be done? Guess he should've paid attention to all the information he'd been given over the past few months.

Chloe's interior design business caught his eye. He paused slightly, looking at her building. He couldn't believe she owned a business. It seemed a little surreal. He could remember high school like yesterday. Now, Guy was going to be Freedom Lake's new sheriff and his other friend, Darryl, was the local pediatrician.

Darryl.

Each time his friend had called over the past few weeks, Evan thought of an excuse not to answer the phone. When Darryl tried reaching him on his mother's phone, Evan refused to talk. If he did, Darryl would want to come over and catch up on old times, but life was different now. *He* was different.

The thought of his healthy, two-legged friend seeing him in a wheelchair, minus a leg, brought an ache to his chest.

"Evan!"

God, please not him.

He squeezed his eyes shut, his stomach dipping as if he rode a roller coaster. Of all the people in Freedom Lake, he had to conjure up the one person he didn't want to see.

Darryl called out his name again and he stopped wheeling. Slowly, Evan rolled around to face him.

"Dude, you've been avoiding me." His friend's brow furrowed, looking like two fighting caterpillars.

"I know." Evan looked down, focusing on his empty pant leg.

"Why? You don't think I can handle hard times?" Darryl ran a hand through his curly mop, frustration etched into his features.

Darryl had always been the comedian of the group, but the look of consternation on his face showcased how hurt he really was.

Evan swallowed. "Man, it's not that. I just...I can't handle it, Darryl." He didn't know how to be normal with people anymore. It took all his strength to be able to look a person in the face instead of staring at their legs. Their two usable, very real legs.

"I get it." His friend stared straight into his eyes.

He wanted to look away but that would just drive the wedge further between them.

"I really do get it, man." Darryl repeated. "Just remember we've been friends since kindergarten. No matter what you look like, you're still my friend."

The pressure in his throat increased. He glanced up, focusing on the clouds, willing himself to ignore the emotion making his throat ache. He'd been shutting everyone out for sheer perseverance. He should have known his friend wouldn't have made him feel awkward. He took a deep breath. "Thanks, D, I appreciate that."

"Anytime." Darryl cocked his head to the side. "So, what's new with you?"

"I just bought a house."

"What? That's great. You're sticking around Freedom Lake, huh?"

He nodded. *What other choice do I have?* "I am. Jo's going to renovate it to make room for me and the chair."

Darryl's eyebrow rose. "Jo? Jo Ellen Baker?" He let out a low whistle at Evan's nod. "Does she still hate your guts?"

Evan laughed. He could trust his friend to cut straight to the chase. "I'm pretty sure she does; we haven't really discussed it. But she's been nice and actually found the place I'm going to buy."

"Is it weird seeing her again?"

"It's a little awkward. When I left Freedom Lake, I never thought I would return, let alone see a bunch of old classmates."

"Well, that's because you were intent on being a professional basketball player. At least your fall-back plan as a coach panned out."

Evan grimaced.

"What? What does that look mean?"

"I haven't worked since the accident."

"Okay," Darryl replied hesitantly. "Why not?"

"They couldn't hold my spot. They wanted a guarantee I'd be back by the start of the school year, but as you can see..." he shrugged. "They needed a coach."

"So what? They could have made your assistant the interim coach and kept your spot open." Darryl held his hands out like it was a no-brainer.

Unfortunately, Evan knew it wasn't that simple. "They didn't keep it." He shrugged.

"It doesn't matter. I can't see myself working now like this anyway."

"Why? You're missing a leg; you're not deaf or blind."

His jaw tightened involuntarily. *Not him too.* His parents hadn't understood why he didn't want to apply for the high school coach position at Freedom Lake High. How could he go up and down the court in a wheelchair and call out pointers? It wasn't feasible.

"Look. Don't get all ticked off. Yeah, I saw you clench your jaw." Once again, his friend met his gaze head on. "I'm not going to let that fly. We've always been straight with each other. So I'm going to say this. Don't waste your talent just because you never imagined yourself doing it one-legged and that's all I'm going to say about that."

"Good."

The conversation picked back up and Evan was glad Darryl avoided topics involving his missing leg. For a moment, time seemed to fade away. It was like returning to basketball practice after winter break. They were a little rusty, but the familiarity was still there. Eventually, he would feel comfortable around Darryl again.

He didn't know how long they talked, but he knew the minute Darryl lost focus.

"Um, Darryl?" The man's eyes held a faraway look. He turned his head to see what had captured his attention. When he saw Chloe locking the door to The Space, he grinned.

"Aww, I see." He turned back to look at Darryl. "You still have the hots for Chloe?"

Darryl scowled. "Man, who says that anymore? Treat her with some respect."

"I didn't mean any disrespect. I just didn't realize you were still interested in her." He glanced back in time to see Chloe turn around the corner, fading from view.

His friend heaved a deep sigh. "Chloe will never know I exist. Oh sure, she sees me. But not *me*." Darryl ran a hand over his five o'clock shadow. "What I wouldn't give for that woman to notice me."

"Dude, you know she's a church girl? When's the last time you sat in a pew?"

"Not since my old man..." Darryl stopped mid-thought, looking at the ground.

Evan closed his eyes. He'd almost forgotten what had happened. "How about we go this weekend?" He clamped his mouth shut, already regretting his words.

Was he even ready to go back to church? Sure he talked to God now, but church was a whole other level of commitment. There would be a ton of people. People who saw him grow up. People who remembered how fast he could hustle up and down a court. And those same people would see him sitting in a chair. *Probably being pushed by Senior if he has his way.*

"You know what, I think I will go with you."

Evan nodded but, inside, dread filled him.

Chapter Nine

$\mathcal{T}$he doorbell pealed through the house. Jo glanced at her watch. Who could be visiting this time of day? She rolled a strip of tape along the top of a cardboard box to seal it and sat the tape down before heading downstairs. Even though she and Michelle hadn't found a new place yet, packing gave her a new level of calm. It signified that she would be soon leaving.

The doorbell rang again followed by the pounding noise of someone knocking.

"Coming!" she yelled. *Good grief, I'm not moving that slow.* She yanked open the door ready to give whoever was on the other side a piece of her mind.

"About time you answered the door." Her sister flounced inside as if she owned the place.

"Good morning to you, too." She shut the door, mentally preparing herself for a drama-filled encounter. Jo faced Vanessa, who was tapping an impatient foot along the foyer's wood floors.

"What's this I hear about you leaving Mother all alone?" She gave her a haughty look complete with a raised arched eyebrow, as if to signify the absurdity of it all.

Breathe, girl. She crossed her arms. Hopefully reasoning would work with her sister. "Vanessa, Mother is barely home. She's always with her friends at the club or in the city shopping. And *I'm* rarely home unless I'm in between projects. Believe me, she'll never miss me."

Her sister rolled her eyes and then sauntered into the

living room, laying her Prada purse on the mahogany end table. She flicked her curly brown tresses over her shoulder as she sat down, crossing her legs in debutante fashion.

"Mother is always out because she can't take the solitude without you here to keep her company. *Of course,* she'd make herself busy with shopping and the club. Would you want to sit alone in a home without your dear husband, focusing on his demise day in and day out?"

Jo rolled her eyes at the drama pouring from her sister like water from a broken pipe. "Nessa, –"

"No, Va-nessa. I'm not your 'homie,' so don't shorten my name."

She barely held back a laugh at Vanessa's use of air quotes. Sometimes she just couldn't take her sister seriously. "Whatever, *Vanessa.* Mother will be perfectly fine without me here. But if you're so concerned with her plight, why don't you ask her to move in with you and Lance."

Her sister threw back her head and laughed. Why she found the suggestion so amusing was beyond Jo. Then again, Vanessa was the baby of the family. She'd always been a little self-centered and spoiled. Marrying a doctor, who was all too happy to meet her every demand and whim, didn't help either. Asking Vanessa to take their mother in was like shooting darts in the dark. Pointless. Sometimes she couldn't believe they were really sisters.

"Jo Ellen, you cannot be serious. Lance is a very busy man and his practice takes up a lot of his time. Not to mention the many conferences he must attend. I'm gone as much as you are; she would have no one in our home to look after her, except maybe the maid."

"You don't even work. How can you possibly be gone so much?"

"I'll have you know that being a doctor's wife comes with many responsibilities. I'm sure someone in your line of work wouldn't understand." Her sister stood up, the tone of her voice dropping a few degrees.

Jo looked at her, taking in their physical differences. They were complete opposites in every imaginable way. She stood at five feet and eight inches and felt like a giant to her sister's five-feet-two-inch frame. Vanessa's hair hung in curls, which were manufactured on a weekly basis at the hair salon. Her own hair hung down straight from her standard ponytail, and the only time she darkened the doorsteps of a salon was to get it straightened. It allowed her to wear a hard hat unencumbered. Chloe kept trying to get her to go natural, but she didn't like wasting so much time on hair.

Besides their physical differences, their maturity levels were vastly different. Vanessa was two years younger but had married a man fourteen years her senior. Whether that made her more mature or not, Jo had yet to figure out. Vanessa was no more than a spoiled child with access to a major credit card. At one point, Jo had tried to make a connection with her little sister, but Vanessa made it perfectly clear they would never be friends.

"Seems sad to hear that you can't make time for a woman you stress is in dire need of companionship. I mean, I did it for over a year." She stared pointedly at her sister.

"Good for you, *Jo Ellen*. I have a life."

"Hmm, obviously one more important than your mother. I'll be sure to pass that along." Without waiting for a reply, she moved to the door and opened it. She couldn't figure out which was worse: arguing with her mother or her sister.

Family.

"As if Mother would ever believe you care more

about her than I do. She understands my commitment to my husband. Maybe one day you'll understand what it means to put your needs aside for someone other than yourself." Vanessa gave a slow perusal of her clothing. "Then again, dressed like that, you'll be lucky enough to get a woman to look at you."

With a smirk, her sister sauntered out of the house, down to the driveway and to her parked Jaguar.

～

Taking an inconspicuous glance out the window, Evan looked for Jo's beat-up pickup. She said she'd be by with the plans, but time crept by. He wanted to see what she had in mind so badly, he almost thought his left foot had been fidgeting. He looked down at the missing member. *Yep, you're going crazy.*

Leaving his parents' house was an important step. Jo probably looked at the plans as blueprints, but they were more like freedom papers to him. He ran a hand down his face. *Be cool, Ev, be cool.*

He looked out the window again. The leaves were starting to fall like crazy. Before he knew it, the frigid winter air would take up residence. God willing, he'd be in his new place by then. Could he handle seeing Jo every day for renovations?

Well, you were friends at one time.

How could he forget the easy friendship that had flowed between them in junior high? They had been in all the same classes together since their last names put them in the same homeroom every year. He remembered how they had joked and laughed. Friendship hadn't been defined as boy versus girl back then. It had been as natural as the changing fall colors.

Yet when he saw her at high school, his world had tilted on its axis. She had shot up a few inches and her body had begun to round out. All of a sudden she wasn't just a friend. She was a woman. He hadn't known how to handle it, so he teased her.

You were a jerk. And he probably still was.

He felt so bad for calling her 'four eyes' that he went to apologize after first period. Unfortunately his boys, Guy and Darryl, came upon them in the midst of his apology. They would have laughed hearing him apologize, so he stopped in mid-sentence and made a comment about her braces. He really didn't care about them, but he knew she hated them.

The soul-crushing look she directed his way had been his undoing. It was no wonder she hated him. He never let up the remaining years of high school. It had become a habit. At first, he liked the laughter, as if they found him important because he could make them laugh. Then it became a way to cement his popularity status. For some reason, he thought he had to surround himself with certain people in order to be somebody. He'd made sure to not let a day go by without making some derogatory comment.

Why in the world would she even take this job?

He turned at the sound of footsteps and saw his mom walking toward him. "Hey, Mom."

"Hey, what are you doing staring at the window?" She looked at him with a twinkle in her eye.

"Just taking in the view." Could she hear his feigned nonchalance?

"Oh...sure. Lake looks beautiful," his mom said as she came to stand next to him. She smiled and then looked down at him. "Now there's a beauty." She pointed outside.

Evan glanced out the window. Jo was here. She looked just as amazing today as she did yesterday.

Wait, amazing? Come on.

Apparently reminiscing had messed with his head.

She had on her standard overalls, but they suited her somehow.

He looked up, realizing his mom had said something. "What did you say?"

"I was asking if you guys are going to look over the plans together?"

"Yes, ma'am. Do you want to sit down with us and offer your opinion and advice?" He held his breath, hoping she would say no, but not sure why. Last time, he'd been more than grateful for her presence.

"No, I need to go to the grocery store. I just got a last-minute reservation for a couple who will be checking in by dinner time."

"Understood."

Upon hearing Jo's knock, his mom walked away to open the door. He remained by the window, listening to Jo's melodic voice, and prayed that God would give him wisdom and the words he needed.

It was time to apologize.

Slowly, he wheeled toward the two women. It sounded like his mom was letting Jo know that she had to leave. He came to a stop, hoping Jo would look his way and give some kind of smile. It would help the apology go more smoothly. She turned and gave him a look that could freeze water.

Okay, a smile is out.

He cleared his throat. "We can sit in the kitchen and go over the plans."

"Sure, that's no problem." The tone of her voice said otherwise. If the dropping temperature in the room was any indication, Jo had no desire to be anywhere near him.

He heaved a sigh. How could he hope his apology would be well received when she kept throwing daggers at him? He turned his chair around and headed for the kitchen. *Was it too late to apologize?*

Maybe if he started the meeting off with an apology it would prevent her from freezing the air. Evan made his way to the breakfast nook, thankful for its bench seating. The seat hugged the corner of the eat-in area, and it left the other side of the table wide open. He never liked the table, but now that he could just wheel up to the open side, it seemed like it was designed just for him.

Jo slid into the seat.

"I just want to say I appreciate the time and effort you've put into these plans." He paused, searching for the words. *Lord, please help me out here.*

The prayer formed quickly in his mind. *Amazing.* It looked like his relationship with God was back on the right track and Evan needed that more than ever. He exhaled and stared straight into Jo's eyes.

Here goes.

"I just wanted to say that I'm so sorry for the way I treated you in high school. I could blame it on youth or stupidity, but neither one of those is an excuse. Frankly, I was a world-class jerk, and I'm sorry for shredding any semblance of the friendship we had with my behavior. I hope you can forgive me."

She stared at him and it took all his power not to squirm in his seat. What was she thinking? Except for the slight widening of her eyes, Jo's face gave nothing away. She didn't even blink. Hadn't blinked since he started talking.

"I'd like to try and be friends again." He continued. "Do you think that could be possible?"

Jo shook her head slightly. "Come again?"

Had she heard anything he said? "I'm sorry for being a jerk. Could we be friends again? Will you forgive me?"

She slowly nodded.

"Is that a yes to the apology or friendship?"

"The apology."

He gulped. What did he expect?

Friendship. "I can understand that. Would it be too much to ask for you to think about the friendship part?"

"Definitely too much to ask." She pulled out the blueprints. "Let's get down to business."

He sighed, but nodded. He didn't know why it mattered, but suddenly he wanted to be her friend. *What can I do to win her friendship back, Lord?*

Chapter Ten

$\mathcal{J}$o hurried into The Space. Chloe greeted her with a smile, which quickly fell once she took in Jo's expression. She could only imagine how the fury altered her looks.

"What's wrong, JoJo?"

"That man had the *nerve* to ask me to be his friend." She flopped into the chair facing Chloe's desk. "Can you believe that?"

"Which man are you referring to?" Her friend's soft voice sounded lower in contrast to Jo's own.

"You *know* who I'm referring to. *Evan*," she seethed as her lip curled. Just saying his name made her tense up. "Evan Carter, the man who thinks he can walk all over someone and then simply apologize like it's water under the sink or whatever the expression is."

Her friend's laughter bubbled up into the air. "Oh, Jo, it was twelve years ago. Shouldn't it be water under the *bridge*? You can't honestly have carried a grudge all this time. Didn't you tell me you wanted to help him?"

She frowned at Chloe. *Was she serious?* The man had put dung in her locker. *Dung!* "I know what I said, but how can he think I would accept his apology and then say 'Sure let's be friends.' Who *does* that?"

Ugh. She jumped to her feet and began pacing.

"JoJo, are you really that bothered by his friendship request? I mean you were friends at one point, weren't you?"

Was she? He had seemed sincere in his request but that's not what bothered her. "It came out of the blue,

Chloe." She picked up a paper weight, jostling it back and forth in her hands.

"How so?"

"We've been arguing and throwing barbs at each other and now suddenly he wants to apologize for destroying my high school years and thinks I want to shake hands and be friends? Seriously, I don't want to overact, but who *does* that?"

She sagged against the wall, throwing the paperweight into the air. The man was infuriating. How could he think a simple apology would undo the years of damage she had suffered at his hand? And then, to add insult to injury, his request that they become friends was a load of…

Well, she didn't want to say what it was.

"Michelle did it to me."

Jo sat up. "What do you mean?" She bit her lip, trying to clamp down the rest of the words begging to be released.

"We haven't talked in twelve years, but all of a sudden she came back to Freedom Lake, apologized and then asked to be friends again."

Jo winced inwardly. Had she been wrong suggesting Michelle apologize? She flopped back into the chair. *You're a hypocrite, Jo Baker.*

No, it was a completely different situation. Wasn't it? She picked imaginary lint from her pants leg. "Did you forgive her?"

Chloe nodded. "What else could I do? It's Michelle, and although our hiatus was longer than our friendship, I missed her as a friend."

Jo stared down at her work-roughened hands. Was she being honest about her feelings for Evan? Could it be she was so upset because her feelings ran a little on the more-than-friends side?

Her finger mindlessly slipped against her necklace.

Should she follow Chloe's lead and forgive *and* be his friend?

Sometimes, life really was too difficult.

~~

Evan nodded in thanks as a patron held the door open for him, allowing him to wheel into LeeAnn's Bakery. His father had dropped him off so he could meet Darryl. Only now, he wanted to back out of the store and hide out at the B&B.

He scanned the eatery, searching for a curly mop of hair. Darryl caught his eye, holding a hand up in the air. Eyes followed his every move as he made his way to the back of the bakery. He bent his head, his chin almost touching his chest, as he concentrated on not rolling over anyone's foot or belongings that littered the aisle. His chest tightened as the stares continued to take in his appearance. Didn't people ever consider how they could be potentially blocking a handicapped person?

His head jerked back. Not once had he put into words what he was. He was handicapped, disabled, in need of aid to get around. His heartbeat raced as he wavered. More than anything, he wanted to be back in that butler's pantry where the world couldn't see him. But the other half wanted, no begged, for life to have some semblance of normalcy.

Swallowing his pride, Evan kept rolling until he got to Darryl.

"Hey, Ev, glad you could make it."

He nodded, still trying to get his emotions under control.

"Got you a coffee and a blueberry muffin."

He could do this. "Thanks, D. Did you get any sugar?" He couldn't stand the taste of coffee without it. His mom always joked at how much sugar he put in it.

His friend pointed to the sugar container on the table and grinned.

"So what's up? Why did you want to meet?" He finished pouring the sugar and looked up at Darryl whose mouth hung open. "What?"

"Dude, do you know how unhealthy that is? Your teeth are going to rot, not to mention the damage you're doing to your arteries."

"Sorry, doc."

"If I saw one of my patients put that much sugar in their coffee—"

"Should kids even be drinking coffee?" he asked, cutting Darryl off.

"No, but that's not my point. You added *way* too much sugar. You're like a poster child for diabetes."

"Okay, I get it." He took a sip of his coffee. *Perfect.* "What did you want to talk about?"

"Church."

"Okay, go on." Evan had avoided going ever since he'd made the offer. He didn't know if he could handle all the looks. Just being in here made him want to climb out of his skin, or at least the chair.

"When are we going to go, and what do I do once we get there?"

Evan wanted to smile at his friend's sober look but kept his face neutral instead. He searched his memory for a time he saw Darryl at church and realized he never had. He leaned forward. "Have you ever been to church, man?"

Darryl shook his head, gripping the coffee mug in front of him.

A whoosh of air parted his lips. "Well, it's been awhile since I've been to church here. But usually, they do worship."

Darryl looked at him blankly.

Right, no church lingo. "We sing songs about God to God."

"Okay."

"After that, they do tithes and offering. A lot of believers give ten percent of their paycheck to God, some offer whatever they can, and there are those that do both."

"Ten percent?"

He nodded at the skepticism in his friend's voice. "It seems like a lot but when you think about it, it's not. God doesn't ask more of one person. He's asking the same from us all. Plus, when you operate under the principle that it's His money and He blessed you with it to begin with, it becomes moot."

"I'll take your word for it. What then?"

"Then the pastor preaches a sermon. It's always based on Scripture from the Bible. He'll use it to show us how we should be living."

"So, do I need to read the Bible before I go?"

"No. I don't know if they announce what will be preached ahead of time, but sometimes they keep it a secret just in case they end up changing the sermon. You'll be fine, man."

Darryl ran a hand through his hair. The boy should really consider cutting it for a more professional look.

"Is that all you wanted to talk about?" Darryl could have texted his questions. Evan felt exposed sitting out in the open with his back to the crowd. It felt like the whole town bore holes into his t-shirt, watching him sit in the blasted chair.

"Well, yeah."

"Man, you could have called me for that." He frowned, trying hard not to roll backward and make a break for it.

"You have to get out of your parents' house, Ev. You can't hide forever."

"What are you talking about?" *How did he know?* Sometimes having a friend since infancy was a pain. He sighed.

"Please," Darryl smirked. "Besides, you get a blueberry muffin out of it."

He stared at the muffin. Somehow it had betrayed him, even if it was an inanimate object. His friends and family knew how much he loved LeeAnn's muffins.

"It's not going to bite you, Ev. And no one's going to bother you either."

The first bite of the muffin was good. He tried his best to blend in with the crowd. Yet, the feeling of eyes following his every move didn't go away. Could he thank God that Darryl didn't bring up church again? It seemed sacrilegious to thank the Lord for not going to church.

I'll get there, one of these days.

Chapter Eleven

*E*xcitement coursed through her. Jo leaned against the porch railing, watching as Michelle slowed her white BMW coupe to a stop in the driveway. They were going to look at places to rent. She wanted to skip to the car with glee; instead she strolled down the steps in case her mother watched. Freedom was a signed lease away. It would be great to be a normal adult once again.

She opened the door and sank into the leather seats. "Good morning."

"It's too early to be good." Michelle sounded half asleep.

"You do know nine isn't early?"

"It is if you don't have to be at work."

Jo shook her head. How had Michelle managed to be the first associate in to work when she was the farthest thing from a morning person? Then again, the girl had been highly motivated. It looked like her motivation flew right out the window when her job ended. "Where are we going?"

Since she wasn't all that particular about where she lived, she told Michelle to pick the places. As long as her mother wouldn't be residing there, she couldn't care less where they lived.

"Did you know they built new townhomes on Second Street?"

"Yes."

"I thought we'd check those out."

"Sounds good."

Jo placed her head back against the headrest and settled in. She eyed the speedometer and glanced at her friend. "Are we in a hurry?"

"No, why?"

She pointed to the speed limit sign. However, the way her girl zipped right past it, she doubted Michelle had had a chance to read it. "You know, now that you're back in Freedom Lake you're going to have to start driving slower."

Michelle laughed. "Says who? Besides who would want to pull over a lady driving a BMW other than a man in want of a date?"

Jo shook her head in bemusement. Sharing a place with Chelle was going to keep the laughter flying. It beat the tomblike silence at her mother's house.

In no time, Michelle pulled into the future-resident parking spot positioned right in front of the leasing office and let out a low whistle. "This looks nice. I never imagined Freedom Lake would have a place like this."

"Well, the town committee is trying to entice people to move back here. I hear they're going to throw a huge Juneteenth celebration next year."

"Why didn't they do it this year?"

"The new hotel on First isn't finished yet. It's supposed to be done in March."

"How come you didn't work on the construction?"

"The town's residents keep me pretty busy with odd jobs here and there. Plus, I don't do commercial construction."

They walked into the leasing office where the sounds of soft jazz streamed through the overhead speakers. Jo loved jazz; of course, she'd rather listen to the pioneers than the contemporary ones they played in every generic office setting. She inhaled, noting the distinct scent of vanilla.

"JoJo, I'm loving the ambiance." Michelle looked like she might explode with excitement.

"It's nice." But a little too high class for Jo's taste. How could she be comfortable in her own skin in a place this fancy?

"Good morning!"

They turned at the sound of a perky voice.

Maybe Chelle is right, it's way too early for that.

"Hi, I'm Camille. How can I help you two ladies?" She beamed a smile at them and offered a hand. Her red hair had been gathered in a French twist and freckles dotted her nose. She had the perfect office look, classy but friendly.

If she had a job like this, Jo would love to wear her outfit. The green silk blouse paired with gray slacks said feminine but business woman. She glanced at the shoes. *Heels.* Nope, she lost her. Jo avoided those death traps at all cost.

"We're interested in renting a two bedroom with a den." Michelle smiled back and winked at Jo.

"Not a problem, follow me this way."

Camille escorted them down a hallway, asking for their drivers' licenses. "As you may already know, we're brand new. If you decide to rent from us, you can rest assured knowing you're the first to live here. We have 24-hour maintenance available via email or our intranet website."

Jo started zoning out as Camille droned on. She was only here as moral support for Michelle. She didn't really need a lot of space, since a home was simply a place to lay her head. Being gone almost all day, from job to job, didn't leave time to enjoy her surroundings. But one day she'd love the perfect home. She'd take time to slow down and smell the flowers…or whatever. Settle in a home she could relax in and be herself without anyone complaining where she put her feet.

Her dream floated through her mind. Perhaps a farm house with a porch. Warm tones throughout the house. A kid or two…nah, just one. And someone to share it with. She frowned as Evan entered her thoughts. Why did he always invade her mind? He was like those subliminal messages they snuck into infomercials. Her mind needed to be retrained.

Jo tuned back in to Camille in time for her to point out some of the amenities, and she took the opportunity to scrutinize the construction. Sometimes people did shoddy work, hoping no one would pay attention. However, it looked like they had hired the right people because everything seemed to be in perfect order.

Finally, Camille led them to one of the townhomes. Michelle had asked for one on the end, so the leasing agent brought them to the last available one.

"Being on the end is a popular request, so if you decide you want this one, you'll need to put a hold on the place right away. They go like hotcakes!" the redhead said with a grin.

She pointed out the two-car garage as they made their way up the stairs leading to the front door. When they stepped in, Jo immediately took in the split-level floor plan. *Ugh, stairs for days.* Nothing like having to climb a bunch after a long work day. But she kept her mouth shut.

"The stairs leading downstairs go to your garage and family room. The stairs leading upstairs go to the bedrooms. And since this is the main area, it houses the living room, kitchen, and guest bathroom."

They moved from room to room and Camille pointed out little features that made it homey. Jo repressed her groan as they climbed another set of stairs.

"There are a lot of stairs in this place," Michelle said with a grimace.

"Yes, ma'am, but it helps maximize the square footage. That way you get the most bang for your buck."

Rolling her eyes, Jo held back a snort. They could probably rent a bungalow for cheaper and have the same space with no stairs. In fact, as soon as they got back in the car, she'd mention it to Michelle.

~~

"When are you going to leave the wheelchair behind, Mr. Carter?"

Evan frowned at Drew as he did his hip abduction exercises. He clutched the parallel bar as he breathed in and out. "I told you to call me Evan."

"When are you going to stop using the wheelchair, Evan?"

He glanced at his chair as he switched legs. "I can't get around without it."

"Why do you think you see me on a regular basis?"

Evan wanted to ignore the man, but Drew was right. Occupational therapy wasn't about strengthening his limbs—it was more about helping him function with one leg. "So I can figure out how to be independent."

"Exactly. Let me hook you up with an appointment with Julie so you can get a prosthetic and start living again."

"I'm living." He hated the implication that he wasn't. He just didn't know how to adjust to life with one leg.

"How? Is your dad still moving you to and from the chair?" Drew raised a bushy eyebrow.

The urge to wipe that smirk off his face was strong, but his therapist meant well. "I told him to stop. I can do it now with no problem."

"Good, what about transferring to a car from the chair."

He felt his face heat up. His dad did it for him this morning. "No."

The quiet tone of his voice barely hid his embarrassment.

"You want me to have a talk with Senior? I know he loves you but he has got to let you find your way. Alone."

"I know." He closed his eyes as he stood there. Standing gave him a rush after so many years of taking it for granted. He wanted to stand and brush his teeth. Stand and take out the trash. Just stand.

Then get the prosthetic.

"Okay," he rushed out. "Make me an appointment with Julie."

"Yes," Drew said with a fist pump. "I'll do it right after we finish."

He nodded. *He was going to get a prosthetic!* Evan swallowed around the lump that seemed permanently lodged in his throat these days. If he could truly get his independence back and regain his freedom, then what did he have to lose? Wearing a prosthetic couldn't garner him any worse looks then the chair did.

Drew was right. It was time for him to live. He stared at his chair and then down to his foot. His left pant leg hung there, oddly flat. Holding on to the parallel bars, he took a step. Then another. And another.

It was oddly exhilarating. Why had he waited so long to consider the freedom a prosthetic could offer him? Why relegate himself to that confounded chair when something could help him stand. *And stand without falling.*

"Have a seat and I'll be right back," Drew stated.

Evan sat down in his chair and shook his head. Stubborn pride had made him think dependence on his parents was the only way he could live. But now he could see how wrong he was. It was time to stop sequestering himself from everyone. Maybe he should reconsider the support group Drew always harped about.

It'd be nice to be around people who understood his plight.

At the sound of footfalls, he looked up. Drew appeared, his eyes crinkling and mouth smiling. *You'd think he just made the decision instead of me.*

"You're all set. I got you an appointment for next week with Julie. She'll walk you through the process. Pun intended." Drew slapped his back and laughed.

Evan just stared.

"You'll get your sense of humor back sooner or later. Hopefully it won't take as long as your decision to get a prosthetic."

"Yeah, yeah," Evan rolled his eyes. "I get the point. I was wallowing."

"Oh, you're still wallowing. But now you'll be standing when you do it."

He shifted in the chair. "How can I still be wallowing? I agreed to the artificial leg, didn't I?"

"Sure, but when's the last time you were around a group of people? When's the last time you went somewhere without caring what people thought? When's the last time you went out on a date, huh?" Drew laid a hand on his shoulder. "When you stop letting fear lead you, then we'll talk."

Not knowing what to say to Drew's insight, he simply nodded. A niggling feeling tingled at the base of his skull. Drew had a point, but it wasn't something he'd admit to freely.

Chapter Twelve

$\mathcal{J}$o pulled into the driveway and hit the garage door opener. She groaned. Her mother's jaguar gleamed in one of the parking spots. Should she go in the house or leave to avoid any possible drama? If she didn't, where else would she go? She was hot and tired but thankful that the Lancaster job was finally done.

"Here goes nothing." She took a deep breath and pulled in next to her mother's car.

After she walked into the mud room, she took off her boots. Quietly, in stocking feet, she headed for the kitchen. Her stomach had been making its complaints all the way home. If she didn't get food into her system soon, she might pass out from hunger.

Loud laughter echoed from the direction of the dining room.

What day is it?

Tuesday. The day her mother's bridge club met. Hopefully the added company would prevent harassment from her mother. Quickly she made a sandwich, thankful for easy meals. *Please don't let her hear me!* Jo tiptoed past the dining room doorway and held her breath.

"Jo Ellen, come in and say hello."

So close. She squeezed her eyes shut at the sound of her mother's voice. Her shoulders slumped as she entered the dining room. Three other ladies turned and looked at her.

"Hello, Mrs. Corneal, Mrs. James, Mrs. Simpson." She smiled at each of them. "Mother."

She tried to keep a false smile in place, but her face threatened to crack from the force of it.

"What brings you in so late, Jo Ellen?"

She glanced at her sports watch. It was only seven. "I wanted to finish a job tonight."

"Whose house did you just make better, Jo Ellen?" Mrs. Simpson asked her.

"The Lancaster's."

A chorus of 'ooohs' and 'aaahs' echoed about. She gave them a smile and waved good-bye.

"Wait a minute, Jo Ellen."

"Yes, Mother?"

"Cassidy was just telling us that her son is moving back to Freedom Lake. He's single."

The sing-song voice her mother used sounded like nails on a chalkboard. As nice as Mrs. Corneal was, her son fell far, far away from the fruit tree. He was a slob and a self-proclaimed ladies' man. She'd always been happy he had been two years ahead of her in school, saved her from sharing any classes with him.

"I'm sure you're happy to have him back, Mrs. Corneal." She smiled at her, hoping it looked sincere.

"Oh yes, it's been awhile since he's lived here. Would you be willing to give him a tour of all the new sites?"

Mrs. Corneal stared at her expectantly, and Jo felt the color drain from her face. Being set up was worse than hearing Chloe talk about God. Suddenly, a friendship with Evan didn't seem so distasteful. Not as dismal as hanging with Joe Corneal.

"I'm really busy these days, but maybe if I have free time." With that, she hurried out of the room and up the stairs. She could only hope Mrs. Corneal wouldn't take her up on her vague commitment.

∽

Senior turned down the street, headed toward Darryl's place. Evan wondered how hard it would be to drive with a prosthetic. Was it even possible? And more importantly, could he do it? His thoughts redirected as his dad pulled up to Darryl's house.

Turned out Darryl lived on the street behind Mr. Joseph's place. If Evan stood in his soon-to-be backyard, it would face Darryl's. Who knew they would end up living so close to each other? When they were in high school, Evan had lived in the B&B—before it had been turned into one, that is—and Darryl had lived in the low-income housing area in downtown Freedom Lake. Funny how growing up changed everything.

Senior unlocked the doors as Darryl walked up to the van. His friend sported a dark gray suit and a purple shirt. His curly hair covered part of his ears. Evan was more surprised the boy owned a suit.

"Good morning, Darryl." Senior gave a nod as Darryl got into the back seat.

"Good morning, Mr. Carter."

"Dude, you need a haircut." Evan turned around to smirk at his boy.

"Good morning to you too," Darryl said, sarcasm dropping his voice down an octave.

"My bad. Good morning, you need a haircut."

"Nah," Darryl said ruffling his curls. "My patients love it. It keeps me from looking scary. They trust me more with a mop of curls."

"That actually makes sense," Evan paused. "If Chloe asked you to cut it, would you?" He looked at Darryl, awaiting his response as his dad drove them toward Freedom Lake Tabernacle.

A weird noise escaped Darryl's mouth, his Adam's apple bobbing up and down. "Um, that would be tough, but yeah I would."

He tousled the curls in question and cleared his throat. "Maybe just shorter, so it's still curly and I look like good ol' Doctor D to the kids."

"They call you Dr. D? I like that."

"Yep, I love my patients. They're great kids."

"Do you get a lot of patients, considering the population is declining in Freedom Lake?" his dad asked.

"Evan's back, right? So there is a slight rise in the population." Darryl laughed at his own joke. "In all seriousness, I do get a lot of kids still. I know the town committee is trying to think of ways to encourage people to move here. Hopefully in the future, there will be a need to bring more doctors in."

His father nodded.

"D," said Evan. "I wanted to thank you for coming with me today. I haven't been inside a church since I left Freedom Lake."

"Oh, and you asked me when's the last time I sat in a pew," his friend scoffed.

"I know, I know. I've recommitted myself to the Lord, so I'm taking the next step and going to church." Evan looked back at Darryl as they came to a stop at First Street. "Why are you going with me?"

Darryl looked at his dad then looked down, fidgeting in his seat.

"Pretend I'm not here like Evan does," Senior offered.

Evan winced. Even though he recommitted himself to God, he still had a lot to make up for. One thing being the uneasy relationship with his dad. "I know you're here, Dad. That's why I don't need to talk. Your presence is enough."

His dad gave a quick nod, a sheen of tears coated his eyes.

Darryl cleared his throat. "Part of the reason is because I want Chloe to notice me. I'm not going to lie, the majority of the reason is for her. But there's a small part of me that's tired of being angry at my dad. Not much, but enough for it to pop in my head every now and again."

"Very mature of you, Darryl," his dad said quietly.

Evan nodded. He could understand anger. "Letting go of anger is very difficult, but God can help you if you let Him."

"Then what takes its place?"

His eyebrows shot up. How in the world did he answer that? *Lord, please help me out here.*

"God," Senior calmly responded.

He let out a sigh of relief. His father had lots of wisdom to share. Most people assumed he didn't have much to say because he was quiet, but Evan knew better. With any luck, he would turn out to be like his dad in that department.

"Well, I'm here, and regardless of why I came, I plan on paying attention."

"Fair enough," his dad said.

The three passed many of the town's folks as they headed inside Freedom Lake Tabernacle. The town only had one church. It used to be a Baptist church before changing to nondenominational in the mid-nineties. Evan heard how it used to be an all-Black congregation but that over the years the racial mix had changed because of the town's growth of other ethnic citizens. Now it was a multicultural congregation. Freedom Lake was no longer a Black-owned resort community, but a place where anyone could call home. Evan liked the change and wondered what Dr. King would think if he was still alive.

His dad headed up the aisle toward his mother. She was on the hospitality committee and had arrived early to set up the snacks for in between services. Evan wheeled himself toward a chair with a handicap sign draped over it. He watched Darryl scanning the crowds, most likely looking for Chloe. "Relax man, she'll be here."

"No, I was just looking at who all was here. I see some of my patients' parents."

Evan parked in the aisle as Darryl took the seat. The place looked different than he remembered it. He realized the pews had been replaced with dark red chairs. "The seats are new!"

Darryl laughed. "Been awhile, huh?" Darryl said.

"Apparently."

He looked around, noting all the people who were there. His realtor gave him a nod of greeting as he walked up the aisle, presumably to be closer to the front. His mom gave him a wave as she caught his eye. He even saw Jo's mom sitting in the second row with a huge red hat with a yellow rose. *Where was Jo?* Her brother and sister sat with their respective families, but no Jo. He'd have to ask her about that. Would she tell him the truth or continue with the hostile treatment?

God, I really want to be friends again, but I know how much hurt I've caused her. Please help her heal. Amen.

Darryl nudged him in the arm. "There she is." He indicated, with a flick of his hand toward the right side of the sanctuary.

There sat Chloe with a peaceful look on her face. Her twists were secured on the left by a white flower. She wore a simple black dress with a white sweater.

"She's so beautiful."

Evan's body shook as he stifled the laughter rising up. The smitten grin on his friend's face told him how bad he had it. Darryl had always had a crush on Chloe but never said anything to her about it. Instead, he had a nervous habit of blurting the first thing that came to his mind. It was often asinine and Evan felt embarrassed for his boy.

Chloe had always smiled politely but never went further than that. Maybe Jo would help him set them up. Could they make a bridge of friendship by getting their friends together? And why couldn't he just let it go and accept the fact that she didn't want to be his friend?

Because you like her.

His nose wrinkled. He wasn't interested in her romantically, but yeah he did like her. She had spunk and didn't pity him. Called him out whether he was handicapped or not.

An image of Jo wearing her t-shirt and overalls came to mind. He wondered if she ever wore anything more feminine. Come to think of it, when they were in grade school, she had worn t-shirts and jeans then too. He couldn't recall a single instance when she wore a dress or even a skirt.

Thoughts of Jo faded from Evan's mind as the sweet melody of "Amazing Grace" filled the air. He hadn't realized how much he missed the sound of a choir accompanying amazing lead vocals. Evan didn't know the young woman singing, but it didn't matter. Her voice sounded like an angel and brought tears to his eyes. God's grace was more than he could fathom, but he wasn't going to let that prevent him from accepting it.

He snuck a glance at Darryl to see how he was processing. Nothing could have shocked him more than to see tears silently streaming down his face. Maybe Darryl's heart wasn't as hardened as he thought. With a smile, Evan closed his eyes and reveled in God's amazing grace.

~

Evan took his time wheeling down the ramp in front

of the church. He had thought the crowd would disperse after the pastor gave the good-bye benediction. Yet people were huddled together in groups, talking and laughing. This was probably the only time some of them saw each other on a regular basis.

He glanced at Darryl. "What did you think of the service, D?" *Please, let him have liked it, Lord.* If he could, Evan would kick himself for taking so long to return to church.

"You know, I went in there with an open mind, and I think I was rewarded. From the very first song to the last prayer, I felt like it spoke to me." Darryl looked at him, a cautious grin on his face. "You know what I'm saying, or do I sound crazy?"

"No, I feel you. Bishop Brown's sermon on the prodigal son was fascinating. I couldn't help but feel like he was talking to me."

"See, I felt the same way. I've heard that story before. My mom used to read me bedtime stories from a little kid Bible when I was young. Once I became a teenager, my father put an end—"

Darryl froze, staring at someone.

Evan looked around to find the source of his friend's distraction. He spotted Chloe speaking to the Bishop, and it suddenly made sense.

The Bishop looked their way and Evan waved. The pastor motioned them to come over.

"Perfect opportunity to speak to Chloe," he whispered.

"Shut up."

He chuckled, then clamped his mouth shut. When they made it to the Bishop, introductions were made.

"Yes, I know who you are. My niece is one of your patients." He smiled. "She thinks the world of you. How did you enjoy the sermon?" asked the Bishop.

Darryl took a step back when Evan, Chloe, and the

Bishop turned to look at him. "I uh…enjoyed it." His shoulders rose and then a slew of words left his mouth, quickly and quietly, "I've heard the story before, but this was the first time I could sympathize with the son."

"Ah, God is always working in us when we begin to have compassion for those in the parables. Reread it when you go home, and if you took any notes, ask God about them. He'll lead you where you need to go."

"Thank you, sir. I appreciate that."

"Do you have a Bible?" Chloe asked.

The softness in her voice had him straining to hear her, but his boy looked captivated.

"Um, no," Darryl replied, shaking his head in bemusement.

Evan was surprised his friend didn't stutter. He swallowed a chuckle as Chloe reached into her floral tote and pulled out a black Bible.

"For some reason I grabbed this Bible today. I usually use the one my grandmother passed on to me, but I received this as a graduation gift. I've never marked in it, so it's practically brand new. Please, take it and enjoy."

"Thank you."

Chloe said good-bye and walked away. A man came up to speak to the Bishop, who excused himself. Before Evan knew it, it was just the two of them again.

"I cannot believe she gave me her Bible." His friend stared at the object in wonder.

"Are you going to read it?"

Darryl seemed to be transfixed. Was it the fact that it was a Bible or that it was from Chloe? He shook his head and began to wheel away toward his dad's van. Who knew how long Darryl was going to stand on the sidewalk staring at the Bible. He had things to do and people to see. Well not people, he wanted to see Jo. It was time to start Operation Make-a-Friend.

Chapter Thirteen

$\mathcal{J}$ o taped the last box, pleased at her progress. Somehow, she'd accumulated a lot of junk in the past year. She had already made a few trips to the community shelter. Now, she was finally able to see what she was going to keep.

She put the heavy box of magazines against the wall. She'd filled it to the brim with her Architectural Digest magazines. Parting with them was not an option. They were great inspiration and worthy of the backache she'd get from lugging them around.

Jo tilted her head. *Did the doorbell just ring?*

Why did it seem like every time she was trying to pack, someone came by to waylay her? She walked out of her room, pausing at the top of the stairs. This time the sound of the bell came through. Hurrying down the stairs, she hoped the person hadn't been waiting long, unless of course it was her sister.

Please don't be Vanessa.

She held her breath and then swung the door open. All the air rushed out of her at the sight of Evan. Not Vanessa. Only time would tell if his presence would turn out to be more welcome than Vanessa's.

"Hello." She folded her arms across her chest.

"May I come in?" He raised an eyebrow and gestured to the foyer.

"Um…sure." She stepped back and held the door open and watched as he maneuvered inside.

At the moment, she felt nothing but gratitude for her mother. She had made a big deal out of their front door a few years ago, until her dad had no choice but to replace it. The wrought iron was a little gaudy for Jo's taste, but it provided ample room for a wheelchair.

"What are you doing here?" Her voice came out stilted and clipped, but she was too unnerved to apologize. Why was he here in her home?

"I didn't see you at church, so I thought I'd come over and say hello."

We're not friends! She wanted to shout it, but didn't. If she truly accepted his apology, at least she could be cordial. "Would you like something to drink?"

"Sure, where's the kitchen?"

"Back here." She walked toward the kitchen and then stopped as she stared at the steps leading to the lowered living room. She turned around. "Do you need help? I can lower you down."

He looked down and for a moment she was afraid she had offended him. Her heart rate increased as she waited to see what he would say or do. *Since when did you care how you treat him?*

His request for forgiveness ate at her. All of sudden, she felt like the one doing wrong. He was now the bigger person seeking her friendship. Sure their relationship could improve, now that she planned to renovate his property, but how could she ever trust him?

She inhaled sharply, trying to find her breath as he lifted his head and looked straight into her eyes. Almost as if he saw into the secret places she kept hidden.

"I would really appreciate that."

The honesty in his voice shook her. She cleared her throat. "Sure thing." Jo studied his chair, trying to figure out the best way to lower him onto the steps.

"It's best if you go down backwards." Evan quirked one side of his mouth.

"Oh, right." She grabbed the handles and tilted the wheelchair back to slowly lower it onto the stairs.

Thankfully, working in construction gave her the muscles needed to help Evan with his chair. After helping him up the steps to enter the kitchen, she looked at him.

"Much obliged, ma'am," he said with a wink and a grin.

Whoa. He had the warmest, most heart-stopping grin ever. She blinked. *Stop it, Jo. You do not like him. You don't even want to be his friend.*

But surprisingly, she did. They were friends once upon a time. Had even discussed their dreams and future hopes. Until high school happened. Her smile disappeared. "No problem."

She tried to mask her emotions but feared the red-hot heat rushing up her face would give them away. Jo whirled around and grabbed a glass from the cupboards.

"So, about church, how come you weren't there?"

"I don't go. That's not my thing." She pressed the water button on the fridge, hoping the conversation would change soon.

"Not your thing? Why not?" His voice was calm with no hint of condemnation.

For some reason, that unnerved Jo more than the stereotypical voice of scorn would have. "I don't want to be another hypocrite. You know the type, they smile and open the door for you, but as soon as it shuts they're spreading your business quicker than a flea can jump on a dog."

A burst of laughter filled the air. She stared, mesmerized by the gleaming white teeth and the crinkles that fanned out at the corners of his eyes. Boy, how he had changed since the first time she saw him, sullen and angry at the B&B. He seemed so carefree now. What happened?

"I know the type. But if you don't want to be one of those, then you won't. Is that the only thing that stops you?"

"Maybe, but let's not get into that now. What brings you by?"

"Besides church?" At her nod, he continued. "I wanted to ask you again if you would consider being my friend."

Her heart stuttered. He asked way too much. "Why do you care so much?"

"Because I know how badly I hurt you, Jo." He wheeled closer. "All I'm asking is a chance. A chance to be the friends we were before. I need someone I can talk to who sees me and not the chair."

She ran her finger against her necklace, but she couldn't think past his big chocolate eyes pleading for friendship. How could she say no to him? What kind of person would that make her?

One who cares about protecting herself.

Wasn't that selfish?

"Please, JoJo. I won't betray your trust again. I'm not the same arrogant kid."

"Or the man who called me high-and-mighty?"

He winced, rubbing the back of his neck. "Or him."

"I can forgive you," she said. *Liar.* "But being your friend, that's a tall order, Evan."

"You've always been a better person than me, Jo. Please," he whispered softly, his brown eyes pleading.

If she said yes, her life would change. For the better or worse only remained to be seen. But somehow, she couldn't deny his request. "Okay," she murmured.

His whole face lit up. She told herself her heart beat had just slowed down, not skipped a beat. How could he look so much better than his teenage self? Age had only sharpened and enhanced his looks.

"You won't regret it."

"I might, because if you keep coming over I'm going to have to build a ramp to save my poor arms from the abuse." She slapped a hand over her mouth. "I'm so sorry. That was so…so insensitive to say."

Evan chuckled. "Refreshingly honest. Besides, I'm not offended. It's nice talking to someone who's not going to bring it up every five minutes, but who also won't treat it like the plague." He winked at her. "I'm shocked you can help me with it. I'm not light."

"Comes from hauling wood and appliances. I'm glad I can help."

"Well, I won't keep you. My dad is waiting for me outside. I told him I'd be right out."

"Oh, duh, of course. I'll see you soon. Now that you've picked the plans we'll meet up again to go over the interior design." She tilted her head. "Or you could have Chloe do the interior design."

"I'd rather you help me." He said softly, gazing into her eyes.

She felt a shiver and crossed her arms as if to keep it at bay. "Sure."

∿

Whistling "My Funny Valentine," Evan wheeled himself into the kitchen. He'd woken refreshed for the first time in a long time. Not one dream about Brenda or the accident tortured him during the night. And, for once, the phantom pain hadn't bothered him. He'd woken up hungry and ready to embrace the day.

His mother turned around at the sound of his tune. "Good morning, Evan. What has you so chipper?"

"A good night's rest. You should try it some time." He winked at her, pleased to hear her laughter.

Since the night of his accident, she'd been worried about him. Although he knew it, it had never tugged at him as he had been lost in his own mind. He took stock of her, noting how the gray hairs had multiplied and the lines on her face had deepened. It made her welcoming laughter that much more special.

"Psssh, listen to you. I'll have you know, since you've moved back home, I've slept like a baby."

"Guess you'll be grouchy like one when I move out again, huh?"

"Nope, because you'll be a couple of minutes away when you do. You hungry?"

He nodded and backed up to the table, so he could face his mom while talking to her. He wanted her advice, but wasn't sure if she was the right person to ask.

"Mom?"

"Yes, baby?"

"Why do you think Brenda was wrong for me?" Ever since she mentioned it, the thought had been burning a hole in the back of his skull.

She propped a hand on the counter. "Brenda's a sweet girl, but your life was way too easy with her."

He frowned. She had said that before, but it didn't make any more sense now than it did before. "Isn't love supposed to be easy?"

"Of course not, whoever said that was lying." His mom laughed.

"But, you and dad…"

"Psshaw, I'm half-tempted to knock him out on a daily basis."

He knew she would never hit his dad, but the thought of her being mad at him was comical. "I don't think I've ever seen you two argue."

"That's what the bedroom is for."

"Say what now?"

Her shoulders shook, and her eyes brightened with laughter. "What I mean was we agreed to never argue in front of you. Now whether or not that was a wise choice,

I can't say. Maybe it wasn't, considering you think love should be easy. If your other half doesn't challenge you, doesn't help you see life in a new way, then you're not *in love* with that person. You can love anyone, but the right person, the one you want to marry, will make you love them even when they're irritating you beyond belief."

He shook his head. Evan didn't know if he believed her, but he knew that loving Brenda had been easy. She never argued with him and always caved to his will. His brow furrowed. Was that a bad thing?

An image of Jo's face appeared. The fire in her eyes when he did something to annoy her sparked something deep inside of him. Being around Jo was far from easy and somehow he knew Jo Ellen Baker wouldn't be easy to love.

Chapter Fourteen

*T*he melodic sound of horns from her iPod soothed Jo's nerves. Today, she and Evan were going to pick out items for his kitchen. Soon he'd have the keys and ownership would be transferred to him. Evan wanted the kitchen remodel to be done first. Thankfully, he wasn't going to move in until all the renovations were complete.

She wondered if he was nervous about living by himself. It had been five months since the accident and he hadn't been on his own since. She looked out the window, noting the trees were almost bare. Although a cold front from Canada had rushed in frosty temperatures and high winds, it left almost as quickly as it came. Maybe winter would stay away for a few more weeks longer.

Before the song ended, Jo pulled up to the Carter's B&B. She took a deep breath to steady her nerves. *Remember be more cordial, but don't forget, this is a friendly, business relationship.* Nodding at her face in the mirror, she slapped the visor shut and got out of her truck.

She rounded the front porch and stopped. Evan sat on the porch in a black peacoat and green beanie. Why did she always seem to notice how handsome he was?

"Hey there, stranger," he called out.

"Morning, you ready to go shopping like a girl?" He laughed and the sound warmed her insides.

"If you mean go to multiple stores," he said, wheeling toward her, "and then return to the first one to get the first pick, not really."

This time she laughed. Was it her imagination or did his grin get wider? "What I mean, *friend*, is that we won't be leaving until you're completely satisfied with your purchase. You'll be surprised how many of my male clients are more indecisive when it comes to picking out faucets and sink inlays than the females are."

He scoffed at her. "Puh-lease. Get in and get out. That's my philosophy." He went down the ramp and headed for the passenger side of her truck.

"Do you need help?"

"No, but if you could put my chair in the back that would be great. There's a lever here that makes it collapse."

After he got settled in the truck, she pushed the lever and watched in amazement as it collapsed. *Why are you so surprised?*

Somewhere in the deep recesses of her brain she had to know the chairs collapsed. She bit her lip. Maybe it wasn't so hard to overcome the difficulties of needing assistance.

The drive into the city went by surprisingly fast. She'd asked if he wanted to stick to Freedom Lake, but Evan requested he be taken to her favorite store to purchase the kitchen necessities. Their laughter filled the cab all the way to the hardware store in Kodiak City.

Why had she been so worried? She had been a little hesitant to spend so much time in his presence, but he made her feel comfortable. When was the last time she had laughed so much or felt more at ease? It was almost like hanging out with her girlfriends, except there was no way Evan could be mistaken for a girl.

He oozed masculinity, from the cedar-scented cologne all the way to his blunt-cut-square-shaped fingertips. She couldn't remember the last time she noticed every detail about a man.

Stop it, Jo. He's not a boyfriend prospect.

The thought caused her joy to dim. It had been awhile since she'd been on a date. Maybe she just needed to go on one and stop thinking of Evan. Pleased with the idea she smiled inwardly.

They got out of the truck and as they neared the store, she pushed the handicap button so Evan could wheel in. She pointed straight ahead. "The kitchen section is in the back."

"Lead the way, oh fearless leader."

She laughed and walked forward. Once he saw the endless possibilities in the kitchen department, would his good mood last? It could be overwhelming to beginners. She'd been in awe her first time here. They had everything you could think of. If she had to pick out things for herself and not a client, she'd probably never leave.

They paused at the cabinet aisle and Jo pointed to the models. "We'll start here. Once you know the style and color of the cabinets, everything else comes together. Too many people think you start with the hardware or the counters." She shook her head. "Not true."

"Okay," he drawled. "They all look the same to me." He looked back and forth between the displays with confusion etched upon his face.

"Right?" She held one of the cabinet doors open and knocked on it. "Hear that?" At his nod she went to a different display and repeated her motions. "Can you hear the difference?"

"Yeah, that's crazy. The first one sounded hollow."

"That's because it's made from plastic laminate. The other one is solid wood."

"What's the difference? Price?" he asked, his voice going up as he read the price tag displayed on the countertop.

"Yes, price is a difference but also durability. The laminate cabinets are something you find in apartments or something you don't plan on staying in for long term. But if you plan on retiring in Freedom Lake, I'd suggest the solid wood because it will last years with all the strain you'll put on it by just using it. Plus, if you decide years from now that you want them a different color, then you can take them off, sand them down and recolor. Easy peasy."

She watched as he rubbed his chin in thought. He looked at her, and she felt a piercing in her heart. How did he look at her like she was the only one around?

"What would you do?"

"I'd use the solid wood." Was her voice breathless? She felt heat creep up her neck. *Get it together, Jo.*

He nodded slowly. "Okay, that's what I want. But I don't like the color. The tan wood seems unmanly for a lack of a better word."

"Great, now we're getting somewhere."

They shopped for a few hours, going over every item he'd need in his renovated kitchen. Whenever he faltered, he'd ask her opinion and usually took her advice. She felt lightheaded from the day with him. Never had she had someone pay so much attention to her, like her words were worth gold. It was a heady experience.

As they drove back to Freedom Lake, Jo couldn't help but wonder about his finances. She knew he'd been compensated from the accident, but didn't he need a regular job? Come to think of it, he hadn't mentioned working at all.

She ran her finger along her necklace. Should she ask him? Jo glanced over at him and startled as his dark brown eyes met her gaze.

He raised an eyebrow. "Penny for your thoughts?"

She faced forward, gripping the steering wheel tightly. "I was just wondering if you still work? I mean you've been back home almost three months. And you've never mentioned a job."

She glanced at him again, trying to gauge his reaction. A look of bitterness stole across his face. *Oh, no, I shouldn't have asked. Way to stick your foot in it, Jo.* The acid in her stomach rose, making her wish for a trashcan. She'd give anything to go back in time, where the conversation had been light-hearted.

"I was let go." The hollow sound of his voice tugged at her heart.

"What happened?"

"My recovery process was slated to take a long time. They didn't want to hold my job while I tried to get back to a new normal. They needed it filled immediately."

"But can they do that? Isn't it illegal to discriminate?"

"It is, but there are ways to work around it. They had a legitimate complaint considering I was in the hospital for a month." Evan glanced out the window.

She wanted so badly to run her hand down his arm to offer comfort. But did friends do that?

He heaved a sigh. "It doesn't matter anyway," he continued on. "It would be pretty odd to have a basketball coach with a prosthetic leg."

"You coached?"

"Yeah, high school."

"Well, maybe you can find a job here. You know us Freedomers love basketball."

He laughed but the sound rang false. She could tell he was hurting and it was all her fault. Why did she always say the wrong things at the wrong times? Knowing nothing else would help, she changed the subject to his mother's cooking. It took a while, but slowly his tone lightened up.

When she dropped him off at the B&B, she couldn't help but think that it wouldn't be long before he weaseled himself out of the business-but-friendly compartment and into something more dangerous.

∽

Evan waited and tapped his fingers against his chair rail. Today, he would be getting fitted for a prosthetic. He was finally ready to regain his independence. *Lord, thank You for pulling me out of my funk and depression.* He ran a hand down his face and let out a huge sigh. So much time had been wasted because of his desire to harbor anger and bitterness. Maybe if he had immediately chosen a prosthetic he'd have kept his job back in Chicago.

"Mr. Carter?"

His head shot up as a blonde nurse stepped into the waiting room. "Right here," he said raising his hand. He slipped his hands over the wheels and followed her.

"How are you today?" She asked, looking over her shoulder.

"Nervous."

She smiled showing a slight overbite. "That's understandable." She gestured to a room and he wheeled in. A woman sat behind a desk and pulled out a stack of papers from a file cabinet.

"Hi, I'm Julie," she said. Her blue eyes stared steadily into his. "I would like to go over the process before we get started."

Straight to the point. Evan couldn't decide if he liked her manner or not, so he simply nodded.

"Since you're an above-the-knee amputee, there will be four parts to your prosthetic. A socket, knee system, shank, and the foot-ankle system. The first step is creating a mold that will be used to create the socket of your prosthetic."

She pointed to the pamphlet. "I'll make one by using wet plaster. Once the socket is created, we have some adjustable legs we can use to figure out the appropriate amount of suction necessary for the socket. I'll also give you plenty of information on the best knee system, shanks, and feet that all have a different purpose. Don't think that you'll only have one prosthetic or parts. Some people use different feet if they want to run, or to go with different shoes."

He raised his eyebrows. Why hadn't he read up on this before coming in? *Because you were overly anxious.*

Evan set his jaw. He needed to stop depending on everyone else for information. There was nothing worse than being ignorant, but that's exactly what his anger and bitterness had allowed him to become. He had hidden behind the shame of missing a leg instead of educating himself.

I won't make that mistake again.

Julie discussed the process at length and he soaked in all the information. "Are you ready to get started?"

He nodded.

"Great. I have a plaster room we're going to go to. It has some parallel bars to hold onto while you're standing, so I can ensure I get the perfect mold."

As she applied the wet plaster to his leg, Evan imagined what his family's reaction would be. His mom would probably cry. She tried not to show how the accident affected her, but she couldn't hide it from him. Her smiles had been less frequent, and her hovering had increased. Every time he had declined her request to go to church, her eyes dimmed.

Last Sunday, tears had filled her eyes when she saw him in church. If he could stand up on two feet—well, one real and one artificial—she'd probably turn into a blubbering mess of a mom. He smiled at the thought.

"Okay, Mr. Carter, just stand here for fifteen minutes until it sets. Do you want me to put the game on?"

"Yes, thanks."

She turned the TV on to ESPN and sat in a chair with her paperwork.

The Pacers were playing the Grizzlies in a preseason game. Man, how he missed the game. The adrenaline of molding high school teenagers to become better athletes gave him a sense of purpose. Now, he spent his days reading biographies of the great African-American men of the past. Not that they weren't interesting reads, but he felt like he was just taking up space.

He watched as the Pacers hustled down the court and called 'foul' a few seconds before the referee did. *I still got it.* Jo's voice filled his senses as he recalled her suggestion of contacting Freedom Lake High. Would they really want him to fill the position? Could he teach basketball?

Isn't that what the prosthetic is for?

Maybe, just maybe, all his dreams weren't lost to him.

Chapter Fifteen

*E*ven though Jo had a grocery list, she couldn't help but peruse every aisle to see what the store had to offer. If she just stuck to her list, she'd be done in twenty minutes tops. But Jo loved food too much to not give it the time it deserved. The teriyaki salmon on display in the seafood department called out to her. She stepped closer.

"Decisions, decisions, huh?" a voice from behind her said.

Her insides stilled. What was Evan doing here? Oh how she wanted to ignore him. Their little excursion to pick out the features for the kitchen had shown her how comfortable she could be around him. But that was dangerous. She didn't want to fall for him. *Just be friendly.*

Business but friendly was her new motto. It *had* to be. She needed to guard her heart, because the last time they were friends, he had crushed her like an ant. She turned and pasted a smile on her face. "Don't tell me you've never debated over a purchase before." She clamped her mouth shut. That had come out with more bite than she'd intended.

"Of course I have, especially when it comes to seafood." He wheeled closer. "Mmm, that salmon looks good but so does the shrimp."

It figured they had the same taste. She had been standing there for five minutes trying to decide between the salmon and shrimp. She sighed.

When they were friends in junior high, they had shared many common interests. *Guess not everything changes.* But he didn't have to know that.

"I was looking at the salmon and chicken wrapped in bacon." *Liar.*

"Can't go wrong with bacon."

Normally she'd agree but the salmon was calling her name. Did she dare get it and risk him seeing it as common ground.

She turned and faced him, trying to ignore the way his eyes held hers. "What are you here for?"

His eyes wandered to the left then back to hers. "I took the community shuttle to the city earlier and missed lunch because of my appointment. I thought I'd eat at the café, but I saw you, so…" He shrugged.

It sounded off to her, but she didn't want to call him out. Wasn't she keeping her own secrets? Her heart ached for him. Every time she saw him, the need to ask what happened pressed upon her. But she kept mute. She knew how frustrating it could be to have people constantly offer condolences. They meant well, but it often drudged the hurt and loneliness up to the top.

An image of her father swam in her mind.

Maybe Evan would want to eat with her. *Whoa, Jo, stop that thought right there. You cannot invite him over for dinner.* Besides, if her mother was at home, she'd ignore the art of subtlety and run him over like a bull. "Anything interesting catch your eye?"

His full lips curved in a half grin.

Her breath caught in her throat. What did that look in his eye mean?

"Sure has."

"What?" Did her voice sound breathless?

"The salmon teriyaki. It looks amazing." He turned and held a finger up at the man behind the counter and then winked at her. "You know you want some."

Jo stood there, her mouth slightly open and slightly confused. Had he been talking about dinner the whole time? She brushed the mental cobwebs away. "I think you're right. I'll get some as well." She motioned to the guy and placed her order. No way would she let him think he got to her.

She took the salmon from the man and thanked him. Jo turned to Evan to say goodbye. For a moment she thought she saw a hint of loneliness flash in his eyes. It was so swift, she wondered if it had even been there.

What should I do? Invite him over? Say goodbye?

"I hope you enjoy your meal." He paused, then grinned at her. "It's nice having a conversation as friends, isn't it?"

She nodded, biting her lip with hesitation.

"See you around, Jo."

"Evan, wait."

He wheeled around, looking at her expectantly.

"Would you like to come over? I'll grill up the salmon and we can continue the conversation?"

What conversation? You've been gaping at him like a guppy for the last few minutes. She wanted to squeeze her eyes shut with embarrassment. Instead, she stared at him waiting for his reply.

"Actually, that sounds great. But I need a ride, if you don't mind."

"Sure."

His smile was full of acceptance.

She walked behind him, following him to the checkout stand. *What have you gotten yourself into, Jo Ellen Baker?*

What if her mother was home? Would she think they were dating? She grimaced. Her mother hated all her past boyfriends. She couldn't imagine what her mother would think of Evan.

Please, don't let her be home.

～

Evan rolled his chair behind Jo as she headed for her truck. He was trying to act nonchalant, but he felt anything but. He couldn't believe she invited him over. In the past, she'd let her guard down and shown her true colors, until he thought they could truly be friends. Then she'd quickly clam up. Her varying emotions were worse than a *Chutes and Ladders* game.

She opened the truck for him and he mentally prepared himself to transfer from his chair to the truck. He hated the height of it. It was awkward and his transition was not as smooth as getting into his father's van. Leave it to him to like a girl who drove a truck.

Are you saying you like like *Jo?*

He paused as he held the interior door handle. Did he like her more than a friend? He had to admit he missed the back-and-forth banter, but he also liked the easy way they conversed. He pushed himself up on his good leg and swung into the cab. Evan wanted to pump his fist in the air. It was finally getting easier and easier to make the transition.

Jo got in the driver's seat and grinned at him. He stared in amazement. When she smiled, it transformed her whole face. The shadows left, brightening her brown eyes. The lines around her mouth all but disappeared, making her look approachable. The need to be closer tugged at him. He shifted in his seat as she pulled out of the parking lot. If he touched her hair would she retreat or welcome his touch?

"How has it been being back in Freedom Lake?"

The soft sound of Jo's voice interrupted his musings. "Weird. They say you can't go back home, and I think they meant you can't live with your parents again. I went from being independent to depending on them for everything."

136

"I know what you mean. I finally took the step and told my mother I was moving back out. She's not happy, but that's not enough to make me change my mind."

He grimaced. Jo's mother had always been demanding. He could only imagine what it was like living in that house without her dad as a buffer. "I'm sorry about your dad. He was a good man."

"Thank you. I miss him so much." She glanced at him and then back at the road. "I'm sorry about your accident."

He drew in a ragged breath. This was the first time she'd acknowledged it. He felt just as confused as when she didn't speak of it. "Such is life."

Jo laughed, but it sounded strangely like crying. Instead of asking her if she was all right, he rode the rest of the way to her house in silence.

Thankfully, the transition from truck to chair was easier. He followed her into the house, pausing at the sunken living room. Whoever thought that was a good idea obviously didn't have any disabled friends. He hated depending on her to lower his chair.

"Sorry, didn't have time to build that ramp." She flashed another grin.

He snorted, shaking his head, but he wasn't offended. If anything, he felt like he did after scoring the winning shot. If she would smile at him like that all the time, liking her would be the least of his worries.

She turned on the light and sighed audibly.

"You nervous?"

"No, just thankful my mother's gone." She held up the salmon. "How do you like the salmon, grilled or baked?"

"Isn't it a little cool out for grilled salmon?"

She smiled at him and removed a grill pan from the cabinets. "That's why I have this. Now we don't have to freeze outside."

He laughed and pulled up to the countertops. He eyed the barstool, trying to decide if he wanted to deal with it. *Yes, you can see her better than sitting in this chair. Remember what Drew said, "Leave it behind, man."*

Once he settled onto the barstool, he watched as Jo prepared the salmon steaks. She threw some asparagus on the grill, squeezing lemon juice and sprinkling pepper on it.

"That smells good."

"And it will taste even better." She looked up at him and met his gaze.

For a moment, he got a glimpse at what life would be like if Jo was his girl. The thought intoxicated him, so much so that he reached over and smoothed a strand of hair out of her face.

Her mouth dropped open and she shifted closer to his hand. Her cheek brushed against his fingers, and he felt the zing all the way to his heart. Stunned by the feeling, he jerked his hand back.

Never had he felt a spark at just a touch.

Jo looked down, but not before he saw her eyes darken.

Lord, please don't let that be the start of tears. He wanted to kick himself and call himself all sorts of names. But what he wanted more was her smile back. "Will you go with me to pick out furniture?"

She studied him, making him feel like a lab specimen. It was all he could do not to fidget. He closed his fist in his lap, stifling the urge to touch her again.

"Sure, when were you thinking of going?"

"Whatever's good for you."

"Okay, how about Friday?"

"It's a…plan." He'd almost said, 'date,' and wouldn't that have been beyond awkward.

Fortunately for him, the rest of the night went smoothly. They fell into the song and dance of laughter and jokes over dinner. When Jo dropped him off at the B&B, it took all of his strength not to lean over and kiss her goodnight. He didn't know how it happened, but suddenly she was more than just his contractor.

Chapter Sixteen

The bitter cold nipped at her cheeks. Yesterday, Jo had gone out with a light jacket and the sun warmed her wherever she went. Today, Mother Nature was intent on breaking her spirit with bone-numbing cold. She rubbed her mitten-covered hands over her face to bring warmth back into it and then knocked on the door again. What was taking Nana so long to answer?

"I'm coming, I'm coming," came a muffled reply.

The door swung open and her grandmother glared at her. "Good grief, child, don't you know I'm not as young as I used to be? It takes a while to get to the door."

"Sorry, Nana, but I'm freezing out here."

"Come in, I'll get some hot chocolate going." Nana looked her up and down. "At least you had the good sense to dress warmly. I'm surprised to see a jacket and beanie on you. You always seem to be wearing a t-shirt and overalls these days."

"What can I say? It gets hot renovating people's homes." She grinned at her grandmother, who rolled her eyes in response. She hung up her jacket and followed her into the kitchen.

Nana pulled a pot out of the cabinet and set it on the gas stove. "Well, it sure isn't hot today."

That was an understatement. Another wind clipper had moved through and left frost and cold in its wake. Jo had a job this afternoon, so she dressed in her overalls but had a pair of long johns underneath. She didn't mind walking around in a t-shirt in the 60s, but the 30-degree weather that greeted her this morning was another story.

"What brings you by my way, JoJo?"

Her face warmed at the affectionate nickname. Evan had used it last night when he thanked her for the meal. When she woke this morning, she'd been surprised she'd slept and even more surprised to have Evan be her first thought. She had to tell someone about the conflicting emotions she'd been feeling. Chloe would tell her she was in love and Michelle would scold her. So she chose her nana.

"That's a mighty hefty silence there, sweetheart. You want to tell me what's on your mind?"

Jo sat on the barstool as her grandmother slowly mixed the cocoa and cream for the hot chocolate. The smell reminded her of the winter evenings she spent at her grandmother's house as a young child. It had been her refuge. The place where she was free to be Jo Baker and not simply Victoria Baker's tomboyish daughter.

"I had dinner with Evan last night." As the words escaped her mouth, her heart picked up speed.

A twinkle entered her grandmother's eye. "I see. And how did that come about?"

Jo told her everything, from the run in at the store all the way up to her dropping him back off at the B&B.

"You seem a little shy with the details." Her grandmother grabbed two mugs and set them on the counter.

Jo picked one up with a grin. "You still have this?" she motioned to the World's Best Nana mug, complete with a picture of the two of them. The mug had to be at least twenty years old.

"Of course. I don't get rid of anything my grandchildren or great-grandchildren gift me with. Now, hand it over so I can spoon your cocoa into it."

Her grandmother returned the mug to her and Jo added some marshmallows and chocolate shavings. She took a sip, careful not to burn her tongue.

"Mmm. You make the best hot chocolate, Nana."

"That's because I have the sense to use cream. None of that skim milk in this house." Her grandmother chuckled, the lines in her face deepening from the movement.

"It's a good thing I'm active."

"Humph. I'm still alive and in great health, which I didn't have to run to maintain."

"I know, I know. You just eat fresh food."

"Don't you patronize an old woman, Jo Ellen."

She winced. Her grandmother rarely used her first and middle name. Only when she was annoyed with her. Grabbing her mug, Jo moved into the living room, sinking onto the floral couch. She took off her boots and settled her feet onto the old brown and white trunk masquerading as a coffee table.

"Now are you going to give me more details other than the fact that you two ate dinner and talked?" Her nana peered at her over the rim of the mug.

Jo sighed. She wanted to tell her but was afraid to give voice to her thoughts. *But that's why you came to Nana and not your friends.*

"Okay. He apologized a few weeks ago and asked to be friends." She stared at her grandmother, willing her to understand the significance of the event.

"Did you accept it?"

She nodded, feeling the tears threatening to escape. "I did." Her voice came out husky from the unshed tears. "I couldn't believe how sincere he sounded. But I didn't want to be friends."

"Why not?" her grandmother fired back.

"Don't you remember how many times I came over after school crying my eyes out?" She knew Nana wouldn't immediately take her side, but it still stung.

"Of course I do, JoJo, but how long are you going to let others steal your joy?"

"Well, that's why I finally caved in. I'm so tired of walking around with the hurt of it."

"You've always been one to lug more than you ought to. Why do you suppose that is?"

Jo took a sip of her drink, hoping it would stall the conversation. She had no words.

"Seems to me," her grandmother continued, "that if you'd let the good Lord do His job, you wouldn't have such a burden upon your little frame."

She snorted. She couldn't help it. No one had ever accused her of being little. Then again, if her Nana was comparing her stature to her beloved God, she guessed she was.

"Do you care for Evan?"

"As a friend." She shrugged. "Maybe more, once upon a time."

"And there's the truth, JoJo. You've carried a torch for that young man so long I'm surprised it's still burning."

"Oh, Nana."

"Don't you 'oh, Nana' me. I know how much his behavior in high school broke your heart. And I know the shock you must have experienced when he returned. But if he has the guts to apologize and the desire to make roots in Freedom Lake, then stop wrestling with 'what-if' and look at what's in front of you. If he's offering friendship, then take that step. If he offers more, follow. Don't be a fool."

Jo ran her fingers through her hair. The weight of her grandmother's words seemed to dance in the air. It reminded her of the caterpillar's floating words in Alice In Wonderland. Except obviously the words were dancing in the steam of their hot chocolate.

"What if he turns on me again?" she murmured.

"Then shame on him. Don't hold out forgiveness or friendship contingent on another's behavior. The good

Lord wants us to treat others the way we want to be treated. You don't want him withholding his friendship, do you?"

"No," she replied with a shake of her head. However, the thought of Evan turning back into the boy who ridiculed her in front of his friends paralyzed her. On the other hand, the thought of him never smiling at her like he did last night made her heart ache.

I still like him.

Okay, maybe it was more than like, but she refused to go down that path. For now, she would concentrate on being a friend. Taking a sip of her hot chocolate, Jo tried to erase the memory of his hand brushing her hair away. The tingle of awareness that had left goose bumps on her arms last night rose again with the memory. She closed her eyes, pleading with whomever would listen to keep her from falling in love with someone who had the power to bring her to her knees.

～

Evan rolled down the hallway to answer the door. He thought he would finally have peace and quiet, but evidently a tourist needed a place to rest. His mother and father had left for a lunch date since they had no guests.

Did they forget someone?

He swung the door open with one hand and rolled back with the other. The shock of seeing his friend filled his being.

Guy looked weary. But the two beautiful little girls holding a hand on either side of him rocked back and forth with impatience. One smiled shyly, while the other wiggled, moving Guy's hand back and forth.

"Hey, man, long time no see."

"Hey, Ev. You looking good, man."

"It's great to see you. Come on in. We can go to the kitchen. I'm sure my mom has some food out we can help ourselves to."

"Thanks, man." Guy shook Evan's hand and slid his palm out with a snap.

They both chuckled, but Evan could hear the apathy in Guy's laugh. What had happened to his fun-loving friend? "Have you moved in or did you just get here?"

"We got in last night. I hired movers. They already unloaded all our stuff at the house. I wanted to stop and say hi before I got too bogged down. Ya know, let ya know I'm in town." As Guy continued, his voice became thick and his words slurred into one another.

His boy was in some serious need of sleep. "How about you chill in one of the guest rooms? I'll keep the girls busy. I could pull a movie up on my laptop or something."

"Nah man, I don't want to burden you, just wanted to say hello."

"Look, no one else is in the house, so you won't be bothering me. Did you drive straight through?"

"No, but I did drive fourteen hours yesterday, so I'm a little worn out."

"I'll say. Go, you remember the green room?" At his friend's nod, he continued. "Great, go take a nap." Evan glanced at the girls and then his friend. "Which one is which?"

Guy chuckled. "Rachel's in the purple and Rebekah's in the pink."

"Got it."

Guy looked at them as they sat munching on cookies at the dining nook. "*Mes petites choux-choux*, Uncle Evan is going to let you watch a movie so I can take a quick nap. Be good, 'kay?"

"Yes, Daddy," they chorused.

He spun around and headed for the guest rooms.

Evan looked at the little girls as they ate, grinning and giggling mischievously. Something told him his friend couldn't nap quickly enough.

Chapter Seventeen

$\mathcal{M}$ ichelle sat on the bench at the foot of Jo's bed. "You really think we should rent out one of the bungalows?"

"Definitely. Those townhomes were nice and all, but you'd be paying more money just because no one has ever lived in them. Is it really worth it? Plus, wouldn't you like to have more money to put into your business?" Jo pulled her boot strings, wrapped them around the top and tied them tight.

"True. But you know how I am about where I live."

"Of course I do. But you also know I wouldn't pick a home that wasn't sound. Many of the seniors in Freedom Lake are moving into the senior community. Because of that, you have a lot of homes going up for sale or rent. Nana knows every senior who's making the switch."

"Okay. I don't want to buy anything, but I'll check out one of the homes for rent."

"Great. We'll take my truck. I found the perfect one, thanks to my nana."

As they drove to the bungalow, Michelle brought Jo up to speed on the progress of her business. She had submitted the paperwork for the permits and signed the lease paperwork that Mike gave her.

Funny how she had the same realtor as Evan. All Michelle needed was a business name. "What? You didn't have one in your business plan?"

"I did, but I don't really love it."

"Well, what was it?"

"Thomas Law Firm."

"Hmm, yeah, it's a little boring, but I've never heard of a law firm not named after its lawyers."

"That's because the lawyer's name has to be in there somewhere. It's the law."

Jo laughed. She glanced at Michelle wondering if she should bring up the subject of Chloe.

"Okay, I see you staring at me even though you're supposed to be driving." Michelle swatted at Jo's leg. *Couldn't hurt.* "Did you talk to Chloe?"

"Yes, I did."

"Well?!" Jo exclaimed.

"Nunya." Michelle stuck out her tongue.

"Get out of here with that."

Her friend made the motion of zipping her lips.

"You're really not going to tell me?"

"Nope. I'm not. Just know that everything is okay."

Jo shook her head. Since when did Michelle keep her mouth shut? She thought she'd want to talk about the healing process. Why wouldn't her two friends tell her about them making up? Well, if Michelle wouldn't talk, she wouldn't talk. Jo concentrated on driving to the bungalow.

They pulled up in front of a bungalow with tan siding. The backdrop of trees arrayed in their autumn glory gave it the look of a storybook cottage. It didn't hurt that the owners had a white picket fence around the home. The windows were framed with dark blue shutters and empty flowerbeds begged for someone to fill them again.

"Oh, Jo, I love this. It's so quaint."

"See, I told you."

Jo dug the spare key out of her pocket. The owner knew her grandmother, who had vouched for Jo. She loved that the residents were welcoming enough to pass around spare keys. Where else could she live that would have the same sense of community?

She opened the door and paused, letting the quiet of the home and the sound of the wind envelop her with peace and calm. Living in the woods would probably give them a sense that they were far away from civilization. As she stepped further into the home, the various shades of brown-and-white décor greeted her.

"A little masculine, but not bad. Are they going to remove the furniture?" Michelle asked as she walked from the living room toward the dining room.

"Yes, the owner's putting them into storage until his kids can come back to see if they want any of it."

"Come look at this table!" Michelle called out.

The black wooden dining table sat in the center of the room with six tan, leather chairs stationed around it.

"Maybe he could let us use this until we get one. I don't have one big enough for this space."

They looked through the rest of the place. It was a nice size at fourteen-hundred square feet. The living room divided the home into a split floor plan. When Jo told Michelle the rental price, her friend's hazel eyes sparkled with excitement.

As they made their way back to the Baker residence, Jo couldn't help but smile. She was entering a new phase in her life and her best friend was along for the ride.

⚬⚬

The trees lined the roadway, swaying back and forth in the autumn wind. Jo took in the beautiful colors, in awe of the splendor. Before she knew it, they would be bare and blanketed in white. She turned onto the gravel road leading to her old apartment. The one Chloe now occupied.

When she had moved out last year, it had been perfect timing for Chloe whose old home had burned down due to faulty wiring. Unfortunately, it had been one of those events that couldn't be prevented.

The home had belonged to Chloe's grandmother, left to her when she had passed away.

Chloe had lived there except for the brief time she left Freedom Lake to attend college. Jo smiled as she saw Michelle's car in the parking lot. For the first time in twelve years, the three of them were going to have a sleep over. Grinning, she grabbed her duffel bag and exited the warmth of her truck.

She'd been surprised when Chloe suggested it and floored when Michelle agreed. Obviously, the two truly had made amends. She hoped it would be fun. If she were a praying person she'd pray that Chloe wouldn't mention God, but that was like asking her not to breathe. Then again, there was the whole absurd point of praying for someone to *not* talk about God. She shrugged and stepped onto the cobblestones leading to the first-floor apartment.

The flowerbeds lining the path were littered with leaves. For a moment, she wished that spring was on its way. The way the blooming flowers brightened this corner of the Freedom Lake Woods always dazzled her. She shook her head, wondering at the sentimentality of her thoughts.

"Nothing ever stays the same," she said under her breath. She knocked on the door.

"JoJo, right on time!" Chloe's dark black eyes lit up as a wide grin stretched across her face. She held out her arms and Jo leaned in to hug her. How she loved this woman. She was the kindest, most genuine and loyal friend a girl could ever ask for.

"Believe it or not, Chelle's already here. She's making fairy juice."

"Oh wow, I haven't had that stuff in years."

"Well, head to the kitchen before she drinks it all."

Jo made her way past the living room, noting the yellow and gray theme. Funny how it fit Chloe. Jo much preferred deeper, rich tones. She walked into the kitchen and felt like she stepped into the 50s.

"Girl, I almost forgot how awful this kitchen was." Jo shook her head. The yellow fridge and appliances were an eyesore.

"It fits perfectly because of the yellow," she protested.

Michelle guffawed, fairy juice squirting from her mouth. She wiped it with the back of her hand. "Chlo," she said, using the affectionate nickname of their past, "just because it's yellow doesn't make it right."

"Are you sure you didn't spike that?" Chloe squinted her eyes at Michelle.

Jo reached for a cup and took a sip. "Nope, not spiked. Besides we promised we'd never do that to one another."

The fairy juice was made from rainbow sherbet and sprite. When they were young, Jo's older brother spiked it. When Nana found out, her displeasure had been swift. As punishment, Darius had to redo her entire garden that summer without any assistance. No one had dared try it again.

"So, what's everyone been up to?" Chloe looked at them expectantly.

"You already know I'm going to renovate Evan's house. And of course, I'm moving in with Chelly here."

Chloe stared at Michelle who was drinking her second cup. "Oh fine, I'm moving in with JoJo and opening my own law firm. Your turn."

"I'm enjoying having my two best friends back together again." Chloe took a sip of the juice and gave Jo a cheeky grin. "I saw you at the grocery store. You looked awfully cozy," she said in a singsong voice.

"Who were you with?" Michelle raised an eyebrow trying to look regal while getting a fairy juice mustache.

"She was with Evan." Chloe continued in her singsong voice.

"What? Doing what with him?" Michelle asked.

"That's what I want to know." Chloe said.

"You're just going to talk about me like I'm not here, huh?" Jo folded her arms as the two talked back and forth.

"Of course, we'll talk to you. How else can we find out what went down?" Michelle rolled her eyes.

"We decided to be friends, and I invited him over to eat. That's it." She grabbed her cup and walked out of the kitchen.

She smiled when she heard their shrieking exclamations. She settled down on Chloe's yellow couch and grabbed a gray chenille blanket. The girl always had the A/C cranked to sub-artic temperatures.

Chloe followed quickly behind, taking a spot on the love seat. Michelle sat next to her.

"You can't walk away after that bomb." Michelle crossed her legs under her. "Since when do you want to be friends and why feed him? You know men are like cats, feed them and they never leave." She smirked at Jo. Only Michelle could make a kindergarten sitting position look regal.

Jo felt like she should curtsy before speaking. "He apologized, and I got tired of holding a grudge. Then we happened to be eyeing the same slice of salmon, so I decided to test the truce and invited him over." She shrugged. "Nothing to it. I doubt he'll show up daily for food." She chuckled at the image to hide the goose bumps that ran up her arms.

"But you like him, don't you?" Chloe studied her.

She tried not to squirm under her gaze. Chloe had a sixth sense about her that had always unnerved Jo. "Sure, as a friend." She winked at Chloe and then quickly changed the subject.

When Chloe's instinct alarm went off, no one was safe. The girl was more rabid than a dog with a bone. Jo slowly calmed as the conversation veered toward shopping and away from her supposed romantic interest in Evan.

◡◡

The room swayed a little as Evan clung to the crutch. He shifted it under his left arm trying to get comfortable. He felt a little disoriented at his current height, but it also brought a sweet familiarity to him. Never again would he tease a short person.

Evan knew the crutch was a necessary evil, but he would be so happy when he could get rid of it. Drew made Evan promise to practice with it daily, so he would be ready for the prosthetic. Apparently, his remaining leg was weak and needed to remember how to walk again.

Which was why he stood in the hallway trying it out. He glanced at his chair, surprised at the longing to just sit in it and wheel around. And to think he thought the prosthetic would be a crutch. He hadn't realized how dependent he was on the wheelchair.

His mother had been so excited when he walked through the door yesterday. He knew it was more so because he wasn't sitting around moping anymore. Come to think of it, he was just as excited. He'd wasted plenty of time being angry at the world.

He hadn't told Jo about getting a prosthetic and wondered how long he could prolong it. They were supposed to meet this Friday to verify everything, since he was getting the keys next Monday.

Evan continued walking back and forth through the hallway with the crutch. *Thank You Lord for knocking some sense into me.* He smiled as peace warmed his heart. He stopped, thinking he heard a knock at the door.

A second passed. Then another.

The doorbell pealed through the air.

Great. He turned to make his way down the hall toward the front door. Since his parents had gone out for a lunch date, he'd have to answer it. He pulled on the door, leaning heavily onto the crutch. He had tried to walk faster, so that whoever was waiting didn't have to do so for very long. Now the exertion weighed him down, and the soreness in his armpit and right leg pained him.

Evan stilled as he met the eyes of the visitor.

Not, Jo! Couldn't it have been anyone but Jo, Lord?

He forced a smile. "Hey, come on in." What was she thinking? Did she think he looked ridiculous?

"Hi, I had some questions for you that couldn't wait until Friday. I hope you don't mind."

He shook his head, thankful she still treated him normally. She looked beautiful in her red beanie and red-and-white puffer jacket. Her cheeks glowed from the cold. He shivered as the Indiana wind made its way inside.

"No problem. Do you mind if we sit?" He asked, gesturing toward the parlor. He didn't think he could make it to the library or kitchen.

"Certainly. That will be perfect." She held up her laptop carrier. "That way I can show you my thoughts and designs on this baby."

Evan stepped carefully. He didn't want her to know he was practicing walking, but she didn't seem to act as if it was out of the ordinary to see him upright. He hated that her face seemed to be an impenetrable mask; he never knew what was going on in her mind.

Jo sat her laptop on the coffee table. He watched as she busied herself. She reached for something in her laptop bag, and he saw her hand shake. Was she nervous?

He'd never seen her any other way but calm and collected. Should he bring up the crutch or ignore it?

Evan slowly sat down across from her and set the crutch next to the couch. He wanted to breathe a sigh of relief as he sank into the cushion, but he didn't want Jo to know how exhausted he was.

Guess Drew's right.

He should have been out of the wheelchair a long time ago. The desire to lean back and rest his head washed over him. Instead of giving in, he leaned forward to engage Jo in conversation. "So, what questions do you have for me?"

"I wanted to make sure I had all your design changes inputted into my renovation software. I put in all the fixtures that we picked out for the kitchen as well as the countertops and cabinets. I also added pictures of the furniture we chose for the bedroom, living, and dining rooms. I thought it would help you to visualize the space, in case you had any questions or wanted to make changes."

She turned the screen around. "Can you see it?"

"Not really. There's enough room on this couch if you want to move over here."

"Sure." She bit her lip and came around.

A feminine scent filled his senses. What was that? She didn't seem like the type to wear perfume. He leaned in a little, trying to get a whiff of it, but she scooted away. Was he making her nervous? The thought sparked his mischievous side. He leaned a little closer, pretending to get a better view of the laptop. Evan had to smother his grin when Jo scooted away once more. If he didn't know any better, he'd believe his nearness was getting to her.

Jo turned the laptop toward him and pointed to the screen as a view of the kitchen came up. "Here you go."

He turned his focus to the screen. "That looks incredible. I love the browns in the granite countertop; however, I've been thinking. Isn't granite high maintenance?"

"It can be. If you want a low maintenance option, you could go for one made of quartz. It's an easy change."

Evan nodded, mulling over the option. "That sounds good. Can I get one with the same brown tones?"

"Definitely." She smiled at him, and he felt like he won a prize. Maybe now was the time to bring up the possibility of a prosthetic.

"Jo, there's something I should probably mention."

"What is it?" Frown lines appeared on her forehead. She looked so worried.

And completely adorable because of it. "I don't think I'll need all of the wheelchair-accessible standards. I'm actually trying to be fitted for a prosthetic."

"Really? That's great! When will you be fitted? Is that why you have the crutch? How come you haven't said anything before?"

His mouth dropped open. Never had he heard Jo ask this many questions that had no relation to her job. He guessed the mask was just that.

"Um, too many questions?" Jo asked cautiously.

"No," Evan leaned back on the couch. "Just surprised you were interested in the process. I almost didn't think you noticed I was standing. You didn't even flinch." Evan stared at her, trying to figure out exactly who Jo Baker was.

"I care. I just didn't know if you wanted to talk about it. You never said anything when we had dinner last week."

Was she angry? "I kind of wanted to surprise you, but then I thought it might affect the plans for the house, so I brought it up."

"Why would you want to surprise me?"

He swallowed, feeling embarrassed. *Why did he?* "I guess I care what you think. You aren't angry, are you?"

"No. I'm happy for you." She laid a hand on his arm and looked into his eyes.

His pulse stammered.

"I'm so glad you turned off the angry-Evan mode."

And just like that, she moved away, putting more distance between them.

He wanted to call her back, but followed her prodding and picked up the conversation. "Angry is an understatement. Thankfully, God helped me let that go." He paused as her body froze and the mask dropped into place.

What in the world is that about?

Chapter Eighteen

*A*t the mention of God, Jo froze. *Not him too!*

Evan continued talking. "He got me to see that the anger was hurting me and those I lashed out at. I knew He would allow me to be angry and not turn His back on me. People who say they'll be there for you don't offer that same guarantee."

Jo tilted her head. In all the years she had known him she had never heard him mention God, let alone with such affection and awe. She studied his features, taking in the slightly bushy eyebrows paired with a nose a tad bit too wide. Yet, the slight imbalance in his features didn't detract from his good looks. And his grin…it made her insides quiver with longing. His perfect smile just added to his charm. The desire to be near him collided with her desire to distance herself from God talk.

Wait a minute, you're not interested. Business but friendly, remember?

She shook herself as his words sunk in. "What do you mean that you could be angry with Him? Why would He allow that?"

That didn't make any sense. Her mother had taught her and Vanessa from an early age that God could strike them down at any moment. As she grew older, Jo had learned that wasn't true. Her mother was the most hypocritical person she had ever known. And still, she remained standing. But the one person Jo had depended on had been allowed to die. As far as she could tell, God seemed to be hypocritical as well.

Evan looked at her as if gathering his words. He ran a hand behind his neck. "Have you ever heard the Scripture 'I will never leave thee, nor forsake thee'?"

"Sure," she said nonchalantly. "But what does that have to do with you being angry with Him and Him just letting that go?"

"Deep down, I knew He would never leave me. I knew, no matter what I did, He would still love me. But life taught me that others who professed to love me could leave me in a heartbeat. So, instead of being angry with those people, I directed my anger toward God. Instead of punishing me, He loved me. He loved me enough to put people in my life to remind me that He has always been with me and will never leave me. Because of that, I was finally able to let that anger go. Of course, I asked for His forgiveness, because what I did was wrong. And God, being the amazing God He is, forgave me."

"How can that be?" she whispered.

Evan leaned close, laying a hand on top of hers. "How can what be, Jo?"

"How can He love you so much that He put those people in your life but didn't put any in mine?"

She heard his sharp inhale but couldn't focus on him through the tears in her eyes.

"Aw JoJo, God has put people in your life. Maybe you just haven't realized it. What about Chloe?"

What about her? She's always preaching at people. Then again, Chloe always told Jo how much God loved her. "She has been asking me to go to church with her since we graduated high school."

"Is that when you stopped going?"

"Yes, once I turned eighteen my mother couldn't force me any longer. Chloe, however, continued to go…still goes. She and the church are like peanut butter crackers, they stick together."

He snorted.

"I know it's corny, but you've never seen how zealous she can be. It's so frustrating! Sometimes, I feel like she's shoving religion down my throat," she paused. "But, I love her anyway."

"Could it be that God put Chloe in your life to remind you that He still loves you, even though you think you've been abandoned?"

Jo gasped. She'd never told anyone how she felt. How was it that Evan could see right into her soul and speak the words of her heart? Tears spilled over, sliding down her cheeks in abandon.

"Aw man, I didn't mean to make you cry." He tenderly brushed away the tears.

"You didn't," she said with a shake of her head. "I just...I mean...how did you know?!" She got up, pacing back and forth. Her finger quietly found its way to her chain despite the racket of emotion going on in her brain. It felt like it was going to implode.

"I've always been the black sheep of the family, but I could handle it because my dad was there to lean on. Then *He* takes the only person who understood me and left me with *her*!"

The image of her mother appeared larger than life in her mind's eye. It was like the billboards on the side of the highway you wanted to ignore. Only she couldn't escape her mother.

"That woman hates my guts and can't stand that I was the apple of my father's eye. Now she wants me to quit 'my hobby,'" she used air quotes as the memory of one of their spats came forward. "And apparently, I need a real job. Or better yet, just marry the next man with a pedigree and pop out a few grandkids so I won't embarrass her. I know she can't stand it that my dad left the business to me."

She sank back on the couch. Her eyes couldn't focus, the parlor resembling a Jackson Pollock painting through the haze of tears. Suddenly, all the built-up pain from her father's death released in a torrent of sobs. Her cries ripped from her chest, one after the other. She felt the couch dip but the reason for it didn't penetrate the noise of her agony.

Warmth came as Evan wrapped his arms around her. She buried her face into his chest and let the pain of the past year flow out.

∽

The sound of a knock slowly penetrated Evan's dream world. Although he wanted to continue dreaming of Jo, the urgency in the knock wouldn't allow him to.

"Come in." He pulled himself to a sitting position, rubbing the sleep from his eyes.

"Good morning, Son. Sorry to wake you, but you'll never believe who's here." His mother beamed at him, her locks framing her face.

"Santa Claus?"

"Oh, you." She shook a finger at him. "Guy's here. Are you decent enough for him to come in here?"

"I just saw him the other day."

"And you didn't tell me?"

"It's been a busy week, Mom."

"Well, come out and say hello anyway. Maybe he needs something."

Evan glanced down at his white tee and flannel pajama bottoms. He supposed he was presentable enough. "All right, just have him sit in the kitchen. Is my chair outside the door?"

"It is. But wouldn't you rather use the crutches?"

"I think I'm a little sore for that. I'll use them later."

When Evan entered the kitchen, he couldn't hide his grin.

Guy was trying to convince Rebekah to stop singing "Let it Go" with food in her mouth. Or was it Rachel? He couldn't remember who wore purple and who wore pink. He wheeled closer to Guy, who looked up and saw him. Guy still had the worn-out look, but not as bad as the other day. Hopefully, he was getting more sleep.

"Daddy! Rebekah is still singing with food in her mouth."

Guy rolled his eyes. "Rachel, stop tattling. Rebekah, stop singing with food in your mouth."

"Yes, Daddy." The girls said in unison.

Evan suppressed a chuckle. "What brings you by, man?"

Guy rubbed the back of his neck. "Do you know anyone who can watch the girls during the day? I have no idea what I'm going to do with them while I'm working."

Shouldn't he have thought about that before moving back to Freedom Lake? The look of desperation on his friend's face kept his mouth shut. *Do I know anyone?*

"I don't mean to eavesdrop," his mother said. "But I do know someone who could help you with the girls."

"Who?"

"Mrs. Baker, you know, Jo's grandmother."

"Jo's grandmother?" Although Guy and Evan said it in unison, Guy's words were tinged with relief while Evan's were full of skepticism.

"Yes, Rosemary Baker is wonderful with children. She works in the church nursery."

"Considering her age, don't you think twin girls will be a bit much for her?" Evan asked cautiously.

At his question, Guy seemed to deflate. His friend sat down on the breakfast bench as if the weight of the world was on his shoulders.

"Rosemary Baker is an older woman, but you would never guess it by looking at her." His mother threw him a look that made him want to slink down in his chair.

Jeez, it's not like I called her old.

His mother continued talking, ignoring him. "She goes to the senior gym at least three times a week. I think she would enjoy watching them and do a fine job. I wouldn't recommend someone I wasn't sure of."

Guy looked up, hope shining in his eyes again.

"I'll give you her number. She's an honest, forthright woman. If she thinks the girls will be too much, she'll let you know. If she can't do it, I'm sure she'll recommend someone else for you."

"Thank you so much, Mrs. Carter."

"Why don't you give her a call now?"

At his mother's prodding, Guy called Jo's grandmother. Evan prayed she would be able to watch the girls. He knew how much Guy needed the help. His boy hadn't been the same since Charlene passed. There was a cloud of sadness that seemed to constantly follow him.

Gradually, a smile began to form on Guy's face. Relief cloaked him like a garment. He hung up the phone and pumped a fist. "She can watch them. Wants me to bring them by tomorrow so she can meet them."

"That's great, man."

"Sure is. One less thing to worry about."

"Guy, honey," his mom said. "You don't have to worry. God's got this."

At the mention of God, a closed look stole across Guy's face. Evan could visibly see the brick wall going up, letting them know God was not welcome in his life. His heart broke for the pain his friend was going through.

Lord, please don't give up on him. Please help unharden his heart. Evan wasn't sure how Guy could get through life without God, but he prayed God would use him to show his friend the pathway back.

Chapter Nineteen

*Y*es! Jo grinned, sliding her truck into a parking spot right in front of The Space. Though Freedom Lake was a smaller town than most, it still had enough people to warrant downtown traffic...or at least what she considered traffic. As she got out of the car, Jo glanced inside the storefront to make sure Chloe didn't have any customers. She didn't want to intrude on her friend's business.

Michelle was there.

She walked inside, hoping to hone in on the conversation. "Morning, ladies. What are you two up to?"

"Hey JoJo," Chloe said. "Michelle wants me to decorate Thomas Attorney-at-Law."

"You decided on a name?" Jo asked.

"Yes." Michelle answered, a beam lighting up her eyes.

"I like that name a lot better. When did you decide on it?"

"Last night, actually," Michelle said with a laugh. "I couldn't sleep, so I was brainstorming. As soon as it came to me, I was out."

Jo leaned forward to look at the color samples Michelle held. "Have you decided what color scheme you're going for?"

"I'm thinking of colors from the purple family."

"That would be pretty. But do you think that would be too feminine for any possible male clients you may have?"

"Why should she have to hide the fact that she's a female?" Chloe said, a hint of steel in her tone.

"Whoa, no one said she had to hide that she's a female. I'm just suggesting the colors be appealing to anyone who may walk in. Just look at this place," Jo threw her arms wide. "Your color scheme draws everyone in." She looked at Chloe, wondering if something was bothering her.

"Hmm, you have a point," Chloe admitted. "What about orange?"

"Orange?!" Michelle and Jo exclaimed.

"That's a bit much, isn't it?" Michelle looked skeptical.

"Not at all," Chloe stated. "Simply pick muted colors to go along with it, so it won't be overpowering. You can go with white and tan accent colors."

"I'm not so sure. I want people to believe I'm the best choice for the job, that I care about their interest, and that I'm not settling or could be doing something better. Does that make sense?" Michelle looked back and forth between Chloe and Jo.

"Totally."

"Perfect."

Jo laughed at how quick she and Chloe were to soothe Michelle's fears. It almost felt like old times.

"Give me a day and I'll pull up some ideas for you, Michelle."

"Thanks, Chloe."

Chloe turned to Jo. "Now, I know you didn't come here to watch me and Michelle pick out colors for her new business."

"Well, no. I originally came to ask if I could go to church with you one Sunday."

"Really?"

"What?"

Chloe squealed while Michelle scowled.

"Of course, you can come to church with me Sunday." Chloe gave Jo a hug. "You'll love it. It's not like it was when we were kids. Bishop Brown is down to earth. He doesn't look down on anybody and I don't know…he's just real. I know you'll appreciate that."

She put her hands in her pockets and took a deep breath. "I can't promise I'll go more than one time, Chlo."

"That's okay, you know I'll keep inviting you until you show up every week."

What would she do without Chloe's friendship and patience? Gratitude flooded her being.

"What brought this on?" Michelle asked, neck craned with irritation.

"Um, I had an interesting conversation with Evan." She shrugged. "It made me curious."

Michelle gazed at her shrewdly. "What kind of conversation?"

She sat down in the yellow chair across from the desk. This would be a difficult conversation. She and Michelle had always agreed that Christianity was ridiculous.

Michelle sat down next to her, peering at her intently. Chloe went and sat at the only vacant spot, the chair behind her desk. Somehow it seemed like an inquisition and not a chat with her two best girlfriends.

"Well, it started out with Evan telling me about his recent decision to recommit to God. Something he said made me think of God and abandonment. Evan pointed out that He hadn't left after all, and that God put people in my life to point me to Him. He brought up Chloe and it all clicked. After that, I may have fallen apart."

"What do you mean?" asked Chloe.

"I cried."

"You trust him," Chloe said softly.

Jo gazed at Chloe, realizing she saw more deeply than Jo would care to admit. She averted her gaze, not sure she wanted to admit something so personal.

"Girl, you must if you're thinking of going to church because of one conversation." Michelle said with an arch of her perfectly drawn eyebrow.

"But that's just it," Jo said, turning toward Michelle. "It hasn't been just one conversation. I grew up going to church so I heard what they said. Even though I stopped attending, Chloe continued going and speaking to me about God. Even Nana and Evan's mom have been quiet witnesses for the Lord. It just so happened Evan was the catalyst." Amazing how she saw it so clearly now.

Michelle sat back as if appraising the situation. Jo knew Michelle had her issues that would make this tough for her to swallow, but she wouldn't drive in the point. Everyone had their own journey and time table.

"So, you're saying this change isn't as swift as it appears, but has been working in your life this whole time."

"Essentially."

"Hmm. Who gave you that idea? *Evan?*" Michelle slowly twisted the silver ring around her right ring finger.

"It's time, Chelle. It's time to stop running from your hurt and anger and talk to Him again." Chloe looked pointedly at Michelle, who in turn glared at Chloe.

Oh no, please don't let them get into a huge fight again. They just started talking to each other again, God! Jo sucked in a breath at the realization that she'd actually acknowledged Him.

"I just can't let years of hurt go, Chloe, no matter how much *He* wants to work it out for good." Michelle said snidely.

Jo cringed inwardly, bracing for a blowup.

"Then don't let it go. But don't use that as an excuse not to show up either. He can handle your anger."

"Oh, my goodness," Jo said. "That's exactly what Evan said to me. He said he could be mad at God, because he knew that God would never leave him. So he directed all his anger at Him."

Michelle's face drained of color, almost appearing yellow. "I need to go."

"Chelle, don't leave."

Michelle turned and gave her a look of such consternation that Jo immediately sat back down in defeat. She watched her friend walk out of the building, praying that the hurt wouldn't swallow her whole.

~

Evan walked down Main Street at a leisurely stroll, letting the crutch take his excess weight. Today, he would get the keys to his new place. It was ironic that freedom was literally a few steps away. Soon his prosthetic would be in, and then he could really be independent.

A movement out of his peripheral caught his eye. He came to a stop, looking up in time to see Michelle Thomas leave The Space.

She still looks the same.

"Hey, Michelle," he called out. She was just about to get into her vehicle but looked up when he called out to her. He waved.

She slammed her car door and stalked toward him. "What in the world did you say to Jo to make her even consider going to church?"

"Whoa." He lost his footing, trying to step backward. Evan gripped the crutch as he righted himself. *What set her off?* "This is the first I've ever heard of Jo going to church, so forgive me for being a little lost."

171

"She informed me about your little talk yesterday. If you want to be brainwashed and think God can solve all your problems, then fine. But don't go around manipulating my friends to believe that hogwash. Jo was just fine without you trying to psychoanalyze her."

"Was she really, Michelle?"

She stared at him, seething with anger.

"I don't think she was," he continued. "She opened up and shared some of her concerns after I shared with her the healing I've received from the Lord. I wasn't attempting to influence her. I was just sharing a little of my life with her." He cocked his head to the side. "If she wanted to go shopping with you and buy a similar outfit, could I accuse you of brainwashing her?"

"Of course not!" she snapped. "Girls bond over shopping, and I wouldn't make her buy anything she didn't like."

"Then why can't I bond with her over God? Why can't I share what He's done for me without forcing her to believe it?"

"Every Christian has an agenda. You people won't be satisfied unless we're all bowing down and letting others walk all over us. I refuse to believe in a God who would let destruction, unnecessary death, hunger, et cetera, go on."

"Yet you do the same thing."

"What!" She stared at him in shock.

"Have you made any effort to stop world hunger? Have you dedicated your life to medicine to help eradicate disease? What are you doing to stop the issues that plague you so much and make you believe God doesn't exist?"

Her mouth dropped open. Evan would have laughed at her guppy look if the topic weren't so important. He didn't know what life experiences made her so bitter, but he recognized it.

If he could help her let it go, all the better.

Lord, please let my words penetrate the bitter wall encasing her mind and heart. Let her see Your truth and what You have to offer.

She glared at him then whirled around, stomping all the way to her car. He watched her go, saddened by the pain she was in. He knew what it was like to harbor such hurt and resentment. To think that God tossed you aside while your life went in a downward spiral. If she didn't let the pain go, Michelle would head down the same destructive, bitter path that he had been on.

Evan sighed and continued to Mike's office. Her life was in God's hands.

He recalled Michelle's words and the sadness abated. *Jo's going to church!* He wanted to jump and shout, but knew he'd probably land on where the 'sun don't shine,' as his mother would say.

Lord, please let the sermon touch Jo's heart so that she can lay her burdens at Your feet. Thank You so much for allowing my words to help her see You more fully. Please give me the wisdom necessary to continue to share about Your goodness. Lord, I especially thank You for getting my attention and reminding me of Your everlasting goodness. I love You.

He cleared his throat, thankful no one was around to hear his thoughts. That was one of the things he loved most about his relationship with God. To be able to unburden himself of all his thoughts, good or bad, and know that not only was he heard, but he was still loved.

God was good.

Chapter Twenty

$\mathcal{T}$he next day, Jo drove to her Nana's house. Despite already committing to attend church, she still wanted to talk it over with her grandmother. If her logic was faulty, Nana would be able to tell it to her straight. Or affirm her decision. Her thoughts evaporated at the sight of a black SUV with Virginia plates parked in the driveway.

Whose car is that?

She pulled in beside it, eyeing it warily. Freedom Lake had its share of visitors, but no one visited her grandmother besides her. Nerves ran up and down her arms as she waited for her grandmother to answer the door. It creaked open. Her forehead scrunched, and immediately she relaxed her face to smooth away the lines as her mother's voice echoed in her head. *"Don't frown so much, Jo Ellen, you'll wrinkle prematurely."*

Jo pushed the thought away. Right now she was more concerned that her grandmother forgot to lock the door. No town was safe enough to leave the doors unlocked, including Freedom Lake. She stepped into the foyer intending to call out for her grandmother, but froze at the sound of giggling.

"Nana?" she called out, cautiously.

"In the kitchen, Jo."

The sight of her grandmother, Guy and two little twin girls greeted her. *Wait, Guy's back in town?*

"Hello," she said guardedly. She couldn't help but remember all the times his laughter had spurred Evan's snide comments.

"Hey sweetie. You remember Guy, don't you? And these are his daughters, Rachel and Rebekah."

"Hello!" the little girls replied in angelic voices.

"Nice to meet you," she said to the girls. "Guy," she responded curtly.

"Hi, Jo." He rubbed the back of his neck, looking sheepish. "Hey, I'm sorry about the way I treated you in high school."

She stared at him, surprised. *That was a fast apology.* Was it sincere? "Technically, you didn't do anything but laugh and be his amen choir."

"And sometimes that's worse than words."

He walked forward and held out his hand. "Bygones?"

"All right, then." She shook his hand as she tried to decide if she was more shocked he'd come right out and apologized or that she had accepted it.

What was wrong with her? Since when did she make nice? *Since you started thinking about God, apparently.* She shook herself out of her reverie. "Are you visiting or back to stay?"

"Back. I'm the new sheriff." He gave her a grin that hinted at its lack of use. "Your grandmother has agreed to watch the girls for me while I work."

She looked at her grandmother in astonishment. "Really?"

Nana nodded.

Jo turned back to Guy. For the first time, she noted the dark circles under his eyes. He looked thin as well. Who would watch after him? "The girls will be in good hands."

"So I've heard. Come on girls, let's go and let Ms. Baker visit with Miss Jo."

"I wike your name," said one of the little girls.

How in the world did Guy tell them apart?

"And I like your overalls." The other one said. "I want some, but Daddy said I have to dress lady-like." She turned toward her dad. "She's a lady."

Jo hid a smile. *Gotta love the guile of a child.*

"Yeah, yeah. We'll talk in the car."

Once Guy and his daughters left, Jo settled down in her grandmother's living room to share with her the conversation she'd had with Evan. She knew Nana would be able to offer wisdom. Though she was willing to go to church with Chloe, she wasn't sure how she felt about running into her mother or Vanessa. She wasn't overly concerned about Darius. Her brother kept to himself. However, Freedom Lake could feel awfully small when all the townspeople wound up in the same church.

"I can understand your concern, Jo. Just remember the reason you're going to church is to learn more about the Lord, not visit with people."

"Sure, I get that mentally, but isn't interacting with the people another reason to go to church?"

"Of course, part of the beauty of church is to be gathered with those who share the same beliefs, but you have to remember we're still people...aka flawed." Her grandmother laughed.

"Wait, how can you be flawed and a Christian?" That didn't make any sense. She thought becoming a Christian was supposed to cleanse you. Perfect you.

"Honey, being a Christian doesn't make you a perfect person. It makes you a redeemed one. You following me, honey?"

"Not really," she said with a shake of her head. She sighed and pulled her ponytail holder out of her head, rubbing her scalp. "Are you saying people still mess up even if they're a Christian?"

"Yes, dear heart, because you're human. We won't be perfected until we're praising our Lord in the kingdom of heaven. But the beauty of His gift is that we no longer have to pay the price for our mistakes – past, present, or future. We're redeemed, baby girl, redeemed."

Jo brought her legs up, wrapping her arms around her knees. *Redeemed.* What would it be like to live life knowing she'd always be accepted regardless of any mistakes she made? The thought was mind blowing in its simplicity *and* complexity.

"You go on to church, JoJo, and experience the Lord for yourself. Not for who's in there, but for you. Go there searching for answers and He will answer them. Believe me."

She got up and hugged her grandmother, noting her thinning body. She hated to see her Nana age but knew it was the reason she was a fountain of wisdom. "Thank you, Nana. I love you."

"I love you, too, baby girl."

Even though her Nana soothed her fears, Jo couldn't help but think church would turn out to be another place where she'd have to avoid her mother.

∽

He was going to get his new leg. Eager to try the prosthetic, Evan rushed behind Julie as she headed down the hall to her office. He tried to breathe slowly, but his stomach twisted like a corkscrew rollercoaster. He was beyond nervous and had to keep reminding himself to breathe.

"Have a seat, Evan."

He lowered himself into the chair, holding the crutch straight up. At Julie's request, he had left the wheelchair at home. Hopefully, he would walk out of the rehabilitation building unaided. Senior had been brimming with excitement, but Evan needed to do this part alone. So, he asked his father to wait in the waiting room. For some reason, Evan didn't want his dad to see him if it didn't fit properly.

"I'm going to fit your prosthetic to your leg to make sure all is well. After that, I'll show you how to take it off and put it on, and then you'll do it. I also have a pamphlet to answer any questions you have about care and maintenance of the prosthetic and your leg as well."

"Okay," he said quietly. His nerves wouldn't let him speak in a normal tone.

"Are you ready?" She met his gaze, blue eyes shining bright. It was obvious she loved her job, but right now he wished they weren't so piercing. He gave a nod.

She took the leg out of the box, removing the plastic bag.

He gulped. It was go time. He was about to walk unaided. At least he hoped he would.

She put the lining onto his stump and then slid the socket on. He watched, surprised at the fit. It reminded him of putting on his shoe, only higher up.

After a few moments, Julie spoke. "That should do it. Stand up, and let's see how it fits."

He sent a quick prayer upward and inhaled. He slowly exhaled as he stood and settled his weight upon his foot and prosthetic. He swallowed repeatedly, trying to choke down his emotions.

It fit.

"It looks great, Evan." She slid backward on the wheeled stool. "Walk to me so we can make sure."

He took a step forward with his right leg and then with the prosthetic. He continued walking as his brain took over, remembering the command and delighting in the response that the left leg was finally moving. Finally, he had something to receive the commands that his brain had been hardwired for since he was a toddler.

He could walk again.

"Fantastic, Evan!" Julie grinned at him and he grinned back. "All right, let me show you how to take it off and on."

The lesson went swiftly. He had watched many YouTube videos in preparation for this day. He was full of knowledge, thanks to some fellow amputees who were not ashamed but empowered and ready to help those who needed direction. Social media really could be used to benefit others.

He walked down the hall, looking down. Once, the sight of the fake foot and steel attached to it would have made him scoff. But all he could see was independence. Never would he take for granted the ability to walk down the hallway. To stand tall. Or do all the things two legs made possible.

The waiting room came into view. His father sat, staring at the clock. Senior must have been anxiously awaiting the passage of time. Evan wanted to call out to him but didn't want to startle him. He stared at him, willing his dad to sense his presence.

It must have worked because his father's head turned toward him. Evan tensed, waiting for a reaction. His father's eyes became glassy as he stood on shaky knees. Evan blinked rapidly. He hadn't seen his dad cry in years.

His father walked toward him, a slight tremor in his hands. The magazine he had been holding fell from his grasp, his gaze riveted to the prosthetic. The last few steps were carried out in a hurry and Evan found himself wrapped in a bear hug. His father swayed back and forth and for a moment Evan was transported in time to when he had broken his arm and his father had wrapped him up in his arms and told him it was okay to cry. For the tears brought by pain cleansed the soul and made way to heal the hurt.

"It's okay," he rasped.

"I know, Son, I know. Thank the good Lord."

"Since the first step."

"I'm proud of you, boy." His dad chuckled and released him.

He dipped his head in acknowledgement. "Let's go show, Mom."

Chapter Twenty-One

*N*ovember. The month of thanksgiving. For once, Jo had a lot to be thankful for. Today was day one of Evan's renovation. She couldn't wait. There was nothing like taking a sledgehammer to the old and breaking in the new. She lived for it. Which was why she was up and ready at seven this morning.

Normally this time of day would come and go without so much as a blink. She'd be living in la la land, letting her dreams carry her wherever they chose. But when she had a renovation project such as this one, she was like a blackbird in search of the worm. Even though she had moved into her new place over the weekend, exhaustion stayed away. The thought of beginning a new project lured her out from under her down comforter.

She peered out of her blinds, grinning when she saw the sunshine. It might be cold, but a few hours of tearing out old cabinets and she'd be warm in no time. Evan and his parents were going to meet her at his place. They were eager to help. Plus, they wanted to take "before" photos.

Jo donned a gray, long-sleeve Henley and overalls. Sometimes she felt like a cartoon character, always wearing the same type of outfit, but it suited her line of work. She pulled her hair into its standard ponytail and grinned in the mirror. It was time to knock out some walls.

The drive to Evan's house took forever. She always thought how funny it was that a ride to someplace exciting seemed to be long and excruciating, but the drive back went by faster than the speed of sound. The first day of a reno always amped her up, definitely better than taking a vacation.

Turning down Evan's street, Jo smiled as excitement drummed through her. Doing a wiggle in her seat to the beat of the music, she cruised into the driveway. She had her iPhone, with her reno playlist all set to go at the touch of a button, and her trusty tool belt. Some of the guys she hired for part-time labor would be coming later in the day, but for now it would just be her and the Carters.

Evan had agreed that gutting the kitchen first was the best plan. It was a wonderful space but it looked like the seventies had thrown up in it. She doubted Mr. Joseph had bought any new appliances since then. The new cabinets and floors were set to come in a couple of days. She just needed the place empty to install them.

As she strolled to the front porch, she took in the staggered sidewalk. It was on the list to fix as well. Evan wanted a level surface that ramped up and flushed to the porch. Even though he was planning for a prosthetic, he wanted to proceed cautiously. She just needed the forecast to call for no rain before she took on the project. No sense pouring concrete that wouldn't be able to dry.

The smile she'd readied on her face froze as Evan opened the door sans crutches. *Where were they?*

"Hey Jo, come on in. We're in the kitchen. Mom brought some breakfast over." He motioned her in.

She walked by, a little too close, in hopes of catching a trace of his cologne.

"I think she made so much due to nerves. The way she's acting, you'd think this was her first renovation."

"She's just excited," Jo said, her voice coming out a little husky. She cleared her throat. Should she ask him about the crutches? Nah, maybe not. "Are you ready for the renovations?"

His eyes lit up with his smile. "Definitely." He shifted, his hands nestled in the bed of his pockets.

She bit her lip, the question hovering, begging for entry.

"Do you want to eat before we start?" He motioned toward the kitchen, looking expectantly.

"Where are your crutches?" She held her breath, not caring that she blurted the question without any kind of class or subtlety.

He leaned forward and grinned.

My heart. She couldn't breathe.

"So you noticed, huh?" He lifted his left pants leg and showed her a steel colored artificial limb. "I don't need them now." He grinned broadly and his cheekbones popped out.

"That's wonderful!" *And so is your smile!*

She blinked. Since when was she noticing his smile? Or his cologne? Or the way his eyes turned to dark amber when he was happy?

"I was a little worried it would be difficult since it's been awhile since my accident and surgery. But so far so good."

"Wow." Jo had never seen him happier. "How do you feel?"

"Redeemed."

There was that word again. "Come again?"

"It's a song by Big Daddy Weave. Listen to it sometime. It describes my feelings perfectly. God is good, JoJo. God is good."

"Okay, I'll check it out."

"Great." She turned to make her way to the kitchen. Before she finished the first step, Evan grabbed her hand.

"Wait a second," he murmured.

She froze, staring at his hand holding hers. The difference in their shades was subtle and oh-so fascinating. She watched as his thumb lazily ran back and forth on the back of her hand. She lifted her eyes as his voice penetrated the longing that strummed a chord in her heart.

"I heard you were thinking of going to church. Is that true?" His eyebrows dipped low.

Was he concerned? Did he care? Not just about her soul but Jo, the person? "Yes, that's true. Where did you hear that?" Why did her voice sound so strange? Why did her mouth feel parched?

"Michelle."

She let out a laugh, humor absent from it. "She's not too happy with me. She gave me the cold shoulder this weekend."

"How so?"

"We moved in together. Temps in the house were pretty frosty." Had been ever since the night he held her and let her cry.

"Oh wow. Do you feel better than being at your mother's house?"

"I will once Michelle stops sulking. You'd think I became a nun the way she's acting. I told her I would try one service. I look at it as investigating, for lack of a better word."

"Well, if you have any questions, please ask. I'd be happy to help you investigate." He winked at her, dropped her hand and headed for the kitchen.

She stared at her hand, noting the sameness. It hadn't changed. Yet the feeling coursing through it staggered her. She felt like her heart had literally been touched. *All because he touched me.* She shook her hand, trying to jar the feeling, but her mind replayed the pattern Evan's thumb had followed while holding her hand.

∾

Evan grabbed a cup of coffee as Jo plopped her toolbox on the kitchen counter. Maybe if he gripped the cup hard enough, his hands wouldn't shake. He didn't know what made him grab her hand like that, but once he had he couldn't let it go. His mind still recalled the softness of her skin. The smoothness of it had shocked him, yet he had still felt the calluses on her palm that came with her job. The dichotomy between the two fascinated him. Jo always represented strength and confidence. But with one touch of her hand, he'd been reminded of the one thing he'd tried to forget: Jo was a beautiful woman.

Sure, she didn't dress like the stereotypical female but that wasn't an issue. When her big brown eyes locked onto his, he felt the need to prove his manhood. He wanted to sweep her off her feet, listen to her and take care of her every need. And he desperately wanted her to see him as a whole man.

Evan heaved a sigh. His feelings could no longer be denied. *I like her, really like her.* She stood there, answering his parents' questions, while his mind tried to wrap itself around his emotions. Instead, he found himself captivated by her. The way her eyes lit up when she talked construction was beyond sexy. What could he do to make her eyes light up like that? Would she laugh at him if he asked her out?

He gulped the coffee, trying to still his thoughts. Just as quickly he spat it out, coughing as his tongue tingled.

"Are you all right?" Jo asked, concern in her eyes.

"You okay, sweetie?" His mother asked.

His dad just grinned in amusement.

"I'm fine. Wrong pipe." He wiped his mouth with a napkin.

Although the women were oblivious to his thoughts, he could tell by the look in his dad's eyes that Senior knew exactly what he'd been thinking.

"So shall we get started?" Anything to divert the attention away from himself.

"I'm ready when you are, homeowner." Jo smiled at him.

It took all his strength not to take the look further. He needed to make sure she'd be interested before he went all soft over her.

She held up a sledgehammer and explained how to use it without injuring themselves. Evan got the first swing since it was his house. He smiled in satisfaction as half of the kitchen cabinet fell to the floor. His dad went next, removing the remaining half. When his mother swung, their laughter couldn't be contained. The small hole left from her swing seemed paltry.

"No laughing," Jo said. "Not everyone is naturally gifted. This next one is for you, Mrs. Carter." She winked at his mother and then took a swing.

Evan's jaw dropped as a few of the remaining cabinets came tumbling down. *She could hit like that?*

"You play ball, Jo Ellen?" His father asked.

"I sure do, Mr. Carter. My dad taught me."

"He was a fine man, fine man indeed. Did he teach you how to swing like that?"

She grinned. "Sure did."

"You'll have to join the intramural league when spring hits."

"Sure, sounds fun." She turned to look at Evan.

He gulped. She really was beautiful.

"I hope your swing will improve by then." She winked at him.

"Oh," his mother said, laughing hysterically. "You've met your match, son."

"All right, all right. It's not my job like it is hers."

He gestured for her to continue.

The rest of the gut job went smoothly. There were some good-natured jabs tossed between the four of them, but Evan didn't mind. It had been awhile since he had enjoyed himself. Surprisingly, he loved watching how Jo interacted with his parents. *But why do I care about that?*

He shook the thought loose. He couldn't help but compare his parents' interaction with Jo and how they had behaved around Brenda. They had always remained aloof, claiming that Brenda was just too hard to get to know. But judging from the instant camaraderie between them and Jo, he had to wonder if Brenda had been the problem.

Had he been too blindsided by her good looks and charm to notice the selfishness running through her veins? He thanked God for opening his eyes.

May I never be blind again, Heavenly Father.

Chapter Twenty-Two

$\mathcal{J}$o opened her blinds. The first snow of the season had arrived. The quietness calmed her and the blanket of white awed her. Snowfall in November wasn't a big surprise, but she wasn't ready for winter yet. It restricted her ability to enjoy the outdoors, since she wasn't overly fond of the cold. If she couldn't go anywhere without access to heat, she didn't go outside. Thankfully, there were no outside projects scheduled for the day because it was Sunday.

As usual, she had the day off because most of her clients were of the religious type and didn't want her working on their homes on the Lord's Day. However, today, Jo would be joining those clients and taking a journey out in the cold to hear Bishop Brown speak at Freedom Lake Tabernacle.

She turned to gaze at her reflection in the mirror. Would her outfit meet with the approval of the elders in church? It had been so long since she'd gone. What was the dress code nowadays? And did they still have elders, now that they were a non-denominational church? They must—she doubted the elders from the Baptist church would have left just because the church came under new leadership.

Jo turned to the side and back to the front again.

"You look just fine, Jo, it's not a beauty pageant."

She turned at the sound of Michelle's voice. Jo couldn't decide what was more surprising, her friend talking to her or the outfit she wore. Michelle stood in the doorway in a black pinstripe suit with a purple silk blouse.

"Wow, don't you look nice and professional. Where are you going?"

"I thought I'd tag along with you and Chloe."

Jo arched an eyebrow. *She was going to church?*

"Don't say anything." Michelle crossed her arms in front of her.

"Okay." Jo paused.

How could she silence her brain when it was screaming in shock? Michelle had been horrified when she mentioned going to church. What changed her mind? Instead of asking, she focused on her outfit. "Do you think this looks okay?" She gestured to her black slacks and red sweater. Her hair lay parted on the side, hanging straight down. No ponytail today.

"You look fine, JoJo. Come on, let's go. And I'll drive of course," Michelle said with a smirk.

Jo shook her head and followed her friend out the door.

～～

The atmosphere of the church was more charged today than last Sunday. Maybe the Holy Spirit was moving through the place but, then again, maybe it was his own excitement. Last week, Evan had been in his wheelchair at the end of the aisle. This time, he stood while listening to the melodic sounds of the choir.

Thank You, Lord.

As the song came to an end, the congregation clapped and sat down. He scanned the crowd, enjoying the look of peace on people's faces. He stilled as he noted that Chloe had visitors this week.

She's here.

Surprise, gratitude, and happiness flooded his being. Jo actually came. More shocking: Michelle sat next to her. He turned to Darryl to point out the girls, but his friend's gaze had already found Chloe. The boy looked like a sad puppy dog.

He leaned close to whisper to him. "Dawg, you gotta stop mooning over her. Just ask her out."

Darryl blinked as if he had just noticed Evan.

"Did you hear me?"

"I heard you. I'm not ready so until then ignore my looks. Besides, I don't see you asking Jo out."

His jaw dropped. He hadn't told anyone of his recent interest in her.

"Man, don't give me that fake look of surprise. You've been sweet on Jo since we were kids. You just thought you were too cool to like her in high school. Your loss." Darryl pointed to Jo shaking hands with one of the eligible bachelors of Freedom Lake.

Deep down he knew the guy was probably just welcoming her to church, but that didn't stop the jealousy from running through his veins.

～

Bishop Brown's message on "Doing Right Regardless" intrigued Jo. Of course, she'd always tried to do right by others, but she never thought of it in the context of religion. He cautioned the congregation on judging a group of people based on the actions of just one person. Everyone was fallible and could make mistakes. He stated that their job would be to do right regardless of whether another person was. This would bring glory to God and be a good testament to those watching.

Jo heaved a sigh. It was like Bishop Brown was speaking directly to her. She had avoided the church and religion like the plague based on one person's actions: those of her mother. If all Christians were like her mother, then Jo hadn't wanted any part of them or their two-faced religion. Now, God was opening her eyes to other viewpoints.

She had the examples of the joyful-and-sincere behavior of the Carters and Chloe—although zealous in her approach—who never spoke badly of anyone. Instead, her friend constantly sought to point others to God. Jo had been so hung up on not ending up like her mother, that in a sense, she had.

Shame rolled over her in waves.

Um, hello it's me. Jo. Well, I don't know where to start, but I will say that I don't know how I feel about church or religion. Evan says You care. He says You put people in my life to remind me of that. And now Bishop Brown is saying I'm supposed to do the right thing regardless of what others are doing. This seems like an impossible task, but I guess following You won't be easy. I'm not sure I'm ready to take that step, but I want You to know I'm listening if You have something to say. Um, Amen?

She looked up and noticed that the service had come to a close. Jo turned to Michelle and leaned in, "What did you think?"

"Interesting." A thoughtful look crept into her eyes. "I've always believed in doing the right thing, but I never equated that to religion. I just assumed most Christians were hypocritical. It never occurred to me that they were struggling everyday like I am. I guess I need to remember everyone can make mistakes."

"Oh, wow, I didn't even look at the sermon from that point of view. I mean I heard him say that, but I was so stuck on doing the right thing regardless if the person next to me was or not."

"Isn't it funny how we heard the same message, but different things spoke to us?"

So true.

The thought that Christians still struggled bothered her for some reason. What was the point of becoming a

Christian if you still wrestled with life's issues? And what did her mother think about the message? Did she ever feel like she was messing up in life?

So many questions and so little answers. Her head hurt from her musings. Perhaps she should contemplate those things later.

Jo got up and made her way down the aisle, with her friends following closely behind. It was surprising to see how many people attended church. She never thought Freedom Lake was that big, but she didn't know half of the people here. Plus, she figured the weather would have kept them in. Then again, Indiana and cold went hand-in-hand for the winter.

"Did you guys enjoy the service?" Chloe asked, looking back and forth between Michelle and Jo.

"Well," Michelle said slowly as if gathering her thoughts. "It did give me food for thought. I don't know how I feel about the music. It was just noise to me really. Sorry." Michelle looked at Chloe cautiously, as if to decide if she had offended her.

Michelle had never been one to believe in religion and after her parents had died she was convinced God didn't exist. What had happened to get her to even step foot in a church? Was she finally tired of hanging on to the bitterness?

"It's hard to get into the music if you don't like the genre or even understand the whole point of worshipping" Chloe stated. "But, I think if you keep coming and get to the point where you believe Jesus is your everything, the music will come together."

"I suppose that makes sense," Michelle said.

Jo wanted to laugh because her tone suggested otherwise.

"What about you, Jo?" Chloe touched her arm.

"I liked the words to the music. It seemed...I don't know...mystical in a way. Like Michelle, I found the sermon intriguing. I'm definitely going to be thinking about it for days to come."

Chloe beamed as if Jo had just won the national spelling bee. They made their way into the hall, although Jo wouldn't call it that. It was huge. It had a café area for people to sit and mingle with one another as well as enjoy the food and beverages laid out on tables situated alongside a wall. The hall even had an information booth with chairs set up behind them for more seating to talk with one another. As Jo looked around, she wondered why she hadn't seen Evan today.

"Good morning, Jo."

Did I just conjure him up?

She turned around. "Good morning, Evan." She took small breaths, trying to calm her nerves. Why *was* she nervous?

"Did you enjoy the message? Do you think it helped clear some things up for you?" He gazed into her eyes as if searching for answers there.

His eyes shined with warmth. *Think, girl!* "Actually, I do think it helped answer some questions I had."

His cheekbones appeared as his lips curved into a smile. She stared, mesmerized.

"I'm so glad. I was hoping you enjoyed the message."

What did he say? She searched her mind. *Oh.* "You saw me? This place is so big. I'd imagine you could lose someone here."

He chuckled. "It is pretty spacious. Hey," he touched her elbow. "If you have any questions, I'd be happy to talk them over with you."

"Would you now?" Michelle interrupted mordantly.

"I would." He answered her, but his gaze never wavered from Jo's.

What was he thinking?

"Would you care to join us, Michelle?" He asked,

finally looking at her. "We could make it a Bible Study."

"That sounds wonderful," Chloe exclaimed.

"I'm in, man," Darryl said, staring straight at Chloe.

Jo did a double take, finally noticing how Chloe refused to return Darryl's stare. *Hmm, what is that about?* She turned back to Evan, who stared at her expectantly. *Oh, yeah, he had said something.* "Are you offering to do a Bible study? And we're all invited?" She waved toward their group, huddled off to the side.

They had never hung out in high school. Did it make sense to suddenly expect them to want to study God's word together? She glanced at Michelle to see if her friend would bow out or cave in.

Her friend arched an eyebrow. "Fine. I'll come. Whose house are we going to have it at?"

"Not mine," Evan said quickly.

Jo laughed in agreement. His was a disaster. The only thing intact was the sidewalk. She'd had a great sunny day a few days ago, allowing her to level it and create the ramp.

"How about mine?" Darryl offered.

Chloe gave him a cautious smile which Darryl returned.

When no one spoke up, Jo did. "Sounds great, Darryl. What day of the week works best for everyone?" Did she hear crickets? What was with this group? "Okay, how about Friday night?"

If they weren't going to respond, then she'd just lead the way. Besides, Friday was her least busy day. Heck, who was she kidding, she never did anything on a Friday night.

The group agreed. After setting the time, the men departed and said good-bye to the women.

"What in the world did we just agree to?" Michelle muttered as they headed for their cars.

Jo got in the passenger side, buckling her seat belt.

She watched as Michelle pulled out of the parking lot. How long could she be silent before bombarding Michelle with questions?

"JoJo, do you mind if I just drive?"

Uh-oh. Michelle only drove when she had something on her mind.

"Not at all. I'll just relax." Jo laid her head against the headrest and closed her eyes, hoping she really could relax. The sermon seemed to echo in her head.

She opened an eye, noticing the car seemed to be picking up speed. Realizing Michelle had turned onto the highway that led to the city, she closed her eyes once again. Hopefully, the girl wasn't planning on driving all the way there. Then again, she didn't have anything planned today so it didn't matter.

"What in the world?"

Jo opened her eyes and glanced at Michelle. "What?"

"You've got to be kidding me." Michelle slowed down and glanced in the rearview mirror.

She looked at the side view mirror and gasped. A Freedom Lake sheriff car was behind them, lights ablaze. Michelle pulled over and rolled the window down, turning off the car in one fell swoop. Jo shivered as the wind whipped into the car. "Girl, you could have waited until the cop appeared before lowering the window."

"Hey, I don't want them saying we didn't cooperate."

Good point.

"Hey, the guy looks black," Michelle pointed out.

Jo glanced back and saw a lanky Black man walking toward the car. She squinted—he almost looked like Guy. Maybe he wouldn't give her girl a ticket. Then again, they had hated one another in high school. Probably more than she and Evan.

He stepped up to the car. "Afternoon, ma'am. Do you know why I pulled you over?"

She wanted to laugh. Cops were the same no matter where you lived. Jo wondered if Michelle figured out who he was yet. His hat was tipped so low you couldn't see his face, but Jo knew that voice anywhere.

"No, officer, why did you pull me over?"

She covered her mouth, holding in a snicker at the lawyer tone of voice her friend used. Yep, Michelle had no clue who she was talking to.

"I clocked you going twenty over."

Guy tilted his hat up and Jo heard Michelle gasp.

"Guy? What in the world are you doing back in Freedom Lake?"

Jo looked down at her hands, wincing at the ice in Michelle's voice.

"I moved back last month. What are you doing here?"

"I moved back last month as well. I just opened Thomas Attorney-at-Law.

"You're *that* Thomas?"

"Yes," she snapped back.

"Then why on earth are you speeding, counselor?"

"I'm sorry. I was…" she stopped.

Jo looked around Michelle's head. Guy looked sick. What was that about? She wished she could see the look on Michelle's face to gauge her mood.

"Never mind. Can I have my ticket, Officer Pierre?"

"Actually, it's Sheriff Pierre."

"What? You're the new sheriff?"

Guy grinned, his white teeth flashing. Jo remembered how often he had flashed that same grin during high school. It had always aggravated Michelle.

"Sure am, counselor."

"Will you please stop calling me that and give me my ticket?" Michelle snapped out.

"Now, Chelle belle, why would I give our newest lawyer a ticket? I'll let you off with a warning." He tapped his notebook against the palm of his hand.

Chelle belle?

"No, thanks, I'd rather not owe you one. Go ahead and write the ticket. I'll wait."

He laughed, his head thrown back. "I promise. You won't owe me one. Besides, it's not like you're the DA."

"Well then, if you don't mind, I'd like to be excused."

He gestured ahead to the empty road. "By all means, go, but drive the speed limit." He winked at her and leaned around her head. "Have a great day, Jo. Tell Nana Baker I'll see her Monday." With a wave, he sauntered away.

She met Michelle's glare and shrank into her seat.

"You knew he moved back?" her friend whispered.

"Yes." Why was that such big news to her?

"You didn't tell me?"

"I didn't know you would care."

Her friend's mouth dropped open and then snapped shut. "You should have told me."

"What's the big deal? It's not like you guys ever dated. He was just one of the guys who bugged us and moved back. I can't call you every time someone comes back to Freedom Lake."

"Whatever, Jo Ellen."

She winced. Michelle only called her that when she was mad. But why on earth would the presence of Guy Pierre make her cool, calm and collected friend go bat crazy?

Jo sighed. So much for a relaxing Sunday.

Chapter Twenty-Three

J o pounded the pavement, letting the rhythm of her breathing propel her forward. Friday arrived on the trail of sunbeams glistening over Freedom Lake. With the lingering snowfall, the lake offered a picturesque view. She normally didn't like to run in the cold, but the looming Bible study had her so full of nerves, she couldn't function. Running would calm her like nothing else could. Chloe and Evan possessed an inner peace that Jo couldn't understand. Maybe she'd ask them how they obtained it.

Peace.

She needed to feel some semblance of calm in this chaotic world. She wanted to be able to talk to her mother or sister and not want to tear her hair out in frustration. In fact, her whole week had been wrought with one frustration after another. The company she had purchased Evan's wood floors from ordered the wrong ones.

Who did that?

It pushed her a week behind schedule. Until they could arrange for the right ones to be delivered, she had no choice but to wait. That meant she couldn't install the cabinets in the kitchen until the floor was in. She wanted to tackle the dining room, but it was using the same flooring as the kitchen. The only places that would differ were Evan's bedroom and the bathrooms. However, those rooms needed to be extended and she couldn't do it with the lingering snow. She was at a stall and it drove her absolutely crazy.

Worse, that was only Monday's sorry state of events.

Tuesday, her mother showed up on the doorstep of her bungalow to object that her wayward daughter had shown up at church without so much as a 'hello.' Jo tried to tell her mother she didn't even see her, but Victoria Baker refused to believe her. Jo had been overwhelmed by the sheer size of Freedom Lake Tabernacle, not to mention the number of people crowding inside. Logically she knew that since the church was the only church in the town more people would be there, she just didn't expect the couple of thousand folks that had appeared.

Of course, that meant that on Wednesday Vanessa had to stop by and throw her two cents into the discussion. Her sister carried on and on about how disrespectful Jo had been by not speaking to them. Jo pointed out that since they saw her, they could have made the first move. Vanessa glossed over that and continued her tirade.

Jo ran harder.

Maybe she should stop trying to be nice. Maybe she needed to start ranting and raving like Vanessa. She looked up trying to keep the tears at bay. *What can I do? Nothing I do is good enough for them.*

Then worry about pleasing Me.

Jo slowed to a jog, looking around her. She stopped running and looked up into the sky. "Is that you, Lord?" she spoke in a reverent whisper.

Yes.

"Wow."

Nothing like this had ever happened to her before. She stared into the clouds, awed at their majesty. If what they said about God was true, then He created this view.

Gradually, Bishop Brown's words scrolled into Jo's mind like a marquee. *"If you do what is right to please God, then He will take care of other people's actions.*

God knows what people say and do to you. The question is what are you saying and doing to others? Are you living out the Golden Rule and blessing those that curse you? Or are you keeping a tally of their wrongs and plotting your revenge?"

"God, how do I do that? How do I *not* focus on their wrongs?"

Jo sat down on a nearby bench. The urge to pray welled inside of her. She didn't know why, but her inner voice screamed for her to pray, to pray through all the headaches and frustrations she'd experienced this week. To pray for her relationship with her family.

To. Just. Pray.

She closed her eyes and every thought that had passed through her mind over the week poured forth. The anger at the floor company, her mother, sister and even her dad for not being around rose heavenward. The more she prayed, the more she found something to say. She didn't know how long she sat there. But when Jo finished, she got up and made her way back to her home, feeling a little lighter. And oddly enough, she hadn't frozen up while praying. It was as if God kept her warm.

Thank you.

◦◦

Senior dropped Evan off for Bible study. As he gave a nod of thanks to his dad, he couldn't help but hope one day he could drive. Then again, Darryl lived right behind his new place, no reason why he couldn't simply walk over. Hopefully, the setbacks wouldn't delay his moving-in date. Jo had expressed her frustration, but he was confident she could get it done.

Evan clutched his Bible as he walked up the driveway. A moan slipped from his lips, his prosthetic chaffing him with every step. He prayed his limb would adjust. The online support groups he joined mentioned that the limb had to adjust to the material, but man, did it irritate his skin.

He looked around and noted the empty driveway. It looked like he would be the first to arrive. Maybe he could answer the door when Jo got here. He'd like to be the first person she saw. With a grin at the thought, he knocked on Darryl's door. A few seconds later, his friend answered, looking frantic.

"Yo man, what's wrong?" He stepped inside slowly, making sure he stepped off with the correct foot.

"Man, I can't figure out what to wear and I burned the bacon-wrapped chicken skewers I was grilling."

"Okay, calm down. First, wear anything. I'm sure she won't care as long as you look presentable."

"Whatever, girls care." Darryl scrunched up his face in irritation.

"How do you know? When's the last time you had a girlfriend?

"A year ago. But trust me, I know they care. They don't want to date a guy who's dressed worse than they are, and not one who is overdressed either. It'll make them feel bad."

That actually makes sense. "Okay then, wear a striped, button-down shirt with your khakis. Did you burn all the skewers or only some?"

"Only some. But I need time to hop in the shower before skewering the remaining ones."

"I can do the chicken while you go shower."

He glanced at his watch. "That'll work. Thanks, Ev." Darryl patted him on the shoulder and raced toward the back of the house.

Evan headed toward the kitchen, passing through the living room. Darryl's house had a great open floor plan. The place had been styled with a lot of black furniture, but it didn't seem too dark thanks to the light yellow walls.

Jo had him thinking about how colors complemented one another. Evan shook his head and looked at the chicken. It was already laid out on the kitchen island waiting to be assembled. He washed his hands and began preparing the food. It had been awhile since he puttered around in the kitchen. His mom had been spoiling him daily.

Just the other day, Evan had told her he needed to eat better before he gained weight. Fortunately, occupational therapy was grueling and helped him work out. What he really wanted was access to an indoor pool. Freedom Lake had become frozen solid, with the last temperature dip into the teens, so obviously he couldn't swim in it. There was a local gym, but it had only the bare necessities when it came to gym equipment. A pool was simply not possible.

Evan walked outside and placed several skewers on the grill. He shivered, glad he had left his beanie on. The sound of the sliding glass door drew his attention. He looked up in time to see Darryl walk outside onto the porch.

"Man, thanks for the help. I feel much better."

"I'm glad." He glanced at his friend with amusement. "I thought only women freaked out over what to wear."

"Ha ha. Go ahead and make fun. You can't tell me you didn't change your shirt a few times, hoping you guessed Jo's favorite color correctly."

"Wrong. I happen to know Jo loves red, which is why I picked this one," he said, pointing to his red checkered, long-sleeved shirt. He thought he looked pretty nice in it too. His sleeveless puffer jacket kept him warm from the winter chill. *Why did Darryl decide to grill?*

"No fair."

"All's fair in love and war, D. Besides, how do you *not* know Chloe's favorite color?"

"It never came up."

He laughed at his friend.

"Yeah, yeah. Hey, watch the chicken. You know what, move out the way."

Evan stepped to the side, amused at Darryl's testiness. Maybe he should just get Jo to set Darryl up with Chloe. Maybe then the boy would get back to being his jubilant, goofy self.

The doorbell rang and his friend's head shot up.

"Hey man, why don't you watch the chicken and I'll answer the door for you?" Evan's palms grew damp at the thought of Jo being behind the door.

"What if it's Chloe? I want to answer the door then."

"All right, I'll look through the peep hole. If it's her, I'll come back and get you or I can just direct her straight out here so you don't burn the skewers again."

The doorbell rang again.

"Fine man, go answer the door."

He grinned in victory and prayed it was Jo.

Chapter Twenty-Four

*T*he moon shined brightly, illuminating the dark street. Thankfully, the front porch light was on. The barren trees swaying in the night gave Jo the heebie-jeebies. It looked like something right out of the Jason movies. If a masked man appeared, she'd pee her pants and die of fright. She knocked on the door and pushed the doorbell again.

Come on, Darryl! Answer the door!

She wasn't really afraid of the dark. It's just that she hated the look of the woods. The hairs on her neck stood on end as she continued to wait. Just when she couldn't take it anymore, the door swung open. She jumped back with a barely suppressed yelp.

"Everything okay?" Evan asked, his eyes filled with concern.

"Yes, sorry, my mind was trying to play tricks on me out here in the dark."

He peered outside. "I guess the woods can be a little creepy. Especially when they're bare. Come on in. Darryl's out back, grilling." He motioned Jo inside.

She took in his appearance. He looked adorable in red. *Wait a minute.* She grimaced. Would her red sweater seem too matchy? Would he think she planned it?

Of course, not! Pure coincidence, Jo.

He held out a hand for her coat and she handed it to him, repressing a sigh as the scent of his cologne greeted her.

"You look great," he said huskily.

"Thanks." *Was it warm in here?* She knew her cheeks were probably red. Lately, she couldn't seem to stop blushing in his presence.

All of a sudden, the foyer seemed incredibly small. She wanted to back up. Instead, she slid her clammy palms down the sides of her jeans and then into her pockets, hoping he would think that's all she was doing. She swallowed as her heart started pounding. It seemed so loud. Could he hear it?

"Do you want to sit outside?

"You look nice, too."

She shook her head when they spoke over each other. Maybe the silence had gotten to him, too.

"I was hoping you'd like the shirt."

He was? "Why?"

"Um, I know your favorite color is red."

So he did wear red on purpose. Before her brain could figure out the importance of it, he cleared his throat.

"I was wondering if you'd like to go out with me tomorrow. There's a nice Italian restaurant in the city I would love to take you to."

He stared at her and she couldn't look away. Didn't she want to keep their relationship purely business? *Yes, but friendly.* Wasn't going on a date pushing the boundaries of friendly? Before she could stop herself, she answered.

"I love Italian."

"I know."

Her mouth dropped open. He wore red on purpose and knew she liked Italian food. How could she say no? "I'd love to go out with you, Evan."

"Great." The grin he gave her turned her insides to mush. She instinctively took a step forward and his grin got wider.

How long they stood there with twin goofy looks on their faces, she'd never know. She only remembered the noise of a throat clearing. It was like getting a bucket of ice water doused on her.

She jumped and turned toward the sound.

Darryl looked at them expectantly. "Evening, Jo. Is it just you?"

"Uh, yeah, Michelle had a late meeting with a potential client. She said she would come as soon as she finished. I haven't spoken to Chloe today, but I'm sure she'll be here soon. She's never late and..." she glanced at her watch. "She has about five minutes before she's on time." She ended the sentence with a grin to ease his worry.

It was so cute how much he liked Chloe. "Are you ever going to tell her?"

"Tell her what," he asked guardedly.

"Tell her you like her, of course."

"You told?" He threw daggers at Evan.

"No, man!" Evan said, holding his hands up.

She rolled her eyes. "Darryl, no one had to tell me. I have eyes. I've seen how you look at her." It was kind of cute.

"Well, I'm not the only one that has a crush. Just ask Evan."

She wanted to laugh. He sounded like a petulant two-year-old.

"As a matter of fact, Jo has an inkling of how I feel, considering I just asked her out."

She looked at Evan who had a smug look on his face. Darryl's look of outrage morphed into surprise.

"What are you two, twelve?" She walked away and headed for the living room. *Neanderthals*.

∽∽

Evan watched Jo's retreating back. Well, he certainly screwed that up. He shook his head, ashamed of himself and how he reacted. Hopefully, she'd forgive him. He looked across the room at his friend. Darryl looked slightly dejected.

"Sorry, man. I don't know what came over me. All of a sudden, I felt like I did in high school. I wanted to prove I could get a girl."

His friend sighed. "I get it. Considering how long you've liked her, I don't blame you for being happy she said yes."

The doorbell rang.

"Maybe there's your chance now. It could be Chloe. I'll leave you to answer the door. Hopefully, Jo will accept my apology."

"Check on the chicken for me too, please."

"Sure thing, D."

Evan headed for the back. He said a quick prayer asking God to help smooth things over with Jo and give him the words he needed to be sincere in his apology. He came to a stop when he saw her in the kitchen. She leaned against the counter, twirling a skewer in her hand.

"Are you going to use that on me?"

She froze and looked at him. "Do I need to?"

"I hope not." He gulped, moving closer to her. "I'm sorry for acting like a jerk."

"I *really* shouldn't be surprised." Her brow furrowed.

"Yes you should. If I've changed like I said I did."

"Evan," she sighed.

The way she said his name curled around him like an embrace. He leaned forward, resting his forehead against hers. "It won't happen again, JoJo."

"It better not." She shoved his chest and walked away.

Evan watched as she greeted Chloe and Michelle. He didn't know if her reply meant she forgave him. *Just gotta pull out all the stops tomorrow, Ev.* If their date went well, maybe it would erase the years of his stupidity.

As the group settled around the dining table, their conversation soon turned into a duel of boys versus girls. In some respects, it was reminiscent of their high school days, which made the evening all the more enjoyable. However, as they put away the laughter and broke open their Bibles, their life issues slowly invaded the light atmosphere.

Evan could only pray the night wouldn't go south.

"So who's going to lead this study?" Michelle asked with a quirk of an eyebrow. Her French manicured nails tapped quietly against the dining room table.

"I'm new to all of this, so I don't think it should be me," Darryl answered.

"Same here," Jo echoed.

Evan looked at Chloe. She was the only steady church-goer here. "Would you like to do the honors?"

"Actually I think you should lead us, Evan. I'll chime in if I have anything to add. Something tells me you know where to go." She gave him a peculiar, knowing look.

The hairs on his arms stood up. Before he had left the house, he'd prayed that God would guide them and lead the study. The first thing that came to mind was Matthew Chapter Eighteen. Now, Chloe was telling him that she knew he had something to share. It could only be the prompting of the Holy Spirit.

He cleared his throat. "Actually I did have a particular place in the Bible I wanted to study with you guys. Let's turn to Matthew Eighteen. It's the first book in the New Testament in case you're unaware of where that is." He cleared his throat hoping he didn't sound pretentious.

Michelle held up her iPhone. "I downloaded a Bible

app on my phone, so I wouldn't hold you guys up."

Evan looked around the table. Jo and Chloe had Bibles open, thumbing through the pages, while Darryl had his phone out. He stared down at his iPad.

Lord, please lead me tonight. "Once you guys get there, look at verse twenty-one through the end. I'll read what it says."

He read in a clear, sturdy voice. When he was done, he set his iPad down and looked around the table. It was interesting to see the various looks on everyone's faces. Darryl looked annoyed. Chloe smiled knowingly. Michelle looked confused. And Jo...well, Jo looked sad.

"What do you guys think?"

Michelle looked up and spoke to the group. "So, we're supposed to forgive someone, no matter how many times they wrong us? Is that the gist of this?"

"In a very simplified way: yes."

"But," she sputtered. "What about someone who murders another person?"

He felt someone stare at him and turned. Jo looked at him, moving her eyes toward Michelle and back to him. Evan didn't know what was going on, but obviously this was important. *Lord, please give me the words.*

"Even a murderer." He answered softly. He paused to gather his thoughts. "Michelle, forgiving another person for such a magnitude of offense is humanly impossible."

"Then why does God ask it of us? It says He won't forgive us if we are still holding onto grudges. What sense does that make if you say it's humanly impossible?"

Chloe chimed in. "That's where the power of the Holy Spirit works in us and helps us to forgive. What I think Evan is trying to say is, without God, we can't forgive another person. But when we trust in Him and surrender our burdens, He can bring us to true forgiveness."

Thank You for Chloe. "Christ has forgiven all of us for every single sin we will or have committed," Evan stated. "It's a done deal, His forgiveness. With that in mind, what sense does it honestly make to walk around not forgiving another person? Of course, most feelings aren't about logic, but just think about the rationality of not forgiving someone who Christ has forgiven."

He looked around the table, taking a moment to look each of them in the eye. When he met Jo's eyes, she looked down into her Bible. He wondered who she couldn't forgive. Her mother? Or her father for dying?

⌇

Jo closed her eyes, thinking about her life. She'd been walking around with resentment and judgment in her heart all because of how her mother treated her. Yet, if Christ had forgiven her mother already for her actions, why was she holding on to it? What good was it doing her?

She looked up and her eyes collided with Darryl's. She sat back, startled by the depth of anger in them.

Ask him.

She froze at the Voice. It was the same one from the running trail. She hesitated, knowing she needed to proceed with caution. Taking a deep breath, she asked the question on her mind. "Darryl, do you think that anger helps you in any way? I'm asking, because it's something I've asked myself." Jo didn't want all the attention placed solely on his shoulders. Besides, she knew she had to work through her own anger.

The others turned toward Darryl, as if unaware of the anger coming off him like heat waves in the desert.

"It...He...why would God forgive bad people?" His hands balled into a fist on each side of his phone.

Jo knew how he felt. That overwhelming sense of injustice. Before she could speak, Evan did.

"What is the definition of a bad person?"

"What?" Shock rang out in Darryl's voice.

It echoed the one in her own head. What in the world did Evan mean? Everyone knew what a bad person was.

"What is the definition of a bad person?" Evan repeated.

"According to my dictionary app, one definition is 'morally objectionable'." Michelle stated, waving her iPhone in the air.

"There you go." Darryl said, gesturing toward Michelle. "If someone is morally wrong or 'objectionable'," he said using air quotes, "why would God forgive such a person?"

"Read Psalm fourteen verse three," Chloe interjected. "Go ahead, do it now, please."

They all reached for their Bibles and silence descended, magnifying the shuffling of pages.

Gasps rent the air.

"So you see, according to the Bible, there is 'none who does good'." Chloe stated it as a matter of fact, without judgment.

"Thanks, Chloe." Evan gave her a smile. "None of us are good; therefore, we're all in need of a savior. The Savior. The One who forgave our sins as He was being nailed to a cross amongst men who were questioning His sovereignty."

Silence roared.

Jo swallowed the lump in her throat. No one was good? What did it mean? She closed her eyes as the information sunk in. "If we are all bad by God's standards, then we're all in need of forgiveness. Am I right?" She looked at her friends.

Chloe and Evan nodded and she continued. "So, correct me if I'm wrong. We should all forgive others to be more like Him?"

Even though she asked it in a question, she knew the words rang true. She could feel the affirmation in her heart.

"Exactly," Evan said with a smile.

They continued on for another thirty minutes hashing out their different understandings of forgiveness and why it was necessary. Evan ended the study with a prayer and Jo knew she was beginning to realize who God really was.

As she walked toward the coat hanger, she felt a lightness in her heart that she hadn't experienced in a really long time. It almost felt kind of peaceful.

It must be a God thing.

Chapter Twenty-Five

E van stared down at his left limb, noting the angry red lines. His prosthetic laid next to him on the bed. He knew there would be a period of adjustment, but now he was beginning to think it was something more.

He rubbed his leg, wincing at the pain. Since it was Saturday, he'd have to wait until Monday to call the office. Hopefully the doctor would be able to tell him what to do to help his limb adjust. The folded-up wheelchair stared at him from the corner of the butler's pantry. Should he use it tonight?

No! Evan wanted to be standing when he took Jo out. He wanted to be able to gaze into her eyes, not crane his neck trying to look up at her.

Lord, I pray that I won't be in pain tonight. I want to enjoy Jo's company. Please bring healing to my leg.

He reached for the prosthetic to begin getting ready for his date.

～～

Jo picked up the rolled carpet to toss into the waste bin outside. She glanced down, noticing the sweat and grime on her clothes. *Date night*, she gasped. The idea to work as long as possible to keep the nerves at bay now seemed foolish. Would she have enough time to be ready by five?

She looked at her watch. *Half past three.* Maybe she should go home to get ready now. She still needed to find something suitable to wear and since denim and t-shirts constituted the majority of her closet, Jo wasn't sure what she would find. What could she possibly wear?

Michelle. Her friend would know the answer.

After closing up the house, Jo stowed her tools in the bed of her truck and hopped in to head home. Progress on Evan's renovation was finally moving smoothly. She loved all the changes. She could only hope…no pray, he would as well.

Her face lifted in a slight smile. It felt weird to go from hoping and relying on fate to praying and seeking God. Did other people think it odd? *I'm trying, God.*

She pulled into her driveway, parking next to Michelle's car. Thank goodness the girl was already home. It was almost four. How did time pass so quickly from getting into the car to arriving at home? Freedom Lake was either bigger than she thought or the clocks weren't using their full sixty seconds.

"Chelle?" She stood in the doorway, listening for a reply.

"I'm in your room looking through your closet."

Thank goodness. She rushed straight back to her room and stopped in amazement. Clothes had been strewn all over her bed while Michelle rummaged through the closet, resembling a mad woman.

"Good grief, did you dump my whole closet onto the bed?"

"Don't give me that look." Her friend snapped. "Your choice of clothing is atrocious. The majority of this crap is overalls and t-shirts." She shook her head in disgust.

"Well, they serve me well at work." Who cared what she wore when she was ripping out walls and tattered carpet?

"Yes, but what about when you're not at work."

Michelle pulled out a blue maxi dress. "Is this the only dress you own?"

"Well, I own a skirt too." She grabbed her necklace. Maybe she shouldn't have said yes to Evan.

"You mean this sad thing?" Michelle held up a long black skirt that was frayed around the edges. "This should have been put out to pasture a long time ago."

"But the frayed edges make it kind of boho chic."

"Uh, no. It's frayed because it's so old. Where is he taking you again?"

"Marcelli's."

"What?"

The look on her friend's face would have been comical if the girl wasn't in such a panic. *Who was going on this date anyway?*

"Okay, we're going to my room to see if you can fit into any skirts or dresses I own. No jeans for you. He always sees you in jeans."

"You know I don't think he minds me in jeans since he did ask *me* out. Besides, I don't want to wear anything too tight or revealing." She stifled a groan as she followed Michelle down the hall. The girl acted like she couldn't hear her.

"Everyone dresses up for a date. He'll be expecting you to as well."

"I wore slacks on my last date."

"And that was when again?" Her friend arched an eyebrow, arms folded in front of her. Her high heel tapped out a steady rhythm against the wood floors.

"A few years ago," she muttered. *Five is more like it.* Who wanted to date men her mother shoved at her? She collapsed on the bed. Okay, maybe she needed to wear something nicer.

Michelle smirked and then tore her closet door open. Once again, she resumed her frenzied rummaging while muttering under her breath. Jo could barely make out the "no, no, no" as she slid clothes from left to right, one after the other. She watched in bemusement.

"You know we don't wear the same size, right?" How on earth would she fit into something of Michelle's? Last time she checked, Michelle wore a size two, a four on her "fat" days. She shook her head. Jo had never fit into those sizes. A steady eight had been her go-to since high school.

"I know we don't. I have a bunch of clothes from when I collected designer dresses to re-gift to those who needed something. You know that charity I did in Kodiak."

"I forgot about that. You actually still have those?"

"Yep, you never know when someone needs the perfect outfit. And I think I just found yours." Michelle pulled a deep purple, sweater dress out of the closet and looked at Jo with a foolish grin on her face.

Jo stood up, taking it in. The color was gorgeous, but she usually stuck to red.

"Well, what do you think?"

"I kind of like the neckline. It's like a loose turtleneck."

"It's a cowl neck, JoJo."

Whatever. "I'm just not sure about it…"

"It's fantastic. You'll look cute and be warm. Don't you have some boots that would go with this? Maybe even a pair of black tights?"

She nodded as the dress slowly grew on her. "I think I may have the perfect ones. But what size is this?"

"It's an eight. Is that good?"

"Perfect."

After getting out of the shower, Jo put on the sweater dress. It fit perfectly, cinched in at the waist by a black belt, then flared out and fell just below her knee. She pulled her black scrunched boots over her tights.

At the sound of a low whistle, she turned toward her bedroom door.

"You're going to knock his socks off." Michelle waggled her eyebrows.

"I certainly hope so." She swallowed as her stomach did the tango. "Thanks for the dress."

"Sure, glad to help. Do you have earrings? And not studs, dangling earrings would go much better. And are you going to wear your hair down?"

"Yes, to all of the above."

Jo grabbed her purple-and-sterling-silver ball earrings and put them in. Her father gave them to her for her sixteenth birthday. In fact, that was probably the last time she wore them. She smiled as the memory warmed her heart. Last, she parted her hair to the side and swept it back over her shoulders. She had added soft waves to it with the curling iron. It wasn't half bad.

The doorbell sounded.

"I'll go answer the door for you. Make sure you come out after a minute or two," Michelle said with a smile.

She nodded and nervously smoothed her hands down over her clothes.

Um, God, it's me again, Jo. I'm super nervous about tonight. I mean, do I even want to take this beyond business? I'm just worried he'll turn back into Mr. Hyde after I've taken the chance to share part of myself.

Jo bit her lip then quickly stopped, afraid to ruin her lip gloss. *I guess what I'm trying to say is, please don't let this date be a mistake. I want to enjoy tonight, but if it turns out we don't click, please help us stay friends. Um, Amen.*

༄

Evan barely glanced at Michelle as she held the door open for him. He couldn't believe how nervous he was. He'd been praying all day that the date would go well.

"How are you?" He looked around, hoping to spot Jo.

"I'm good. Jo's finishing up. She should be out in a moment."

"Great." He stared at the back hallway, then realized he was being rude. He slowly turned to face Michelle, being careful not to fall. He wasn't great at pivoting on his prosthetic yet and the pain made it more difficult. "Sorry, I was being rude."

"I understand," she said, her hazel eyes twinkling at him.

He nodded, feeling his face warm under her scrutiny. He prayed she kept her mouth shut and didn't make any jokes. Footfalls echoed on the hardwood floor. *Great, now I have to turn back around.* When he did, he knew that it had all been worth it. His heart stilled at the sight of Jo.

She was gorgeous.

He didn't know what was more shocking, her wearing a dress or the way her hair cascaded around her shoulders in waves. He never realized how thick and long her hair was. All he wanted to do was touch the soft-looking waves.

He stepped forward, his eyes never leaving hers. "Right about now I wish I had my wheelchair to hold me up." His eyes did a slow perusal. "At least I know which leg won't buckle at the sight of your beauty," he said with a wink.

Her laugh mesmerized him. "Laying it on a bit thick aren't you, Evan?"

"You ain't seen nothing yet, JoJo." He grinned at her.

Tonight would be a great night.

On the drive into the city, silence enveloped them like a canopy of trees. Except, all it did was increase his nerves. It would be better if he could drive. Instead, Jo did. He gestured toward the radio.

"Is it okay if I turn it on?"

"Sure."

Soulful notes of Miles Davis filled the air. He glanced at Jo out of his peripheral vision and noticed she toyed with the silver-rope chain around her neck.

"How long have you had that? I don't remember you wearing jewelry that often."

"I've only been wearing it since my dad died. He never wore rings or anything because of his job, but he always had the chain on underneath his shirt. It was a sign to my mother that he loved her and would stay faithful."

She paused and he glanced at her again. She inhaled, her brow wrinkling in the moonlight. It was evident the death of her father still grieved her.

"Anyway," she continued. "I asked him why a rope chain and he said a 'three strand cord isn't easily broken'."

"That's awesome. I didn't know your dad was a Christian. I don't remember seeing him in church when we were younger."

Jo cleared her throat and he concentrated on her voice. "How did you know he was a Christian?"

"The three strand cord phrase is in Ecclesiastes from the Old Testament. It's part of a passage that explains why two is better than one."

"Do you believe that? That two is better than one? What if the two aren't compatible?"

"How boring would it be if they were? Now, I'm not saying people should be different in, say, their beliefs. However, what people mistake as incompatibility of personality is the beauty of a complementary relationship."

"I never looked at it that way. I always wondered how my parents got together, because they're as different as night and day. My dad told me he knew from the moment he met her that she was the one for him.

He wanted to be able to make her laugh and lighten up. And he always did."

Her voice faded as if she had been caught up in the memories. His mind raced as he tried to figure out a way to turn the conversation to prevent the downward turn of her mood. *Think!*

"What do you think about us? Do you think we're compatible or complementary?" He wanted to take back the words as soon as they left his mouth. What if she didn't want to look that far ahead? He stole a glance out the corner of his eye.

A look of concentration settled on Jo's face. "I don't know. We used to get along great until high school, and then you stopped talking to me. Now, it's like I'm discovering who you are all over again."

"So what have you discovered so far?"

"You love getting to know God more. You have a positive outlook on life, despite losing part of your leg. You love your parents and you're a good friend."

"I'm not sure if my outlook is completely positive, but God and I are working on it."

"I have been curious about one thing."

"Yeah? What's that?"

"What have you been doing since you graduated high school? I'm assuming you went to college and got a job, yet you never talk about anything from that part of your life."

He tapped his hands against his right leg. What should he say about it? It was filled with good, but the accident seemed to have overshadowed any joy in his previous years. "I don't know where to start."

"Okay, start after high school graduation. Where did you go?"

"To the Air Force."

"What?! Really? I didn't know that." She laid a hand on his arm and his skin heated from her touch.

He cleared his throat. "I did four years which was enough for me to know I didn't want to make a career of it. It's not that there was anything horrifying that happened to me or anything like that. I just like being my own boss, having a little more freedom than the military lifestyle allows."

"I can understand that. What did you do in the Air Force?"

"Security Forces. That's the name of the Air Force police force."

"Wow. What happened after you got out?"

"I knew I didn't want to stay in the Air Force, so I took a few college courses while I was in and got an associate's degree in Criminal Justice. When I got out, I decided to go to Purdue to pursue my bachelor's degree."

"You went to Purdue?"

He looked at her noting the incredulous tone of voice. "I did."

"That's awesome. Did you get your bachelor's?"

"I did and was able to play some basketball as well."

"Wait, you played basketball at Purdue?"

"Yep, I was a point guard. Even though I didn't get all the press, I was just happy with the opportunity to play. It's always been my dream to play, but I thought my chances were gone when I went to the military instead of college right away."

"What did you get your degree in?"

"Sports Education."

"Wow, Evan, I'm proud of you." She paused. "I take it the accident changed things," she said softly. "How did it happen?"

"Ahh, the accident. Are you sure you want to hear this story?" Because he didn't really want to tell it.

"I do. Isn't that part of getting to know one another?"

"True." He took a deep breath. He hadn't talked about it to any of his friends. "The night of the accident, my ex-girlfriend Brenda was driving. I had just bought a new car and she wanted to drive it." He shrugged. "So I let her. We were headed out to eat, only we never made it. A truck hit us head on. He was drunk."

Jo gasped, still managing to keep her eyes on the road.

Evan continued when he realized she kept glancing over at him, waiting to hear the rest of the story. "The truck veered off into our lane and hit my side of the car, which took the brunt of the impact. Brenda broke her right leg, but my left leg was basically crushed. The doctors did all they could, but it couldn't be saved."

"I'm so sorry, Evan. I can't even imagine what that must have been like." There was a slight pause before she continued. "How come you didn't return to Freedom Lake sooner?"

"I had to wait until I could heal completely. I had some internal injuries that aided in my long hospital stay. My mom and dad took turns coming out, so that one could stay behind at the B&B. Their visits kept me from falling off the edge. I don't know what I would have done if they hadn't come." He snorted. "This is great date conversation, JoJo."

"Well, how can we know if we're 'complementary' if we don't discover who we are?" She winked at him.

"Indeed."

From that moment, he made a point to make the rest of the conversation light. Despite the awkwardness of the conversation, he was thankful that the story was out and he wouldn't have to repeat it.

∽

Jo stared at the porch light illuminating the front of her house. She swallowed as Evan opened her truck door. She'd had a wonderful time tonight, but now the anxiety of being walked to the door weighed her down. Would he kiss her or would that be considered going too fast? Would he hug her and if so, what kind of hug? A date hug or a church hug, leaving a wide ol' space between their bodies? She blinked rapidly as his cologne drifted toward her.

What *was* that scent? It had driven her crazy all night. It was like woods met spice in a tantalizing mixture. He offered his arm and she hooked hers through his as they walked up the sidewalk.

"I had a wonderful time tonight. I hope you'll go out with me again." He stopped and looked at her, the porch light casting a warm glow over them.

She glanced at his mouth then quickly back at his eyes. "I'd like that."

His face lit up. Heat flushed her face. Should she smile back? Lean closer? She took a step forward. Evan let go of her arm and stepped back. "Good night, JoJo."

She watched, bewildered by his abrupt departure. *No kiss?* Did her breath stink? She had wanted him to kiss her, but at the same time she was afraid the nerves would threaten to choke her. Had he picked up on her anxiety? She watched forlornly as he made his way down the street toward Darryl's place, where Senior would pick him up later.

He waved again, and she turned and went inside.

What an anti-climactic night.

Chapter Twenty-Six

$\mathcal{E}$ van pulled up to his house and grinned. He'd passed his driver's license test. With his new home almost ready, independence was a fresh coat of paint away. Well, maybe Jo had more to do than that. His cheeks felt like they could touch his ears he was so happy. Was it the fact that it was his house or that he drove here? Never again would he take driving for granted. Fortunately, driving with a prosthetic had been easier than he expected.

Thankfully, Jo had already leveled the sidewalk. She said she would be working on the laundry area since the kitchen had finally been completed. He opened the car door, pulling his prosthetic out before swinging the rest of his body, so that he could stand.

His gait faltered a bit in his rush to see the state of repairs. Of course, knowing Jo was inside fueled his movement. Their date had been great and he kicked himself all weekend for not kissing her goodnight. The way her hair had fallen gently on her shoulders, the porch light illuminating her rich brown skin...she'd been stunning, but the timing felt off.

Who was he kidding? Evan snorted. He'd been afraid of losing his balance. What would happen if she kissed him and he had fallen backward? Was that even possible? He proceeded in the house and walked past the foyer. He stopped when he saw Jo.

She ran a hand across the quartz countertops, looking pleased with her handiwork and completely unaware of his presence. He studied her as she stood back, hands on her hips. Today she was back in her standard overalls with a Henley sweater, but it didn't detract from her looks. She was still beautiful, but he would never forget the sight of her in that dress.

He groaned. *You're an idiot. You should have kissed her last night.* "Hey JoJo."

She looked up and paused, a pensive look on her face. Whatever she had been thinking went away as a calm façade covered her face. "Hey, Evan. Come look at your kitchen." She held her arms out Vanna White style.

Evan walked toward the brown quartz kitchen island. She was right, it would look great with some barstools. "This is fantastic, Jo. I can't wait to see the barstools in here."

She smiled at him. "What do you think of the cabinets?"

The empty frosted cabinets looked back at him. Would it matter what kind of plates he owned? He never cared before, but all of a sudden the details mattered. Especially, since he valued Jo's opinion. She had assured him the frosted cabinets would enhance the look and value of the house. He stared at her, struck by an idea. "Come pick out plates with me?"

"What?" she asked with a laugh.

"The cabinets need plates. Will you come?"

"I don't think so." She turned around, her laugh quickly replaced with a frown. Was she mad at him?

"Hey, what's wrong?"

"Nothing." She stared at the counters.

Since there was nothing on them, he knew something was up. Why did women always say 'nothing' when it was obviously something? "Come on, JoJo. What's up?"

"Fine," she snapped, whirling around. Her hands gripped the island. "Why didn't you kiss me the other night?"

His mouth dropped open. Never in a million years would he think she was upset about that. Besides, wasn't it gentlemanly not to kiss on the first date?

～

Jo stared at Evan, wishing she could reel her words back in. She hadn't meant to blurt it out, but it had bugged her all day Sunday.

"I didn't want to rush things."

"Oh." Of course he had a good reason. Now she really wished she could take her question back.

She turned toward the cabinets, trying to hide her embarrassment. Should she go shopping with him? Visions of aqua plates danced in her head. They would look perfect in his kitchen. The light color would contrast perfectly with the dark brown wood. *Or red plates.*

Jo turned around to say 'yes' and yelped. Evan had walked right up to her. *How does he move so quietly?*

"Sorry, didn't mean to scare you." His dark brown eyes danced in merriment.

"I just didn't expect you to be so close." She doubted he was that sorry.

"Why not? Isn't that how one kisses?"

"What?" she squeaked, taking a step back. He wanted to kiss now? Now, when she was covered in dust from the plaster of the walls? Now, when her hair had been pulled into a haphazard bun?

"I really wanted to kiss you last night, but I was afraid it was too soon. I didn't want to appear foolish."

She stared at him in disbelief. He'd been nervous? She cleared her throat to reassure him. "It's okay, Evan. We can take our time. I'm sorry I said anything." Her pulse jumped in the base of her throat.

"Are you?" he asked, taking a step closer.

Jo stepped back and stopped abruptly as the counters hit the back of her legs. Did she make them too low? *No.* She vaguely remembered lowering them to check the wheelchair height. Obviously, she forgot to press the button to raise them to standing height. She licked her lips. "I'm fine now. You made a very good point about—"

Evan leaned forward and gently pressed his lips to hers. They were soft, as if asking her permission. With a small gasp of delight, she slid her hands up his arms and around his neck and kissed him back. *He was kissing her, dust-covered-overall-wearing Jo Ellen Baker.* Her body warmed as his hands cradled her head. Vaguely, she realized her hair flew free and his hands were threaded in them. She breathed in his scent as she stepped closer, putting into her kiss all the longing that had been building in her since he asked to be friends.

"*Excuse* me."

They jumped apart as the sound of Michelle's voice penetrated their kiss-induced haze.

"Sorry to interrupt," she said with a smirk.

Jo glanced at her friend, hoping her eye daggers were finding their intended mark.

Michelle rolled her eyes. "Your mother's looking for you. She says you need to come home ASAP."

Of all the rotten timing!

Evan stepped back, holding her loosely.

"Did you tell her I was working at Evan's house?"

"Of course. She said she couldn't come down here and that you needed to make your way home now."

Jo groaned. Why was she summoning her now? She looked at Evan and he gave her a reassuring grin.

"It's all right. I'll be here when you get back."

"You sure?" She whispered the question since he still held on to her waist.

"Positive. Go, I'll be waiting."

"Thanks."

He bent down and kissed her forehead. A flush started at her neck and went up to the top of her head. She ignored Michelle's look as she grabbed the keys to her truck. Her mother had better have something important to say.

"JoJo wait up."

She turned as Michelle followed her outside.

"That was some kiss." Michelle wiggled her eyebrows.

The girl was a clown sometimes. "We'll talk later. Apparently, the great Victoria Baker summons."

Michelle stepped forward, a note of seriousness replacing her early playfulness. "It sounds bad, whatever it is."

She bit her lip. "She always sounds like that."

"I think it was something more."

"Okay, thanks for the warning."

Five minutes later, Jo pulled up to her mother's house. She grimaced and laid her forehead against the steering wheel. "Do I really have to go in?"

God, it's me again, Jo. I have a situation here. I don't know if I can handle my mother today. Please, guide my words. Help me to be nice and not let her get to me. Amen.

Jo got out of the truck and headed inside. She paused, listening for sounds. Not a peep. She glanced around. All the curtains were still drawn. Her brow furrowed. *What is going on?* Maybe her mother was in her room. She'd probably find her in the sitting area of the master bedroom.

She climbed the stairs, trying to keep the dread at bay. The house was eerily quiet. Could Michelle have been right? Could something truly be wrong? Jo knocked softly on the door to her mother's suite, wincing as the sound seemed to echo upstairs.

"Come in."

Please, be with me, Lord.

She went in and stopped. The room was pitch black. Blackout curtains hung from the windows. Most likely, the blinds had been closed as well. She blinked, trying to get her eyes to adjust. When they did, she made out her mother's figure lying in bed with an arm over her eyes. "Mother, it's Jo."

"Don't you think I know the sound of your voice?" her mother's tone was laced with disgust.

She crept closer to the bed. "Sorry, Mother. What's going on?"

"Don't you know what day it is?"

Jo frowned. It was the first Monday after Thanksgiving. Christmas cheer had descended like a madness. She searched her brain trying to find any other significance than that. "I don't know."

"Really? You of all people?"

What in the world? It wasn't the anniversary of her father's death. None of the Baker's had a birthday in December. How was she supposed to know the significance? "I'm sorry, Mother. I don't have a clue."

Her mother heaved a sigh and threw back the covers. She sat up, tightening the sash on her pink silk robe. She swung her legs over the side of the bed and slid her feet into a pair of fuzzy high-heeled slippers.

"Of all my children, I thought for sure you would remember our wedding anniversary."

Jo closed her eyes. How could she forget? But then again, why did her mother care?

Her mother walked toward her vanity and sat down. "I was depending on you to remember, Jo Ellen."

"I'm sorry." She stared at her mother, not sure she had heard correctly. Since when had she ever depended on her, and not to simply run errands for her.

Her mother waved her hand. "Spare me the sorry. I knew Darius wasn't going to remember. If it weren't for his wife, he wouldn't remember his own birthday."

Jo wanted to laugh but, judging from the tone of her mother's voice, that would *not* go over well.

"And Vanessa," her mother shook her head. "That child is oblivious to anything that doesn't involve her. But you," her mother turned and stared at her.

Although it was dark, Jo felt her piercing gaze.

"I thought for sure you would remember, considering you picked out the anniversary presents."

"How did you know that?" Though she barely spoke above a whisper, the harsh silence magnified her voice.

"Oh please, Jo Ellen, you really think I thought your father bought those things? He hates shopping."

True. But the thought of her mother knowing all along flabbergasted her. Jo thought her mother would hate the gifts if she knew who had picked them out.

Her mother reached for a tin jewelry box and opened it. Holding it reverently, she pulled out a man's wedding ring. "Every year, you two would go out the day before and on our anniversary he would present the gift with such pride."

Tears spilled over. She wiped them away, shocked at their presence. Shopping with her dad had been great. Neither one of them cared to do it, but spending time together had brought them both pleasure. He'd always buy her an ice cream cone after they had picked out the gift. Jo had always thought her brother and sister had missed out on the fun. And her mother knew the whole time?

"Why didn't you tell me you knew?"

Her mother looked up from the ring, her gaze meeting Jo's in the vanity mirror. "Why else do you think I kept the gifts, Jo Ellen?"

"What? But…but you hate me!" The words tore from her mouth, and all the hurt and anger from the past ripped open her heart. She wrapped her arms around her stomach as if she could hold herself together. But her wounds were too deep, too fresh.

"Jo Ellen, how could I hate you? You're the first child I've ever been proud of. I may be a Baker, which I became out of respect to your father, but I have always been and will always remain a Holliday. And Holliday blood runs strongly through your veins, my dear."

Jo collapsed onto the floor. This was too much. All the years she thought her mother hated her. How could Jo believe anything she said? "Do you even know why you got the jewelry box?" she asked her mother, skepticism coating her words and sending them flinging like arrows.

"Of course I do. It was for our tenth anniversary. The first year you started helping him buy gifts. The ones before that were hideous." Her mother shuddered delicately.

Jo stared, flummoxed. Her mother knew all these years? "But you hate the way I dress. You're always trying to change me."

"Of course I do, dear. What mother doesn't want to dress her daughter up?"

"But you hate that I renovate homes."

"Do I need to repeat myself?" Her mother arched an eyebrow. "That business killed your father. Don't you think I want better for you?"

The question hung in the air, but her mother continued, giving Jo no time to measure the weight of her words. "The doctors asked for your dad to take it easy, but he refused to listen. In the end, it killed him. I want more than that for you."

"But, you're always asking me why don't I get married like Vanessa." She wanted to pull her hair out. Who *was* this woman?

"Well, of course I am, Jo Ellen. The years I had with your father were the happiest years. I want that for you as well."

She wiped a hand over her face, erasing the tears. This was too much. She couldn't comprehend what her mother was telling her. She made it sound like she'd been a saint all those years and Jo knew better. "And having kids like Charlene?"

"Grandkids from my favorite child? Need I say anymore?"

Jo shook her head, although whether it was in response to her mother or the confusion was anyone's guess. She couldn't believe it. This had to be some ruse. No way would her mother actually call her the favorite. She felt like she was in the twilight zone.

Her mother walked toward her and gestured for Jo to stand.

Reluctantly she did, looking at her mother as if seeing her for the first time ever.

Her mother placed her hands on Jo's cheeks. "My mother wasn't demonstrative. She didn't hug and she didn't kiss. I'm set in my ways too, so I do the same. But just so you're not confused: I love you, Jo Ellen."

Her mother clumsily patted her on the cheeks. With a small smile, Victoria Baker walked back to her bed, slipping her heels off. She swung her legs under the covers and laid back down as if nothing momentous had happened.

Jo stared, unsure of what to do with all this new information rolling around in her brain. She looked at her mother and then at the tin jewelry box. *What do I do?*

She looked down at her shoes and decided to take them off. A moment later, she crawled into bed next to her mother and reached for her hand. Quietly, she began sharing her favorite memories of her parents' anniversary.

Chapter Twenty-Seven

G radually, Evan made his way up Guy's sidewalk. He inhaled sharply as pain shot up his left limb. He kept forgetting to call the doctor, but knew he would have to do it soon. The redness was worse and his limb had started to swell. Every movement caused his prosthetic to chafe against his skin.

He knocked on Guy's door, rubbing his hands together to warm up. He hadn't seen him since the day he came to his mom's place. He knew his friend was in a difficult stage of life, but that was no reason to sequester himself. Evan laughed at the irony of his thoughts. Fortunately, he knew better and wanted the same for Guy. Hopefully, his friend would accept his invitation to attend church or join their Bible study group. *Lord, please give me the words I need.*

"Hey, man," Guy said, opening the door and motioning Evan in.

"How are you?" He glanced around, noting the wreckage in the living room.

The place looked like a tornado of girls' toys had made its way through the entire house. He looked at Guy, noticing his bloodshot eyes. The man looked like he was drowning in sorrow and exhaustion.

"Man, I'm hanging in there. It's been weird adjusting to life without my mother's help. Nana Baker is wonderful though." He rubbed the back of his neck. "I don't know what I would do without her." He gestured around.

"Sorry my place is a mess, but the girls just crashed for their afternoon nap, and I haven't had time to clean up. Follow me to the kitchen."

"No worries." He followed his friend into the kitchen, taking care with each step. "How are you dealing with everything?"

Guy heaved a sigh as he sat down in a chair. He stared down at the floor as if deep in thought. Finally he shrugged. "I don't even know where to begin."

"Fair enough. Have you started the sheriff's position already?"

"Yeah. It's been interesting running into people I used to know."

"I hope not literally," Evan joked.

"Ha. No, I gave a couple of tickets to former classmates, but for the most part it's seeing people at the grocery store and what not."

Evan nodded. He looked around the kitchen. Dishes were piled in the sink. The place wasn't much cleaner than the living room. He glanced at his hands at a loss for words. *Lord, please help me offer words of comfort.* He cleared his throat. "Could I pray for you?" he asked cautiously.

"No, thanks," Guy said with an emphatic shake of his head.

Evan chewed the inside of his lip, wondering if he should ask about church or the Bible study. But he wouldn't know unless he tried. "So Darryl, Chloe, Michelle, Jo, and I started a Bible study to help us navigate through the Word. Would you like to join us? Maybe something in there will offer you comfort. At the very least, being around other people might help."

"Evan, I know you mean well, but I'm done praying, studying the Word, and all things related to God. He didn't see fit to answer my prayers for Charlene, so I don't really have anything to say to Him."

He tensed at the bitterness in Guy's voice. What could he say to help him through this? Evan knew what it felt like to believe God had not answered your prayers. "Guy, I know how you feel—"

"Actually, you don't know how I feel." Guy stood. "You've never seen your wife die in front of you. You've never had to make the decision to choose between your daughters or your wife. You've never had to bury a family member, let alone someone you pledged your life to. So forgive me if I don't believe a word of what you're saying. All I hear are mindless platitudes that make me want to—"

His friend whirled around, rage pouring forth in a torrent of words too delicate for anyone's ears. His shoulders shook as he slowly looked Evan's way, careful not to look him in the face. "You know, man, I think it would be better if you just leave."

Evan stood up slowly, the ache of failure heavy in his chest. He didn't want to leave like this. "Man, G, I didn't mean to offend you. I just wanted to help."

"But you didn't." His friend motioned toward the door with his head.

He stared at Guy. His eyes had gone cold, the irises melding perfectly into the black of his eyes. Evan didn't want to leave but if he stayed, a fight might break out. He would just have to continue praying for his friend and to keep showing up in his life. He couldn't let Guy believe he'd been forsaken.

As Evan turned, a sharp pain shot up his leg. He cried out, a wave of dizziness washing over him. He tried to still himself, but the pain was too great. Vaguely, he realized Guy was calling out to him, but he couldn't make out the words. Instead, the black oblivion enveloped him in its snare.

~

Humming to herself, Jo pushed the paint roller up and down. The cream color would add the perfect complement to the maroon colored washer and dryer. Evan's laundry room would look absolutely perfect. Even though Evan no longer used his wheelchair, he wanted to keep the extra space in the room.

She let the sounds of her iPad wash over her as Wynton Marsalis' trumpet crooned in her ear. Life was finally looking up. Since the day she heard the Lord speaking to her during her run, Jo had become firmer in her belief that God truly loved her. Her mother had seemed to soften toward her as well. No longer did she have to duck her phone calls. Besides, didn't God ask for her to honor her parents? It was time she did her part and stop complaining about those who didn't do theirs.

In a steady rhythm her arm went up and down, the color showing up smoothly in the path of the paint roller. Jo stepped back, surveying her handiwork. Hopefully, Evan would be pleased with the renovations. With her work.

With me.

Although they'd had a few setbacks, the rest of the renovations were going smoothly. Soon, Evan could move in and enjoy life as a homeowner. She smiled, remembering when they'd shopped for plates. She had found the perfect set in aqua. He hadn't batted an eye when she suggested it. And she had to withhold how much it pleased her when he had agreed with her suggestions.

At first, she'd tried to get him to seek Chloe's advice for furnishings and overall décor; after all, the girl was an interior designer. But he'd seemed a little put out. She remembered how the lines around his mouth dragged his lips downward.

"Evan, I'm not trying to pawn you off on someone else. However, Chloe does make her living picking the right furnishings for a space. She takes in mind all the colors you have in the walls and the floors, et cetera. I'm really not that knowledgeable."

Jo had been exaggerating a little bit, but really, Chloe had her own business, why not seek her advice? She remembered laughing and hoping that it soothed the wounded look on his face. He had smiled back at her, but it was forced. Could it be he wanted her opinion for a different reason?

She shook her head. Surely not. They'd only been on one date and kissed that time in the kitchen. Then again, they did hold hands when they went shopping. The feel of his hand pleased her more than she'd let on. He made her feel safe. The hairs on her arms stood up at the memory. Her body vibrated with awareness.

Wait a minute, that's your cell, Jo girl.

She pulled out her earbuds and answered the phone.

"Jo, it's Guy."

"Hey, what's up?" she frowned at the sadness in his voice. Would he ever sound happy again?

"I'm at the hospital in the city."

"What are you doing there?" *And why was he telling her?* "Wait, is my Nana okay?"

"Yes, she's fine."

Relief flooded through her and her shoulders sagged.

"But Evan's not."

"Wait, what?" A roar filled her ears as her heart picked up speed.

"He was over at my house, and he passed out. He was feverish, so I called for an ambulance. They rushed him to Freedom Lake and the doctors there had him transferred to the city hospital."

"What's wrong with him?" She gripped the phone, afraid it would crumble in her grip. *He has to be okay.*

"They don't know. They're doing a bunch of testing. His mother is here, and Evan asked me to contact you."

"Okay, I'm on my way." She dropped the paint roller and ran out the back door, barely remembering to grab her parka.

God, it's me again. Jo. Please don't let something happen to Evan. Please, let him be okay, please!

She couldn't lose someone else. She just couldn't. They were just on the brink of something wonderful. The ease in which she could talk to him made her feel valued and cared for. Never had someone watched her with such attentiveness. Evan made her feel special, because *he* was special. What would she do if something was seriously wrong? She sniffed, and she realized tears were coursing down her face.

As she drove to the city, worry ate at her. She wished she knew some Scripture to calm her, but she didn't. She didn't even know if Freedom Lake had a Gospel or Christian radio station. So she talked to God as if He were in the seat right next to her. Somehow, the action—which would seem insane to most—kept her sane.

"Lord, please make him better. I don't know what's wrong, but please let the doctors figure it out. Let it be curable or easy to fix. Whatever it is. And please, please," she pleaded, gripping the steering wheel in her gloved hands, "please let his spirits remain high. Don't let him spiral into that anger and depression he had when he returned home. It seems like he just overcame it."

Fear gripped her. Thankfully, the signs for the Emergency Department soon popped up. She followed the directions toward the parking garage. Guy had told her they were in the emergency room, but she had never been to this hospital. If it weren't for the red signs, she would have been lost. After parking she headed inside, slowing to a brisk walk when she spotted the nurses' station.

She gripped the counter. "What room is Evan Carter in?"

The older woman sitting behind the desk peered over her eyeglasses. "Are you family?"

Jo bit her lip. She didn't want to lie, but she wanted to know how he was doing.

"Jo!"

She whirled around at the sound of her name. Guy motioned for her from the other end of the hallway. She dashed toward him, worry clogging her throat. *God, please let him be okay.* It didn't register that she didn't say 'Amen' or mention who she was. They had been talking ever since she'd left Evan's house. There was no need to end her prayer. She'd finally understood the concept of "praying without ceasing."

"How is he? Where is he? Can I see him?"

Guy lowered his hand. "Calm down. He's stable. He wanted me to come get you and bring you to his room. This way," he gestured down the hall.

The litany of "please, heal him," played over and over in her head until she entered his room. His mother looked up with red rimmed eyes.

Please, don't let him be dying.

Jo turned to look at Evan and her heart stopped. He looked so weak with an IV hooked up though the vein in his arm. His six-foot frame was dwarfed by the hospital bed. She smiled, hoping he wouldn't notice the way her lips quivered. She didn't know how she managed to hold back the tears. All she knew was that she had to be strong for him.

His face looked wan, the chocolate tone of his skin had lost its luster. But the smile he gave her filled her with relief. *If he could smile, all would be okay, wouldn't it?*

"Hey JoJo."

"Hey, Ev." She tried to say it in a light tone, but the barely suppressed sob probably gave her away. She gulped. "What's going on? What happened?"

245

Evan closed his eyes for a moment, and then opened them slowly. "I've been feeling some pain in my left leg. It's red, and I thought it was just part of the adjustment period."

"It's not?" She gazed into his eyes, praying he wasn't going to make light of a bad situation. She needed to know the truth of whatever ailed him.

"The doctor thinks I may be allergic to one of the materials in the prosthetic."

She walked around the other side of the bed to sit next to him. Mrs. Carter gave her a brief smile, from the other side. Jo looked at Evan. "So, what does that mean?"

"Well, they have to do allergy testing and depending on what they discover, I will either have to get a new prosthetic or I may not be able to wear any of them."

What?

How would he feel to have to depend on the wheelchair all over again? He had been so excited about driving and being able to do things on his own. She knew how much Evan valued his independence. *Lord, please don't take it from him.*

"Have they started the testing? What can I do to help?"

His eyes lit up and he gave her the most gorgeous smile she had ever seen. Her heart tripped and fell right into love.

"Just pray for me, Jo." He grabbed her hand and kissed it.

The tears that had been threatening an entrance since she got to the hospital made their way down her face. "I haven't stopped praying since I got the call."

"Then you've done enough."

Chapter Twenty-Eight

$\mathcal{E}$van wiped away the tears from Jo's face. He was so proud of her. He knew that trusting in God was difficult for her, but the fact that she'd prayed for him made his heart swell with love. He knew they'd only been on one date, but apparently that was enough for his heart.

He wanted to beg her to love him and not leave him. Now he understood what his mother meant. What he felt for Brenda paled in comparison with his feelings for Jo. Could he handle it if she walked away too?

A knock sounded, startling him from his contemplations. He looked away from Jo and stared as the dermatologist, Dr. Benson, walked in the door.

"How are you feeling, Mr. Carter?"

"Better now that the pain meds kicked in, Doc."

"I'll bet." He held up some paperwork. "Got the results from your lab tests. It confirms my prognosis of an allergy to the material. The antibody test they conducted is positive. The count is pretty high. I know wearing a prosthesis is new for you and that's why you didn't contact your prosthetist sooner; however, you should always err on the side of caution. Your contact dermatitis is severe."

He gulped. Why had he been so foolish? He should have called the moment he started noticing the redness. And this contact dermatitis was the reason it had been so painful to wear the prosthetic lately. He'd let his pride rule. In searching for independence, he had become dependent on the prosthetic.

"It'll be a few days before you can go home. We need to make sure the leg starts healing and that there is no damage from the allergy."

Evan nodded, still too stunned to speak.

"Visiting hours end at eight, please be sure to leave before then." The doctor pointed to Jo, Guy and Mrs. Carter.

"Thank you, Doc."

"Not a problem. I'll stop by tomorrow. We'll do some patch testing of common allergens and also add in the materials your prosthesis is made of to determine the specific allergy."

"Thank you so much, Dr. Benson," his mother said. She shook his hand as she dabbed at her eyes. His mother had been sniffling since she'd arrived at the hospital.

"Hey man, I'm going to let you get some rest." Guy looked at him. He could tell from his expression that he was sorry about their earlier conversation.

"Thanks for getting me here, G."

"Of course. That's what friends do, right?" Guy looked at him expectantly.

Evan smiled at him, hoping to reassure him that he wasn't angry. Relief flooded his friend's eyes. Guy waved and left.

"Well, I'm going to mosey on out too, son. Your dad will want to have a chance to see you before eight o'clock comes."

"Okay, tell him not to rush."

His mother laughed, relief turning the sound light and airy. "I will. Plus, I'm sure you two want some privacy." She waggled her fingers between him and Jo.

Evan glanced at Jo just in time to see her cheeks turn a rosy shade.

"I can leave and get Mr. Carter for you, Mrs. Carter."

"Now Jo Ellen, I told you to call me Marilyn. But don't worry. I haven't seen my son smile so much since he started talking to you, so I'll be the one to leave."

His mom leaned down and kissed his cheek and whispered in his ear. He laughed and watched her go.

"What did she say?"

He turned to Jo, her eyes dark brown with curiosity.

"She told me to behave or she'd make sure the nurses checked in on me."

Jo laughed, but her cheeks became redder.

"You're cute when you blush."

"Cute, Evan Carter? A woman never wants to be thought of as cute. Puppies are cute. Babies are cute."

"I get it, I get it." He tried to laugh, but he barely had the energy to let it out.

"Why don't I come back tomorrow so you can rest?"

"No, I want you to stay." He grabbed her hand and held it to his chest.

"But you're obviously tired."

He closed his eyes in contentment as she rubbed a hand across his forehead. "Then stay until I fall asleep." He didn't know how long she would be with him, and he wouldn't let her go until he had no choice.

"All right. Hey, I have my iPod. Why don't we listen to some music?"

He nodded and soon the soft sounds of jazz filled the air. He held her hand until sweet sleep captured him.

∽∽

Firelight danced across Jo's face. Although, the fire warmed the entire living room, she couldn't seem to warm up. All she could think about was Evan lying in the hospital. They wouldn't let her stay once visiting hours had ended. She couldn't blame them. She wasn't family. She wasn't his wife.

The thought of being Evan's wife made her heart skip a beat. Could she even think about that? Besides the one date, what more did she have to measure the status of their relationship? One date did not constitute a roadmap to marriage. *Right?*

Then again, didn't the idea of marriage grow from an ember? Some spark that said there could be more than one could imagine? If she could imagine laughing with him, talking with him, being cherished and loved by him...wasn't that the spark one needed to start them on their journey toward happily ever after?

What was marriage anyway? Sure, some would say it was two people committing to one another for a lifetime, but was that it? Her own parents' marriage remained a mystery to her. She had no idea what her father had seen in her mother. And on some level she had no idea why a blue-blooded woman would be attracted to a blue-collar man.

With the need for answers pressing upon her, she picked up the phone to call her mother.

"Hello?"

"Did I wake you, Mother?"

"What do you think, Jo Ellen?"

For once the sting of her mother's words didn't penetrate. "I'm sorry to wake you. I don't know if you heard, but Evan's in the hospital. He might be allergic to his prosthetic."

"I did hear. They passed his name along in the prayer chain."

"Oh." Her mother was in a prayer chain? How little she knew about the woman who raised her. "Mother, I was wondering what attracted you to Dad? I mean, how did you know you wanted to marry him?"

"Really, Jo Ellen. Can't these questions wait until a decent hour?"

"I...I just need to know."

Her mother sighed into the phone. "Your father was the life of a party. He had this charisma that brought out the best in everyone he met." Her tone lightened. "No one ever had a bad thing to say about him."

Was her mother smiling while strolling down memory lane? Jo thought about her father. He had been friendly to everyone he came into contact with. If there was a person nearby, he would interact with them as if he had known them forever. "Is that what made you fall in love?"

The answer seemed to hang in the air for a silent moment. Jo looked at the phone, wondering if her cell had dropped the call. She opened her mouth to speak, but stopped as her mother's voice came through.

"I fell in love with him because he saw the worst in me and still thought me magnificent. When you find that person willing to overlook the worst in you, hold on to him."

She closed her eyes, trying to hold in the tears. It almost sounded like her mother truly loved her dad. She wanted to cement this moment in her memory. It would go right next to holding her hand and talking about her dad. *Thank you God for this moment.*

"Thank you for sharing, Mother."

"You're welcome, Jo Ellen. Now, can I go back to sleep?"

She smiled as her mother slipped right back into her no-nonsense tone of voice. She could only thank God that her harsh tone no longer seemed to grate against her skin. "Sure thing, good night."

For the first time in history, her mother had given her some motherly advice not laced with condemnation. She didn't know what brought about the recent change in her, but Jo would always hold this memory in her heart.

~~

The sounds of a hospital at night were eerily rhythmic. The beeping of the machines in his room. The frequent whirring noise as the blood pressure cuff squeezed his arms. The squeaky sound of rubber soled shoes walking down the halls. None of it helped Evan sleep so instead he stared at the ceiling, the sense of déjà vu overwhelming.

He couldn't count the number of times he had been laid up in a hospital bed, looking at the ceiling to search out life's answers. When he got the prosthetic, he thought it would be an answer to his prayers and an end to the soul searching. Wasn't it supposed to give him the independence he so desperately sought? Now an allergy to the components in his prosthetic put him on his back once again, and here he thought life altering moments were supposed to bring him to his knees.

Evan snorted. Apparently, his humor was intact. He counted the black dots in the ceiling tiles, hoping that doing so would lull him to sleep. Instead, the words of Psalm 121 scrolled in through his mind's eye. *"I will lift up my eyes to the hills—From whence comes my help?"*

Had that been the purpose of lying flat on his back? Would he have been aware of the sovereignty of the Lord if the accident had never happened? He'd like to think so, but he knew the path he had been heading for.

The first time he ended up in the hospital, frustration and anger were like a black curtain masking the light of God. He now knew why it was so important to renew his mind. The flesh constantly struggled to get in line with the Spirit. This time, while lying on his back, he saw the majesty of God. Whatever happened would be God's will and the Creator truly would work it all for his good.

But what about, Jo?

If she left him, would he still believe something good could come of it? Evan sighed, hating the downward turn of his thoughts. He could see the break up with Brenda as proof that something better would and could come along, but he didn't think he could feel that way if it happened with Jo.

He didn't know if she was strong enough to stay with him if the wheelchair was his future. Sure, she put on a brave front when she came to visit him, but what choice did she have? Their relationship was just beginning to develop. She had no incentive to stay with him. One date. One kiss. That wasn't enough to engage the heart.

Or was it?

Would she be able to treat him with the same respect and care she had when he had walked? He really shouldn't compare his time in the wheelchair with now, since they had both been angry with each other. Truthfully, he had no clue as to how she felt about the chair.

Lord, please, don't let my relationship with Jo be over.

He heaved a sigh. He would have to release his relationship to the Lord's hands. For if he held on too tightly, he would squeeze the life right out of it.

Chapter Twenty-Nine

As the morning dawned, Jo pulled into the visitors' parking lot at the hospital. She'd made sure to awaken early so she could bring Evan some blueberry muffins from LeeAnn's Bakery. She couldn't imagine the hospital food would be anything very appetizing. Before she got out of the car, Jo smoothed away some hairs threatening to stick out in an unseemly way.

She had borrowed a long, denim skirt from Michelle's closet to go with her cerulean cable-knit sweater. The outfit kept her warm and hopefully would catch Evan's interest. Of course, he wouldn't be able to see anything if she didn't take off her parka.

The sound of her boots echoed in the silence as she walked down the hospital corridor. Although morning had arrived, the halls seemed devoid of life. She shivered as a chill ran down her spine. "I hate hospitals," she grumbled. They reminded her of the day her dad had died.

Her mind flitted back to the memory.

"Why do they leave the walls so stark? Shouldn't a waiting room be comforting?" Jo asked.

"It's not a house," Vanessa rolled her eyes. *"It doesn't have to be inviting, just get the job done."*

"Will you two please act like the civilized women I know you to be?"

"Sorry, Mother," Vanessa said, smiling angelically.

Her mother turned to face forward and Vanessa sent a snide look Jo's way.

"Excuse me," the doctor cleared his throat, getting their attention. *Before he even opened his mouth, Jo knew the news would be bad.*

"I'm sorry, Mr. Baker didn't make it."

She shook the memory away, trying to ward off the gloom threatening to take root in her heart. If what the Bible said was true, her dad was in a better place. There was no need to worry. But what about Evan?

Lord, please heal him.

If she could combat the darkness with the light of the Lord, she would pray all day long. She walked into Evan's room, a smile ready on her face. But the sight that greeted her, struck fear in her heart. The bed had been freshly made and, judging from the smell, freshly cleaned. And remained empty.

"Evan?" she called out, looking around. Her heart thudded as her palms grew clammy.

"In the bathroom."

Sweet relief flooded her heart. She leaned against the wall, closing her eyes in gratitude. He was just in the bathroom. The door opened and he came out, using crutches to hold him up.

"Hey there, JoJo." His eyes lit up, crinkling at the corners.

Today, he didn't look as pale as before but his mouth grimaced with pain as he navigated to the bed.

She stepped forward. "Morning, brought you a blueberry muffin." She held up the brown paper bag from the bakery.

"My favorite." He grinned at her and her heart fluttered.

Jo looked down. She didn't want him to know she had asked his mom what his favorite was. The question that had been burning in her mind since yesterday soon took the forefront of her thoughts, begging to be released.

She placed the bag on the hospital tray, watching as Evan settled into the bed. "How are you feeling today?"

"Much better. Whatever medicine they're giving me is working wonders."

"Is your leg still red?"

"Yeah, I suspect it will take a while before it looks normal. Do you want to see?" he asked, staring at her expectantly.

Jo gave a slow nod. She needed to know if she could handle seeing his limb. It didn't make sense to continue their relationship—whatever it was—if she couldn't handle it. He pulled up his hospital gown and a gasp escaped from her lips.

"Oh, Evan, that looks painful. Are you sure the meds are helping you?"

Despite the coloring of his dark brown skin, there was no mistaking the awful red streaks running up his thigh. Instinctively she moved closer, laying a hand against his skin, trying to soothe him. She looked up at him and caught her breath. The look he gave her was enough to heat the entire hospital floor. Desire darkened his eyes to molten pools of chocolate.

She stepped back and calm reentered his eyes. *Had she imagined the longing?*

Evan looked down at his leg. "It looked much worse yesterday."

"What? And you thought it was from your prosthetic?"

He gave a sheepish shrug. "What can I say? It's not like I've ever worn one before."

"True."

She had no words to convey the emotions coursing through her. Could she voice them? Did she have any right? And, worst of all, would he balk and become defensive?

∽

Evan stared at Jo, taking her in. She looked beautiful in her sweater and skirt. He'd gone his whole life without seeing her in a dress and now, in a matter of weeks, he'd seen her dress up twice. Did she do it for him? He'd like to think so, but didn't want to get his hopes up.

But the more important thought: she touched his limb. He couldn't believe it. The hope and attraction had collided in an inferno of longing. He'd wanted to swoop her up and kiss her senseless, but she had stepped back.

Had she read his mind?

He reached for the muffin, breaking the silence and his musings with the crinkle of the paper bag. He looked up from the bag and gazed into her soft brown eyes. "I'm glad you're here."

"Me, too."

Her cheeks bloomed and her eyes darted away as if she was suddenly shy. He didn't want her to turn skittish. Not when he felt their relationship could make a turn. For better or worse, only time would tell. He patted the space on his right. "Come sit with me."

The bed shifted as she settled next to him. He tilted his head and leaned it against hers. "How did you know I liked blueberry muffins?" He took a bite, contentment coursing through his being.

"I asked your mom."

"Thanks for thinking of me." For some reason, they were whispering. There seemed to be a silent agreement to savor the moment. He held out his hand, hoping she would grab hold.

He sighed when she clasped her fingers with his. They sat in silence, save for the soft sounds of chewing. When he put the wrapper back in the bag, Jo broke the silence.

"I have a question, but if it's none of my business then please tell me." A pause. "Did they do the prosthetic allergy test already?"

He traced his fingers along hers, noting the subtle differences in their complexions. He wanted to ask her if she loved him. Wanted to know if she'd stick by him, for better or worse? But he knew, deep down inside, that their relationship was too new.

So instead, he cleared his throat to answer her. It was time to see if she would flee like Brenda had done. "It's definitely an allergy."

"I know, but did they pinpoint what kind? Will you be able to wear another prosthetic?"

He winced as the questions hit him like darts. He knew that wasn't her intent, but the anxiety of having to provide answers gnawed at him like a dog chewing a bone.

"They had to send the results for the patch test kit to the company who made my prosthetic. Once it arrives, they can do the testing to see if I'm allergic to any of the materials." He drew in a breath before continuing. "And as far as another prosthetic, I first have to let my skin heal. Depending on what allergy I suffer from depends on what type of prosthetic I will need in the future. Most likely one made from different materials than the one I was wearing. If the same thing happens, it will be best for me not to use a prosthetic." He felt her head shift in a nod.

"Are you okay with that?"

"I'll have no choice but to be okay with it."

"Right," she whispered. "Let's pray for your leg to heal. Okay?"

Her voice came out softly, like a gentle breeze. He'd liked to imagine there was love in her voice. *If only.* "Sure." The corners of his mouth lifted into a strained smile.

The smile dropped and turned to disbelief as Jo bowed her head and laid a hand on his leg.

"Hello God, it's me Jo. This time I'm here with Evan. I wanted to ask that you bring healing to his body. God, you know all that He's been going through. His life is a better testament than my words could ever be. Yet, I wanted to try and speak to you. He needs Your healing touch upon him. Please restore his skin and take the pain away. Please remove any potential complications. And please help him get through this time with the grace You supply us with. I guess that's all, Amen."

The last word was uttered in a whisper, but he didn't mind. He ran his hands across her face and held on, hoping to convey his gratitude with the emotions gathered on his face. Only he could barely see her face out through the tears he was trying to hold back. So instead, he leaned forward and kissed her lips softly. His hands slipped from her face to cradle her head.

"That was the most beautiful thing anyone has ever done for me, JoJo," he said as he rubbed his lips across hers. "Thank you."

Her arms slid around his back and he hugged her to his chest, thankful for finding calm in the midst of a storm.

Chapter Thirty

$\mathcal{J}$ o stood back, surveying her handiwork. The laundry room had turned out nicely. The frontloading washer and dryers made it look complete. The shelving space she added almost made her want to do laundry. *Almost.* The dining room had also received a new coat of paint and wainscoting to complete the look. Now, all she had to do was finish the master suite and Evan would be set to move in.

A picture of his face filled her mind as her memory traced over his features. The crinkles at the corner of his eyes when he smiled. The white flash of teeth. The prominent cheekbones. The care that filled his eyes when he watched her. For his sake, she hoped he wouldn't be allergic to another prosthetic. She liked the new Evan. The one intent on letting God handle his life.

The angry, bitter Evan had nothing soft in his expression. Bitterness turned his mouth downward. His dark brown eyes had seemed lifeless with resentment and rage. She didn't want him to go back to that dark place.

The doctors had discharged him from the hospital a couple of days ago. His limb no longer had angry welts running the length of it, but it was still red and a little swollen. She made sure to visit him every night. It allowed her to get closer in a more comfortable setting. She didn't have to worry about impressing him like she would on a date.

Time had shown her how easy he was to talk to. They talked about everything from favorite foods to their beliefs about God. Most importantly, they ended each night with a prayer. She had never dated a guy who prayed, let alone prayed with her. It seemed to connect them on a deeper level. Evan wasn't just concerned about her everyday well-being, but her spirit as well.

And that was so attractive.

Jo wanted to do something special for him, so tonight she planned to make him dinner. Michelle promised to hang out with Chloe for the evening, so she didn't have to "watch you two make googley eyes at each other." Jo had laughed, but mentally agreed that was probably what she'd do.

Nana had given her the Baker family recipe for fried chicken, macaroni and cheese, and collard greens. For dessert she would make red velvet cake. She prayed it all turned out well. She'd never been good at making fried chicken.

Lord, please don't let me mess tonight up.

～

The sounds of a saxophone filled the living room with its haunting melody. Evan sat back in the leather recliner, letting the notes flow over him. He knew Jo liked jazz, but not like this. This was truly a throwback to the beginning of the movement. When he was a kid, Senior would play jazz whenever he worked on their vehicles or did repairs around the house. The music soothed him, reminding him of a simpler time.

He looked up as Jo entered the living room.

"Dinner's almost ready. A few more minutes on the chicken, then we can eat." Her lips curved upward.

He swallowed, trying to resist the urge to rub his hand over his heart. Jo had no idea what she did to him. Evan smiled back while etching her face into his memory. He never wanted to forget this moment.

It made him think they could have a future of nights listening to jazz and talking about their day.

Jo looked at him expectantly.

Right, dinner. "Sounds fantastic. The chicken smells delicious, too."

"Wait until you taste it. Nana finally gave me her recipe. She wouldn't give it to me before—"

He looked at her, puzzled. Why did she stop mid-sentence? "Why wouldn't she give it to you before?"

She looked away, but not before he caught a blush blooming against her skin. "Because I wasn't seeing anyone." She sighed and turned to face him. "Nana has a policy regarding recipes. She doesn't give them out to single people."

He laughed. He couldn't help it, especially since she looked so put out. "You mean to tell me she never gave you a single recipe until now? I can't believe you've been single that long."

"Well, no, I haven't. But, she didn't like any of my past boyfriends and refused to give me the recipes, because she told me the relationships wouldn't last." She said it in a hurry and then whirled away, disappearing into the kitchen.

Huh. Does that mean she thinks we'll last?

Evan grinned so wide his cheeks ached. He'd been worried about how Jo would feel now that he was back in his wheelchair, but maybe he didn't need to. He maneuvered himself from the recliner to his chair. When he wheeled into the kitchen, Jo finished plating the food. "Do you need any help, JoJo?"

"No," she said with a quick smile. "You can go to the dining room. I thought we'd eat in there."

"What's wrong with the kitchen?"

"Oh, Evan, just go to the dining room." She shooed him away and he chuckled softly.

He wheeled into the room and stopped. *So that's why she wanted to eat in here.*

The lights were dimmed, but a soft glow from several lit candles illuminated the room. The muffled sound of jazz carried into the dining room. The table had been set for two, although there was only one chair.

See, it doesn't bother her.

He wanted to believe being relegated to a wheelchair didn't matter to Jo, but how could he when it bothered *him*?

Jo arrived shortly, placing the plates on the table. "How about you lead us in prayer?"

He held on to her hand and prayed for them. He didn't know how long she would continue to date him, but he was going to thank God for every day with her. As he thanked God for the food and the hands that prepared it, he silently added on thanks that she was still with him. He squeezed her hand then reached for a drumstick.

He took a bite, chewing slowly. Nana Baker's recipe was awesome. It might even be better than his mother's.

"Well?"

He winked at Jo. "Fantastic. Be sure to thank Nana Baker for sharing the recipe."

"Definitely." She took a bite then looked at him when she was done chewing. "I was afraid the chicken was going to be awful. I never make it right."

"You just needed your grandmother's recipe."

"Or the right man."

They laughed in harmony.

"We should schedule another Bible study now that you're out of the hospital."

"That would be great." He really missed the group. "I just wish I could convince Guy to join us."

"He seems to be hurting pretty badly. What happened?"

"His wife died giving birth to the twins."

Horror filled Jo's eyes. "Oh, no! I can't even imagine."

Evan thought about his friend's words about 'platitudes.' How did you console a friend when you truly didn't know their pain? That would be a question he'd have to seek God for.

"I can't either." He cleared his throat. "I'll call Darryl and see if he's up for it Friday."

Jo put her spoon down and wiped her mouth. "I'm sure the girls would be interested. I'm not sure why Michelle has continued to go, but I'm praying the change sticks."

"And add Guy to your prayers, too, would you?"

"Of course." She squeezed his hand.

Thank You, God, for this woman.

Chapter Thirty-One

$\mathcal{J}$o rang the doorbell again, shivering from the subzero temperatures. What was taking Darryl so long? She turned to Evan. "Do you think he's okay in there?" She still couldn't believe they had ridden together. Like a couple.

"JoJo you already rang it twice, give the man some time to answer."

"But I'm freezing." She frowned, hating the whine in her voice but unable to stop it. Mother Nature had doused the entire state in frigid temperatures.

At the sound of a lock unlatching, she swung around. Darryl stood with the door wide open. She turned to Evan, "Can you maneuver inside?"

He nodded and she rushed inside.

She proceeded straight to the kitchen, hoping it was the warmest room in the house. She came up short when she noticed Chloe. "Hey Chlo, what are you doing here already?"

Chloe's cheeks turned a lovely shade of red. The poor girl's light complexion did nothing to hide the tell-tale flush. Jo bit the inside of her lip, trying to keep from laughing.

"Hey, Jo." Chloe picked up a mug and sipped from it, as if nothing unusual was going on.

Why did she get the distinct feeling her arrival had interrupted something? She looked at Darryl as he walked into the kitchen, talking nonstop to Evan. *He doesn't look guilty.*

She turned back to Chloe, who quickly averted her gaze. *Yep.* Something was up with these two. If it wasn't so cold, she'd make an excuse to take Chloe to the porch and investigate. She shivered. No, she didn't want to help her friend that badly. She'd just have to find out what happened later.

The doorbell rang again. "I'll get it," she offered. If it was Michelle, she wanted a chance to talk to her about Chloe and Darryl.

Jo made her way to the front door, rubbing her gloved hands together. Why couldn't she warm up? She opened the door and smiled as Michelle hurried inside.

"Brrr. It's freezing out there. What took you so long to answer?"

Jo laughed. "Stop being a baby. It took me two rings to get inside."

"Well you know my body can't handle the cold." The girl was so melodramatic.

"Then why haven't you moved down south yet?"

"Because you haven't. You know I love me some JoJo."

She chuckled, giving Michelle a hug. The girl was certifiably crazy, but made the best friend. She laid a hand on Michelle's arm as her friend started to move away. "Hey, when Evan and I got here I didn't realize that Chloe had been the first one here." She took off her gloves since her hands were finally warm. "Girl, she wouldn't look at me and her face is all red. I think something's going on."

Michelle's eyes widened. "I've been wondering about that." she whispered. "Do you think Chloe likes him?"

Jo wanted to laugh at the fact that she didn't even ask about Darryl's intentions. Everyone knew he liked her, except maybe Chloe. "Why else would she blush?"

"She is pretty proper. Maybe she was embarrassed at being in the house alone with a guy."

She snorted. Sure Chloe was straight laced, but Jo doubted that had anything to do with the current situation. "Nah, I think she likes him."

"Well, I'll keep an eye out."

They walked to the kitchen and the gang greeted Michelle warmly. Jo couldn't wait to hear what today's topic was. Every Sunday, she had listened to the sermons with an open ear and was beginning to believe that God truly had great plans for her. She was close to committing herself to Him, but something held her back.

～

Evan glanced around the table at his friends. His heart was a little heavy at the thought of Guy's absence. He prayed his friend would resolve his issues with God, sooner rather than later. He clapped his hands together. "Are we ready for the study?"

Everyone nodded and pulled out their various forms of the Bible.

"I hope no one minds, but I actually prepared a study today." He shrugged. "It hit me in the middle of the night." He passed out a sheet of paper to everyone.

"You wrote it out?" Jo asked, her eyebrows arched in surprise.

"I just wrote a few notes and a list of Scriptures I want to look at." Evan stared at his handout, trying to keep the heat from rising to his face. He wanted to run a finger under his collar but didn't dare. He already felt everyone's eyes on him.

"You picked anger?"

He glanced up at Michelle. He couldn't tell from her tone if she was upset or surprised. She met his gaze with a blank expression on her face. *Great, that doesn't help me any.* Yet, he instinctively knew he needed to tread softly. "Yes, I thought it would be good to look at righteous and unrighteous anger."

"There's such a thing as righteous anger?" Darryl asked.

His boys had been the main source of inspiration when he studied the Scriptures related to this topic. He knew how much anger Darryl had toward his father and how much anger Guy felt toward God. He even had his own past to pull from.

"Yes, let's dive right in. Turn to John chapter two, verse thirteen. I'll read until verse sixteen."

He cleared his throat and began reading. After reading the last verse, Evan looked up. Surprisingly, Michelle and Darryl were equally fixated on him.

"So that's righteous anger?" Darryl asked.

"Yes, exactly. They turned the temple into something it shouldn't have been. How can people worship the Lord or draw closer to Him when people are busy selling goods? Can you imagine the noise that would create?"

He had prayed long and hard over this study. He wanted God to give him the words, because he knew this would be a sensitive subject for most of them to examine.

"Why is it okay for Jesus to act like that?" Michelle asked. Her words came out measured.

"Think about it. He didn't hurt anyone. Instead, He appropriately admonished those who turned His Father's house into a 'den of thieves.' Sure, He made a whip and turned some tables over, but Jesus didn't use them to hurt the people. Think of it like a punctuation mark. They were in the wrong and needed to know it."

"Okay, sort of like punishing criminals here," Michelle stated. "We have a judicial system that makes sure people who break the rules are punished."

"Right."

He glanced at Darryl out of the corner of his eye. His friend's brow had furrowed and confusion marred his features. Evan knew a question would be coming, so he braced himself.

"Let me get this straight." Darryl replied. "Suppose I see a guy hit a girl. If I get angry at him for his lack of respect and horrible treatment of women, then that's righteous anger." Darryl stared straight into his eyes. "Right?"

Lord, please give me the words. Evan knew what his friend hinted at. However, he doubted anyone else at the table did. "Yes, that's righteous anger. God doesn't want any of His children to be harmed."

"Then how does that jive with forgiveness?" Jo asked.

Evan was surprised she'd kept quiet for so long. Then again, Jo liked to observe and come to her own understanding before jumping in with questions. "Great question, JoJo. It's okay to be angry at something that angers God. It's an honest emotion. What's not okay is to let that anger fester and rot inside. It's not okay to let anger lead your action, when that happens you entertain the possibility of righteous anger turning into unrighteousness." He paused, gathering his thoughts. *Please don't let me make a mistake with my thoughts. Please, steer me in the right direction.* "I just want to state this is how I've understood it. I'm not an expert, I just felt this was where God was leading me." He looked around to make sure everyone understood.

The group nodded, so he continued. "Think about it. How do you treat someone you're angry with?"

"Rudely," came Chloe's quiet reply.

"I agree, but God wants us to be loving to someone. If we're harboring anger in our hearts, then it becomes impossible to love our neighbor."

"But you just said there was righteous anger." Darryl pointed at his phone in disbelief. "Which is it?"

"The two do exist, Darryl. Sometimes, our righteous anger fuels us to make a change for the better. Like Michelle," he gestured toward her. "She prosecutes drunk drivers under the umbrella of Indiana state law."

Evan paused for a moment. "If she were to allow her emotions to turn into hate and prosecute someone unjustly, or more harshly than necessary, then that is not righteous anger."

Darryl ran a hand through his mop of curls, a look of frustration on his face. "How are we supposed to know when we cross over into unrighteous anger?"

"When the sun goes down and you're still angry." Evan shrugged. "But that's just one example. We have to be in constant communication with God so that the Spirit leads us and not our flesh."

"What do you mean, 'when the sun goes down'?" Michelle asked. Her eyebrow arched like a question mark.

"Ephesians four twenty-six says, 'Be angry, and do not sin': do not let the sun go down on your wrath." He cleared his throat. "When we let anger take root into our hearts, we give the devil a foothold to lean us toward the direction of letting our flesh rule instead of the Spirit."

"Why are there so many rules?" Darryl looked at him, frustration emanating from him like steam in a sauna.

"But are there really?" Chloe's soft question caused Darryl to blink rapidly. "Jesus told us there are only two rules and that any other rule falls under them. Love God and love your neighbor as yourself. It's the principle of the golden rule."

"How are we supposed to do that? It seems humanly impossible."

"By trusting God." Jo said. She appeared nervous, but kept talking. "We can't do any of it ourselves, I think that's the whole point. In order to do any of what He requires, we have to rely solely on Him. On His Spirit to guide us."

"Exactly," Evan stated. "It's a daily process. We have to take each moment as it comes and ask God to direct us. We're going to mess up, but the point is to seek Him regardless."

Chapter Thirty-Two

*E*van wheeled to the door. It never failed, whenever his mother or father were out running errands, someone knocked. His hands glided over the wheels, propelling him closer. He knew his mother wasn't expecting any guests, so maybe it was Jo. He grinned at the thought. Maneuvering in the wheelchair, he managed to open the door and slowly roll backward. One glance told him it was not Jo.

"Hello, Evan. May I come in?

What was she doing here?

"I know it must be a shock. I just wanted to talk."

"Brenda?" His voice reached an octave higher than normal, but it didn't register. Just like the sight of his ex-girlfriend-almost-fiancée didn't penetrate his brain.

"May I come in?" This time her voice held more timidity, enough to bring him to reality.

"Um, sure." He moved aside and shut the door behind her.

Brenda was here. Really here. In the flesh. But why?

"Evan, who's at the door?"

Evan froze at the sight of his mom coming down the hallway. He thought she was gone. He glanced at her then to Brenda. His mother stopped, midstride when she saw their guest. *This is not going to go well.*

"Hello, Brenda." The tone of his mother's voice added a distinct chill to the air.

"Hello, Mrs. Carter." Brenda straightened up but kept the contrite face.

Was she really sorry or was it all an act?

"To what do we owe this *pleasure*?" His mother stepped forward, wringing the kitchen towel.

Evan couldn't help but think his mother was imagining Brenda as the towel. This needed to end before it even started. "Mom, would you please bring me and Brenda some hot coffee? We'll have a seat in the parlor while we catch up."

"You want me to do *what*?" Each note increased with incredulity, until his mother ended up staring at him like he had two heads. Her hands fisted at her waist.

He stared at his mother, willing her to be cordial. *Please, don't make this worse.* Evan prayed his pleading look conveyed his thoughts.

"Fine," she snapped. She stomped down the hall toward the kitchen.

Moments later, he heard the pantry doors slamming shut. He gestured for Brenda to follow him. He took his time, letting the wheels move slowly under his hands.

Lord, I have no idea why she's here. Or what she could possibly want to talk about. Please, don't let my anger rule me, because I'm ready to let it loose.

Evan knew his mother still carried a grudge against his ex-girlfriend, but it paled in comparison to how he felt right now. She had left him, left him stranded in a hospital with a missing leg. Granted, she hadn't waltzed out of the place but she certainly never looked back.

Brenda sat down, pulling her black-and-white purse onto her lap. Her cropped-style hair made her appear more angelic and petite. Evan recalled from memory how small she was. She barely made it to his shoulders...when he stood, that is.

He stared at her, trying to find the words to begin.

"I'm sure you're wondering why I'm here." The softness of her words grated against every nerve in his body.

"It crossed my mind." The harshness of his tone echoed.

"I wanted to see how you were doing." Her eyes dipped downward in sadness.

Her doe eyes were accented by white eye shadow which made them all the more piercing. *Why was he noticing these details?* "Wow, you care now, huh?"

"Evan, you know I care."

"Do I? How do I know that? Was it the many calls you placed to my room? The daily visits?" He snapped his fingers. "I know. It was the time you took to bring me my favorite foods." He made a tsking noise. "I'm sorry. That wasn't you. You didn't come except to say you were breaking up with me. Well, you're about six months too late."

"I can see that." She looked away as if gathering her thoughts. When she looked back, resignation filled her face. "I just wanted to be sure that you're doing well."

Evan snorted. "That's the only reason you came? To see if I'm doing well?" He couldn't believe her. He never had a reason to distrust Brenda before, but that was before she decided she couldn't handle a 'cripple' for a boyfriend.

"Well, no." She stared at her hands. "The real reason I came was because I miss you." She looked back up and made direct eye contact. "Since you moved back here, I've become aware of this gaping hole in my life. The one you used to fill." Her voice had gotten softer as she continued, ending on a barely held back sob.

I'm going to be sick. Disgust filled his being. He couldn't help it. Her tears weren't going to work on him. In the past, this would have been the point he would rush to her and console her. But all he felt now was anger and betrayal. She'd professed to love him, and when the going got tough she left. *That* wasn't love.

～～

Jo jumped out of her truck, eager to see Evan. She'd stopped at the local deli to bring him his favorite sub. Of course lately, she'd use any excuse to see him. It seemed like days instead of hours since they last talked.

She walked up the B&B's front porch and rang the doorbell. Excitement, or maybe the cold, shook her body. She stared at the spot where the hole used to be. She'd finally plugged it the other night. Right before Evan had kissed her good night. Who knew he found a working woman in overalls so desirable. Her face warmed at the memory.

Mrs. Carter opened the door. "Good afternoon, Jo Ellen. What brings you here?"

Her brow wrinkled in confusion. Mrs. Carter always ushered her in with a warm hug. Why was she blocking the doorway? Her features seemed strained, the smile false.

"I brought Evan a meatball sub." Unease tingled her spine.

"Oh, how nice, dear. I'll make sure he gets it." Mrs. Carter reached for the bag.

Jo backed up. "How about I give it to him myself, Marilyn?"

"Oh honey, now's not a good time."

"Why? Is he feeling bad? Did something happen?"

The older woman's eyes softened. "He's fine. I just don't think now's a good time."

"Excuse me, Mrs. Carter."

Jo raised an eyebrow as a woman's voice spoke behind Evan's mom. Did they have a guest? She thought they took the month of December off?

Marilyn threw a worried glance at Jo then moved aside. A petite woman stood behind her, clearly startled when she saw Jo. Her eyes were red-rimmed, but that was the only sign that she wasn't composed. Her black-and-white-checkered peacoat had been cinched tightly at her waist, and a white scarf spilled over at the neckline. The whole ensemble seemed to match which, guessing from the gold label, also cost a pretty penny. She looked like she had been shopping in Michelle's closet.

Suddenly, Jo felt very self-conscious in her jeans and giant red parka. She shifted to the side as the woman slipped out. Her eyes fixed upon the woman's retreating back. When she faded from sight, Jo turned back to the house. Evan sat in his chair, looking troubled, and there was no sign of Marilyn.

Jo stepped inside, closing the door. "Hey, Ev, you okay?"

"Long day." He rubbed the back of his neck.

The atmosphere felt oppressive. What had happened since the last time she spoke to him? Jo cleared her throat. "Brought you a sub." She held out the bag, no longer feeling jubilant, but not sure why. Did that woman have something to do with his downcast face? "Who was that? I thought your mom didn't take guests in December."

"She doesn't." He sighed and ran a hand down his face. "That was my ex-girlfriend."

What? Jo stepped back, suddenly feeling lightheaded. "What was she doing here?" Her voice sounded shaky to her ears. She swallowed.

"Apparently, she wanted to 'check on me.'" He rolled his eyes, then rolled around, presumably headed for the kitchen.

She followed, but her steps felt unsteady. His ex must want him back. That was the only logical explanation for her to travel out here to 'check on him.' Jo wanted so badly to ask Evan if that's what his ex wanted, but a part of her was afraid to hear the answer.

Although, if the woman's red-rimmed eyes were any indication, she didn't get what she came for. The thought added a small measure of comfort.

Evan grabbed a plate from the counter and put it on his lap. He wheeled to the table. "Are you going to eat with me? I know there's more than a sub in that bag."

"Sure." She sat down on the bench seat. Eating no longer sounded appetizing. Not when her insides churned, imagining the conversation that had happened moments before.

"Hey, why the long face?"

"Does she want you back?" The words flew free as a bird. Jo couldn't grab them back and didn't want to either. She needed to know what she was up against.

"So she claims."

"And you don't believe her?" Her hands fisted in her parka pockets. Was Evan just saying what he thought she wanted to hear?

"I believe her as far as I can throw her." His lip curled in disgust. "And if she is telling the truth, then I don't care. You don't walk all over someone and then expect them to just give you a second chance."

The bitterness flowing from his mouth shocked her. She had no idea he harbored such resentment. Did that mean he still cared for his ex? "You wanted me to give you another chance."

His eyes widened in surprise. "Come on, that's not even the same thing."

"Why not?"

"I was a teenager for heaven's sake. And furthermore, the two of us weren't even dating, let alone engaged!"

She jumped back as he shouted.

Engaged? They were engaged?

"I thought she was just a girlfriend?" How she managed to croak out the words she couldn't even fathom.

"Jo," he sighed wearily, rubbing his forehead. "I was going to propose that night, but got my leg chopped off instead."

"Don't give me attitude, Evan Carter. You know good and well that's something that should be disclosed in a relationship."

"We've only been on one date." He held a finger up as the words echoed in the air.

"What?" she whispered. A tear slipped out before Jo could stifle it. She swiped at it, angry that she had let him see how much his words hurt.

"Jo, I didn't mean that like it sounded."

"Sure, forgive me if I don't believe you or want to give you another chance right now." She stalked out of the kitchen.

Stupid!

How could she have believed that he would ever truly change? She stormed past Mrs. Carter, eyes cloudy with unshed tears.

"Jo, come back."

She kept walking, ignoring Evan's pleas, and slammed the door shut. Jo didn't stop until she made it into the cab of her truck. As she shut the door, tears fell freely and sobs wracked her body.

Chapter Thirty-Three

E van stared up at the ceiling. Once again, he'd ended up in a bed. But this time, he had the strength to hobble to the hallway where his chair waited for him. This time he wasn't plagued with the nightmare of his crash.

No. Instead, his nightmare had been the look on Jo's face when he mentioned they'd only been on one date. He squeezed his eyes shut, trying to block out the image. Unfortunately, the look of hurt on her face became more clear. The sheen of tears glossing over her beautiful brown eyes took a prominent place in his mind's eye. No matter what he did, he couldn't escape the hurt that he'd caused Jo.

He called her repeatedly, but she wouldn't answer. Her voicemail was registered as full and no longer accepting any messages. Which left him alone, in the butler's pantry, to stare up at the ceiling. It always came down to him and the ceiling.

Alone.

With his thoughts.

Why did Brenda have to come back? If she hadn't arrived, he and Jo would be just fine. But no, she wanted to ask for a second chance. And what was with Jo reminding him of his own second-chance request. The two weren't even on the same playing field.

One night. One drunk driver. And poof. His life as he knew it had been over. He lost the job, lost the girl, and now he was in danger of losing Jo. The one who really mattered, judging by the ache in his chest.

He knew loving her wouldn't be easy.

A knock sounded.

"Come in," he heaved out. Talking was just a waste of energy. If his mother wasn't knocking to tell him Jo was here, then he didn't want to hear anything else.

"Ev, you want something to eat?" His mom peered at him as if assessing how severe his pity party was.

"No, thanks, Mom."

"Good." She nodded briskly. "Because Brenda's back. Now, you won't have to worry about losing your lunch."

"What?" He sat up straight. Why was she back? What more was there to say?

"She's in the parlor." A look of sympathy flashed across her face. "Do you want me to leave her there or what?"

Evan ran a hand over his face. It was bad enough she came yesterday. Two days in a row was a bit much. "Yeah, fine. I'll be there in a few."

His mother nodded and left the door open. He took a deep breath and stood up, leaning on the dresser. Evan stood there, indecision warring through his mind. Should he remain in the chair? Would he feel better if he could look down on her? Taking a chance, he grabbed his crutches that Julie had recently given to him. He hobbled into the parlor on them.

Brenda looked up, startled. "You're…you're walking." Her mouth dropped open and the wide, doe-eyed stare got bigger.

"They're just crutches," he huffed.

"Have you tried a prosthetic?"

He clenched his jaw. "How is that your concern?"

"I'm sorry. I just…I just want to make sure you're doing well."

"Yeah, you said that yesterday. I'm fine." He indicated toward the door with his head.

"You can leave now."

Brenda stood, wrapping her hands around the strap of her purse. "I didn't get to tell you everything yesterday."

Ugh. "Just get on with it already."

"Fine," she snapped. "I'm so sorry I can't move on as swiftly as you can."

"Are you kidding me?" By the shocked look on her face, he knew she was serious. *Unbelievable.* "You left *me*. Me, the one you'd been dating for two years. Two years! But as soon I got more than half my leg chopped off, you left. So *excuse* me, if I don't join your pity party. You've disrupted my life enough, so just say what you have to say and leave me alone."

His heart pumped so fast, Evan thought he might fall over. He could feel his pulse pounding in his head. His eyes glazed over as the anger swelled and took over his body.

"Thomas called me. He didn't know how to get in touch with you. They want you back."

He blinked. *What?*

Evan blinked again, staring down at the empty pants leg. *They wanted him back?* But…he was missing a leg. How useful could he be as a coach?

Brenda continued. "He wanted me to pass the information on to you and ask that you call him."

Her words stunned the beast inside and his anger fizzled out. *They wanted him back.*

"He gave me his card with all his contact information." She pulled a business card out of her purse and held her hand out.

He took it, but it was like he watched the scene from above. *They wanted him back.*

"Evan, I know how you feel about me and I understand. But don't let that stop you from getting your old job back. I know how much it meant to you to coach basketball at the high school." Brenda looked down as if she didn't know what else to say. A sigh escaped her lips. Everything she did had a gentleness to it. Always had.

And now he wondered what she hid with it.

"Anyway, just call Thomas. I'll stay out of your hair." She sidestepped him and headed down the hallway.

"Brenda, wait."

"Yes?" She whirled around, almost falling from the speed of it.

"Is that why you really came? To deliver Thomas' message?"

"No, that was just the excuse I needed."

A pause.

An inhale.

"Goodbye, Evan." A look of resignation filled her face, and she walked away.

∽

Jo was supposed to be at Evan's house finishing his master bathroom, but she couldn't go there. Not today and not after what happened yesterday. She stood on her Nana's front porch, legs jiggling to keep her warm.

She knocked again. What was taking her so long? It never took her this long to answer. She frowned as her upper thigh vibrated. Jo reached into her jeans pocket and pulled out her cell.

"Hello?"

"May I speak to Jo Ellen Baker."

The man's voice was kind, but she had no idea who it was. "Speaking."

"Miss Baker, this is Dr. Daniel Philips at Freedom Lake Hospital. I'm calling you regarding your grandmother, Rosemary Baker. She asked us to contact you."

"What? What's wrong with her?" She glanced at Nana's front door. No wonder she wasn't answering.

"First you need to know that she's in stable condition. She's had a heart attack. We're in the process of doing some tests to get a full prognosis." He continued on, but it didn't penetrate the fear roaring in her ears.

"I'll be right there." She jumped into the car.

Please, Lord, please. Don't let her die. Please, she's the only other person who loves me.

The key shook as she tried to get it into the ignition. Why wouldn't her hand stop shaking? "Come on!" She slammed her hand against the steering wheel. Sobs racked her body as her control slipped precariously. She was in no condition to drive. She dialed Michelle.

"Hey, girl."

"Nana just had a heart attack. The doctor called. I need to get to the hospital right now, only my hand won't stop shaking and I can't get my truck to start." Her last words ended on a sob as her body once again began to shake.

"Where are you?"

"At her place."

"I'll be right there, don't move."

Jo hung up, her hands still shaking. Her pulse pounding. Tears ran down her face, and she knew any minute her nose would join the disaster.

Please, Lord, please. Don't let her die.

Trust Me.

A sob escaped Jo and her hand flew to her mouth to muffle the sound. *She's my grandmother! She's more of a mother to me than my own. Please, don't take her.*

Trust Me.

"Open the door, JoJo."

She glanced at the window and noticed Michelle. Her friend motioned for her to get out. Jo complied and

Michelle immediately wrapped her arms around her. "I'm here, girl. I'm here."

As Michelle drove to the hospital, Jo couldn't contain her tears. They fell without restraint as she pleaded with God the entire way.

Once at the hospital, Jo walked up and down the halls. She couldn't sit. Couldn't remain in the spot where she'd received the news that her father had passed away. Nana had gone into surgery over an hour ago. The doctor informed her that her grandmother had hardened plaque in her arteries. They were going to do bypass surgery.

She was so scared. It was like the nightmare of her dad's death repeated all over again, sort of a depressing twist to that movie *Groundhog's Day*. And she desperately wanted to call Evan. The desire to hear his voice, to hear his words of comfort, called to her. Except, every time she went to dial his number, the echo of his words greeted her. *We've only been on one date.*

The words hit her like a punch to the gut. It took her breath away. She hadn't told anyone what had happened. It had been the reason she went to see Nana Baker. Now the one person who could offer comfort was lying on an operating table, fighting for her life.

Life was so unfair.

Jo glanced over at Michelle. The girl had refused to leave her alone at the hospital. She wanted to unload and share her anxieties, but Jo didn't know if Michelle was the best person to help her. Why couldn't she trust anyone?

What's wrong with me, God?

A tear dropped and she wiped it away, turning to face the window. She felt so alone. She felt…forsaken.

Trust Me.

She heard the words, but her heart felt closed off. How could she trust Him when she was so alone?

Chapter Thirty-Four

A few hours later, the sound of footsteps jolted Jo from her slumped-over perch in a waiting room chair. She straightened up, looking around to get her bearings. Her mother sat in a chair and, if that wasn't shocking enough, Darius had shown up. Jo hadn't wanted to call them, but Michelle had insisted, then promptly left upon their arrival. Vanessa was, big surprise, out of town. Dr. Philips strode down the corridor, headed their way.

For a moment, time froze as Jo remembered the last time a doctor delivered news. Her throat seized and her heart stuttered. Her mother rose and Jo held her breath, waiting for the results.

"Mrs. Baker, Ms. Baker, Mr. Baker," Dr. Philips said, nodding to each one of them. "The surgery went just fine. We ended up fixing two arteries. Your grandmother is in the recovery room. Once she leaves, we'll place her in ICU for round-the-clock observation as a precaution."

A tear slipped down her cheek. Relief flooded her soul. God hadn't forsaken her. "Okay," she nodded.

ICU.

"How long will she have to stay there?" her brother asked.

"One to two days. I'll check on her tomorrow when I make my rounds. If her labs and vitals all look good, then we'll move her down to the medical surgery floor. She'll stay there for a few days before I discharge her to go home."

"Once she does go home, will she be able to live by herself or will she need help?" her mother asked.

For once, Jo was thankful for her presence. She had no mental fortitude to think of pertinent questions.

"She'll need help for a couple of weeks. I don't want her driving for at least four weeks. Once we do more tests and follow-up appointments, I'll be able to give you a better idea of when she can resume normal activities. She'll need to change her diet," he cautioned. "I'm guessing she eats a lot of fatty foods."

Jo nodded. She'd never thought of Nana's cooking as fatty. She'd just been happy to get a plate. All the memories of her grandmother's famous soul food dinners came to mind. Obviously, they were the culprit of her hardened arteries. Jo wanted to be mad, but she didn't know anyone from her grandmother's generation who didn't overindulge in that kind of food. Maybe she could find a healthier cookbook to give to her.

"Will I be able to see her tonight?" she asked. Her voice came out raspy from unshed tears and lack of use.

"Once they have her settled in ICU, they'll probably allow you to visit for five minutes. Visiting hours are over, but they'll make an allowance considering how late we did the surgery." Dr. Philips paused, looking at each of them. "Tomorrow, you'll be able to visit during normal hours, but ICU doesn't have long visiting periods due to the severity of the patients' health issues."

"We understand," her mother responded. She held out a hand. "Thank you so much, Dr. Philips."

"My pleasure." He shook her hand, then turned and walked away.

All of a sudden the words that God had been whispering to her came through, loud and clear. *Trust Me.*

She closed her eyes in guilt. She'd been so anxious that she questioned His trustworthiness. Jo bowed her head and offered thanks to God for her grandmother. Gratitude filled her heart.

God, it's me, Jo. Thank You so much for my Nana. I'm so sorry for doubting You. I thank You that You're ever patient with me. That You are with me. I'm sorry for believing You'd leave me alone. Thank You for loving a sinner like myself. Thank You for Your saving grace. Thank You for welcoming me home. Amen.

Jo exhaled, letting all the stress out. For the first time in a long time, she finally believed everything would be all right. God just wanted her to trust Him with the details. She felt like she'd finally returned to the kingdom of God.

∾

Evan rolled down the hall to the front door. Last night had been rough, and he didn't have the energy needed to exert himself with crutches.

The bell rang. He groaned. It seemed like it was always ringing. He wished he could move in to his own place right now; he was so very tired of the many visitors the B&B received. In fact, he tired of being in this house with no privacy. He wished Jo would hurry up and get the renovations completed.

An image of a smiling Jo, complete with overalls, flashed in his mind. He blinked, trying to erase the image, but it remained even though his eyes were wide open. She wouldn't return his phone calls. Wouldn't answer the knock on her bungalow door. He had known she was home because her truck had been parked outside. How could they resolve this if she never picked up the phone?

Maybe, if you hadn't cheapened your relationship to one date, she'd answer. He scowled. If he could take those words back, he would. But how?

Evan opened the door, rolling his chair backwards as he pulled it open.

Brenda.

Again.

"What do you want, Brenda?" He ran a hand down his face. *Lord, I don't think I can take anymore.*

Her mitten-encased hands twisted the strap of her purse. She looked cold as her body shivered in the winter wind. A peacoat wasn't going to do much in the dead of an Indiana winter. Reluctantly, he motioned her inside. If she got frostbite, she may never leave Freedom Lake.

"I just wanted to say one last thing and then I'll leave you alone," she breathed out. Her soft voice which used to seem like a warm caress, now paled in comparison to Jo's soothing tone.

"Fine, state your piece, then leave me alone."

"I want you back," she stammered out. "I miss you and I kick myself daily for breaking up with you. But I didn't know how to handle everything that had happened. My parents wanted me to focus on healing. They encouraged me to go back home and get away from it all."

"Get away from what exactly? Me?" He pointed to his chest, anger coursing through him. Did she think he would let her cast the blame on her folks?

"Did you forget I was injured as well? Did you forget I needed healing, too? Or did you think you were the only one who needed to get away from it all?" Bitterness coursed through him. "I sure hope your mommy and daddy picked up the pieces of your shattered life." The words spewed from his mouth like a fire hose. He was beyond disgusted. How did he ever believe that he was in love with such a selfish person?

"Of course, I knew you were hurt. Evan, I love you. I wanted to be with you, but my parents…"

He cut her off. "You're a grown woman, Brenda. If you can't make decisions on your own, then you have no business being in a relationship. What would you do if we ever got married and life became too much? Would you run back home then?"

"Evan, please, don't be like that."

Evan sighed. This was getting him nowhere. *Lord, I'm losing my cool. I'm so mad, I want to spit! Please, give me the words to make her realize how much she hurt me.*

Forgive.

What? He blinked. How could he? She'd left him alone in the hospital.

"Evan, please, say you forgive me. Please, take me back."

He stared at her as she pleaded. The anger left the instant her eyes glistened with tears of obvious hurt. He'd dated her long enough to know when she was faking and when she wasn't. Too bad her love hadn't been strong enough to withstand the pressure from her parents.

Then you wouldn't have fallen for Jo.

Realization dawned on him. He and Brenda weren't right for each other. And just like that, the fight left his body. There was no reason to hold a grudge. "You're right. I shouldn't be acting like this. The accident wasn't your fault and you did what you thought was best."

"Yes, exactly. I was just so confused. I never meant to hurt you." She shook her head, relief shining in her eyes.

"I believe you." He sighed, taking in a cleansing breath as he gathered the necessary courage. "I forgive you, Brenda."

Tears slipped down her face as a whispered "thank you" fell from her lips.

Evan wished he could prevent further pain, but he knew the next words would be a blow to her delicate nature. "I forgive you, Brenda, but I don't want to resume our relationship."

"What?" The words came out on a rush of air. Her tears seemed to stop in their tracks. "What do you mean? You love me, Evan, I know you do."

"I thought I did. I really did." He swallowed, wishing he could lessen the impact. "But going through this, healing from the loss of my leg *and* you. Well, it all taught me that we weren't right for each other."

"How can you say that?" she cried out. Brenda stepped forward, her hand out before her as if she was trying to grasp for help. She laid a hand on his arm, then immediately pulled it back as if burned, when she glanced at his chair.

"Brenda. You don't want to be with me. I think you have some idea in your head that you wronged me leaving like you did. I think you have a sense of…" he paused, searching for the right word. He ran a hand down the back of his head, pausing at the nape of his neck. "Obligation. You feel obligated to be with me considering what happened."

She shook her head in denial, backing up with every shake of her head. "No, that's not true."

"It is. If it wasn't, you wouldn't be trying so hard. When it's right, it's right. But you're forcing something that shouldn't be."

"I…" she stopped and looked at him. "I'm sorry." Her shoulders slumped downward. She looked defeated and beaten down by life.

"I forgive you. Truly."

With a wave of the hand, she walked out, without a backward glance.

Evan's heart ached for her, but he knew there was no love lost. They had been together because it had been easy and, when it wasn't, going their separate ways had been just as easy. He had never tried to call her when she walked out. Yet, Jo had been gone for two days and he was going stark raving mad from the loss.

∽

Evan groaned. He refused to answer the door again. The doorbell had pealed shortly after he made it to his room. His mother would just have to get it.

"Knock, knock," she called out.

"Yes?"

His mom stuck her head through the doorway. "You have a visitor."

"Please tell me it's not Brenda." No one could be that oblivious.

"Nope." She opened the door to show Michelle standing next to her.

"What are you doing here?"

His mom walked away and Michelle walked in. "I should be asking you the same question."

"What? I live here." *What was wrong with her?*

"I know that." She rolled her eyes. "But why are you here instead of at the hospital with Jo. She's been so sad."

His heart dropped to his stomach. "What do you mean? What's wrong with her?" He sat up and reached for his crutches.

"Wait a minute," Michelle arched an eyebrow, her hand in the stop position. "You haven't heard? Nana Baker had a heart attack and has been in ICU for two days. Jeez, I thought you two told each other everything."

Oh, no. Jo had to be frantic with worry. "She isn't talking to me." And maybe this was why.

Michelle stared at him, confusion darkening her hazel eyes. "Why isn't she talking to you? What happened?"

"It's just a little misunderstanding. If she would return my calls, then it could be cleared up."

"Jo doesn't misunderstand things. Are you sure you didn't misspeak?"

He sighed and ran a hand over his face. "I did say something and it came out wrong. I tried to apologize, but she hasn't spoken to me since then. It didn't help that my ex came by as well."

She let out a whistle. "Then I suppose you better get to the hospital and fix it."

"Can I get a ride?"

"Let's go."

The ride to the city was quiet, but Evan didn't mind. He needed time to pray.

Lord, I don't know what's going on with Jo's grandmother, but please bring healing to her. Please give wisdom to the doctors. Please strengthen Jo and let her cling to You and draw closer. Lord, I know she's so close to trusting You, but this will set her back. It's her grandmother. Her last link to her father, please help her. Amen.

Michelle pulled up to the hospital and he turned to her. "Are you coming in?"

"No, I'm not who she wants and I'm okay with that. Go be there for her. Chloe and I will bring her truck up later, so you'll have a way to get back once she's ready to leave."

"Thanks, Michelle."

She nodded. "I'll get your chair."

After settling into the chair, Evan rolled inside the hospital. *Lord, I forgot to ask that You pave the way for me. I'm not sure how upset she'll be to see me. Please, just let me be a comfort to her.*

Chapter Thirty-Five

$\mathcal{J}$ o stared out of the hospital window. It was odd how often life mirrored the seasons. The winter wind seemed fierce as it whipped the trees. She could feel the cold seeping from the window seal, trying to sink its frigid talons into her skin. The overcast skies and lifeless trees depressed her, reminding her of the inevitability of death. Then there was the other side of winter.

The fresh coat of snow ensconced the earth like a blanket, turning the dark dead of winter into something wondrously majestic. Something to admire. Something to hope in. Would her life mirror a fresh start or choose the dark path? So far, God had healed her grandmother and kept her from death's door. But the prognosis seemed tenuous at best. She wasn't ready to lose her last beloved family member. If Nana left, who would remain?

Her mother. The woman who admitted she couldn't love like Jo needed to be love.

Her sister. The one who hated her guts from some unknown reason.

Her brother, who remained full of apathy when it came to family.

Once Nana had been moved to ICU, he'd left and hadn't visited since. Jo rarely said two words to him unless it was his birthday or a holiday that her mother forced them to celebrate together. Darius had made his own family and there was no more room for anyone else.

Leaving her to go through life alone…if God called Nana home.

Trust Me.

She brushed a stray tear away, hating that she had given in to the pity party, but unsure of how to stop. She trusted God, but her grandmother was still sick. They wouldn't let her leave ICU. Jo seemed incapable of preventing worry from gnawing at her stomach like termites who had joyfully found wood to dine on.

She was scared.

"Jo?"

She froze. What was *he* doing here? What more could they possibly have to say to one another? Jo stared out the window, willing Evan to leave her alone.

Alone?

She drew in a ragged breath. If he was here, was she truly alone?

"JoJo, please talk to me."

She turned around, her heart aching from the sound of desperation in his words.

"I'm so sorry about Nana," Evan said softly, wheeling closer to her.

The gulf between them seemed to disappear, but she still felt miles away from him. How ironic. She went from wanting to hear his voice with each passing second to dreading the much needed conversation.

Only one date.

"How is she?"

Finally Jo met his glance, trying not to flinch under his scrutiny. "She's in critical condition. It looks like she may be developing pneumonia from her stay." She almost startled at the sound of her voice. It sounded dead, stripped bare like the trees outside.

But they are covered by Me.

She shook her head. Did it matter when they were stripped and left with nothing? Jo drew in a ragged breath. Could she reign in her emotions? What happened to the peace she had felt the other day? With one negative word from the doctor, she had gone back to worrying and feeling alone. But she refused to wilt in front of Evan.

Never again.

"I've been praying for her since I heard."

"How did you hear? I didn't tell you." Jo frowned. "How did you get here anyway?" *And why do you care*, her soul cried out. He'd said his piece. Made it abundantly clear where they stood.

"Michelle told me and gave me a ride. I came as soon as I heard."

Of course. She'd have to have a word with her roommate. First, she needed to sort through the feelings warring inside her. Should she feel grateful that he came over right away? Did he care as a friend or something more?

"I've been trying to call you."

Jo touched her pockets, going through the motions as she searched for her phone. "I must have left my cell at home."

A flash of emotion passed through his eyes. She almost thought it looked like relief, but what could concern him? She turned to look down the hall leading toward the ICU corridor. It remained dark. One nurse said it helped the patients get the best rest.

Jo disagreed. It felt like they were ushering death into the place. But what did she know? She wasn't a nurse or a doctor, just someone desperately wishing for life to remain.

"Do you want to sit down and tell me what happened?"

"Why? You already know she had a heart attack. What more do you need to know?"

Why was her voice so flat? Where had the hope of the day before gone?

Away with her grandmother's promised recovery. She hated the seesaw ride that her emotions put her through. They felt so precarious. She needed them to be stable. Desperately needed stability.

Trust Me.

"Oh, God, I can't," she mumbled. "My grandmother's lying on a bed, in a dark room, fighting for her life and you want me to trust You? Bring her back to her vibrant self and I'll trust You." She sank onto the nearest chair, sobbing her heart out.

She had snapped. She couldn't even be brave in front of Evan. Why must that man always see her crying?

The sound of his chair briefly penetrated as he drew closer, but her tears refused to stop. Jo startled as Evan lifted her up and cradled her in his lap. His arms wrapped around her as he tucked her head against his chest. With a moan, Jo gave into her fear and the sorrow poured out like water running down a gutter.

∽

Evan held onto Jo as if his life depended on it. Violent sobs shook her body as she let out all of her emotions. She was still rambling and speaking of trust and the dangerous state of her grandmother's health. It was like he wasn't even there.

God, guide me. Help me help her.

He ran a hand down her hair in soft strokes and started crooning the soft words of *Amazing Grace*. Evan sang to her until her sobs calmed to quiet sniffles. He continued stroking her hair while rubbing her back. Even though he did it to calm her and show her he was there for her, it affected him more.

How he wanted to be there for her every day. Calming her fears. Cheering on her accomplishments. Evan wanted to love her in every way possible. He wanted to be with Jo for a lifetime. He wanted to love her and commit himself to her and her alone.

Evan knew he loved Jo Ellen Baker with his entire being and would for life.

The thought slammed into his body so forcefully it shook with the emotion. When he had said they had only been on one date, he wasn't trying to minimize their relationship. He'd just been so shocked at the strength of feeling he had for her, considering how very little time they'd been together.

What about all the other times you spent with each other?

Jo had been there every day of his hospital stay. Brought him his favorite foods while his body healed from the toxins of the allergen. She'd talked with him over jazz, sharing her hopes and dreams.

No, their relationship went far deeper than a mere date. It had evolved into a partnership without him even realizing it. And before he made the move to date her, his psyche had already started down the path with a simple crush that began in his teenage years. He could only pray that she would forgive him and give him another chance, because he had used up his second one.

Please, Lord, let her forgive me and give me chance after chance for the rest of our lives. I pray that she is the woman You have for me. I love her and want to take care of her and cherish her for as long as You have me here on this Earth. In a wheelchair or not.

He thanked God for listening and for hearing his prayer. Jo moved slightly, struggling to sit up. She looked into his eyes, and he stilled his hands.

"You just let me cry." Her eyes searched his.

For what, he wasn't sure. Did she see something positive? Had his action shown her how sorry he was?

"I haven't cried like that in years."

"Thank you for trusting me with your tears." He wiped a stray one away. Her skin was so smooth. Her eyes reminded him of a sweet truffle.

"Why would you reduce our relationship to one date?"

His eyebrows rose up in surprise. He hadn't expected that. He thought she would want to talk about her grandmother. To think, he had just been pondering the exact same situation. "My feelings for you took me by surprise. I thought voicing my thoughts would show me how ridiculous it was to feel so strongly for you after one date."

Her eyes widened in surprise. He prayed it meant a good surprise and not a bad one.

"So then why didn't you just say *that*?"

"Ah Jo, you know I'm not good at sharing my feelings. Look how I tormented you in high school. Do you think it's because I hated you? It was because I was so shocked to be attracted to you."

"But I had glasses and braces." Her brows wrinkled in bewilderment. She looked adorable.

"True. But it's never been about your looks."

The clearing of a throat startled them both and Jo jumped off his lap. He stared down at his empty hands, missing her presence already.

"Ms. Baker, I have an update on your grandmother."

Evan rolled toward the doctor so that he could take his place next to Jo. He wished he could stand next to her and tuck her into his side for safe keeping, but just being next to her would have to suffice. He reached out for her hand and sighed in relief as she linked her fingers through him.

"How is she, doctor?"

"I'm afraid the news isn't good, Ms. Baker. The pneumonia is progressing rapidly and an infection has developed at her incision site. At her age..." he trailed off, a frown marring his features.

"At her age," Evan prompted.

"At her age," he cleared his throat. "It's unlikely she will recover. If you're praying people, now would be the time." The doctor relayed his regrets and then turned back down the hall toward ICU.

Evan couldn't believe it. The doctor all but stated that they were waiting for her to die.

Lord, please bring healing to Nana Baker. And please let Jo feel Your presence. She's going to need You if healing Nana on this earth isn't in Your plans.

He could only hope that Jo would allow him to be there for her as well.

Chapter Thirty-Six

*J*o watched as Dr. Philips walked away. She couldn't believe it. He seemed so defeated, so prepared for her Nana to die. *She can't die, Lord.* Nana had to live. If she died, who would be there to cheer for her when she got married? Who would tell her children stories of their ancestors? Or better yet, make them cookies?

Who would encourage her to trust God and look to Him for answers? Who would remind her that she only had one sister and needed to become friends with her? Her grandmother had practically assumed the role of her conscience. Without her, who would she be?

Jo sank into the nearest waiting room chair. How had life taken such a turn for the worst? Suddenly last week's Bible reading flashed in her mind. She had been reading the first chapter of Job after he had lost everything. What had he said? Oh yeah, *"The LORD gave, and the LORD has taken away; Blessed be the name of the LORD."* Even in his anguish, Job had sung praises to the Lord.

Was that where she went wrong? She'd been ignoring His whispers of trust and, instead, focused on the what-ifs. Jo closed her eyes, ashamed, feeling the tenuous trust slowly building like a brick wall.

God, it's me, Jo. I'm so sorry I've been ignoring You. You've been telling me to trust You and I know it's because I don't trust anyone. Look at how easily I pushed Evan away because of that.

God, please help me trust You and remember that You are holy and worthy to be blessed, no matter what's going on in my life.

"You okay?"

She looked up, startled from her prayer. For a moment, she had forgotten Evan even existed.

"Yes, just praying and praising God for being worthy."

Evan blew out a breath of air. "You're amazing."

"What? No, I'm not. I had to be reminded that no matter what's going on in my life, He's still worthy of praise."

Evan laughed, but there was nothing comical about the noise. It sounded weary and slightly bitter. "It took me a few months to remember that."

"Some people are slow learners." She grinned at him.

His laughter warmed her heart. It felt much better to share joy with him instead of pain.

"Evan, please forgive me for ignoring you and shutting you out. I shouldn't have done that. All it allowed me to do was wallow in self-pity. You didn't say anything that wasn't true."

"JoJo, I forgive you if I must, but I'd rather you forgive me." He caressed her cheek. "I shouldn't have reduced our relationship to nothing. It's been a long time coming and I let my fear keep me from admitting we have something special." He traced her lips with a soft touch. "Go out with me, JoJo. Let's make this a two-date relationship?"

She grinned, lightness pushing out the darkness. She didn't know what was going to happen with her grandmother, but she knew she wanted Evan to weather the storm with her. "It's a date." Jo leaned forward and brushed her lips against his.

∽

Silence filled the hospital chapel. Evan looked around, thankful that Darryl, Chloe, and Michelle had all gathered to pray for Jo's grandmother. He had invited Guy, but his friend wanted no part in the "farce." Instead, he wished Jo and her grandmother good thoughts. Evan wanted to shake some sense into his friend, but that would most likely cause him to retreat further.

"Thank you so much for coming, you guys." Jo looked at them all with gratitude.

The group nodded.

"I'll start," Evan offered.

They joined hands and bowed their heads.

"Father, we come to You today to lift up Nana Baker. Lord, You know how many days she has here on this earth, and all we ask is that it not be in the near future. Lord, please heal her body and give the doctors wisdom to treat her adequately and fully."

He paused. What else could he say?

"Lord," Chloe chimed in. "We thank You for giving Jo the strength to get through this. We know that You are here with her, no matter what happens."

Chloe's soft voice faded, but the silence didn't last long.

Darryl began talking. "Lord, um, I'm rusty at this, but I wanted to ask that You would help those caring for Nana Baker show her Your love. I have to believe that Your love would be better than all of ours combined, so please shower her with it as well as Jo, so they can get through this. Thanks."

Evan wanted to clap his friend on his back. He was proud of D. The boy was trying.

"I guess it's my turn," Michelle said quietly. "Lord, You know how I feel about death.

Even though I understand no one can escape it, I wish no one had to endure it. Please, don't take Nana Baker. Not now, not yet. Please," she whispered.

The sound of sniffles broke through.

"Lord, it's me Jo. Thank You for surrounding me with people who care about me and Nana. I can't thank You enough. Amen."

"Amen," they chorused.

Evan looked around and met Jo's gaze. He crooked his finger at her and she walked up to him.

"What's up?"

"I have to go see Dr. Benson. He consulted with the allergist regarding my results. I'm going to go find out the results now."

"Do you want me to come with you?" Her eyes darkened with concern.

Man, was he thankful for her. "No, you worry about Nana Baker. I'll be back once the appointment is over."

She leaned forward and placed a kiss on his lips. "Okay."

He said his good-byes to the rest of the group and headed for the orthopedic floor.

~~

"I'm allergic to plastic?" Evan couldn't believe what he was hearing. "How is that even possible? Wouldn't I have figured that out by now?"

"Doctors and researchers are just now discovering polypropylene allergies. It's quite possible you've had reactions in the past, but they weren't severe enough to alert you."

A plastic allergy?

"Also, if you think about it, your skin rarely comes into contact with plastic. However, since you were wearing the prosthesis day in and day out, it aggravated the contact dermatitis on a daily basis. Some allergies develop over time and others are more instant."

"Can I get another prosthetic?"

"Yes, if it can be made without plastic. I would also encourage you to look into forearm crutches. They're another means of mobility. A lot of patients who have problems wearing a prosthesis decide to go with those. They have some high-end ones as well, not the kind a doctor hands you for a sprained ankle. You can buy ones that are made to walk on ice, survive tornados, etc. And of course, without plastic."

He could get another prosthesis. He wanted to shout with joy. *Thank You, God!*

"I need to caution you," the doctor continued. "If you go with another prosthesis, you *need* to let me or your prosthetist know of any abnormal skin changes. Don't let it get bad like this again."

"Understood." Evan knew he was grinning from ear-to-ear, but he couldn't help it. He could get another prosthesis and get out of the chair.

Why he'd even depended on it as much as he did was beyond him. The underarm crutches had been uncomfortable. He'd never even thought about forearm crutches. But none of that mattered, because he could get another prosthetic.

～

Jo picked up her cell phone. The hospital's number flashed on the caller id. She took a deep breath and answered.

"Ms. Baker, could you please come to the hospital?"

"Yes, how's my Nana doing?"

"She's off oxygen."

"Wait, what?"

"She's off her oxygen, Ms. Baker. She's able to breathe on her own."

"Thank you, Lord!"

"Amen."

Jo blushed. She hadn't realized she thanked Him aloud. "I'll be there as soon as I can." She wanted to jump and shout. "Yes!"

"What is all that racket?" Michelle said, peering in her room.

"Nana is off oxygen. She can breathe on her own. They want me to come to the hospital."

Michelle clasped her heart. "I'm so happy for you, girl. Mind if I tag along?"

"Of course not. Let's go."

Jo opened the front door to the bungalow, eager to get there and stopped.

"Hello, Jo Ellen." Her mother looked prim and proper and not the least bit chilled. How the woman always looked put together was beyond her.

"Mother. What are you doing here?"

"I came to see if there is anything I can do to help out with your grandmother. We've been praying for her at church."

Tears sprang to her eyes. Despite the issues she had with her mother, the thought of her actually praying for Nana made her forget every single grudge she'd harbored against her. Without thought, she wrapped her mother in a hug. "Thank you so much."

Her mother cleared her throat and patted her awkwardly before removing herself from Jo's embrace. "It's the Christian thing. Plus, your father would be filled with worry if he were still alive to see her go through this."

Agreed. "Well, I just got a call saying she's doing better. I'm headed there now." She stopped, searching her mother's gaze. "Would you...would you like to come with me and Michelle?"

"I don't want to impose." Her gaze darted away and then returned.

If Jo didn't know any better, her mother was actually nervous. "I would like the company."

"Yes, Mrs. Baker. Why don't you and Jo…Ellen go and I'll stay here." Michelle directed a smile toward her mother and squeezed her arm.

"Sure." Her mother looked over her shoulder at the driveway. "Why don't I drive?"

"Sounds great, Mother." Jo tossed a wave to Michelle and headed for her mother's Jaguar.

Jo settled into the leather interior, intent on making the drive pleasant. She didn't know what made her mother extend an olive branch, but she would accept it.

"How have you been dealing with this?"

She looked at her mother, surprised at the question. Was her mother trying to do better at showing she cared? "It's been rough. We held a prayer meeting at the chapel yesterday. I was praying that it would turn her toward the better, but before I left the hospital her status remained the same."

"Well, your prayers worked, just not as quickly as you hoped."

"Yes, I'm getting the hang of this prayer thing. Or rather more importantly, trusting in God."

Her mother glanced at her. "Good. No one can make it through life without Him."

"Amen," she whispered.

Chapter Thirty-Seven

E van walked down the hall, his crutches barely making a sound. After the good news from the doctor, he decided it was time to ditch the wheelchair. He'd become lazy and too dependent on it. It was time to take back his independence, regardless of his mode of transportation. He shifted the crutches under his arm, so that he could open the door.

A lady glanced up from her computer screen, her eyes squinting behind her glasses as she tried to focus. "Good morning, may I help you?"

"Yes, I'm here to see Principal Parker. I have a two o'clock appointment."

She glanced down at her computer screen and he noticed the pencil sticking out of her bun.

"Are you Mr. Carter?"

"Yes, ma'am."

"Have a seat and I'll notify the Principal."

Evan sat down and straightened his tie. He couldn't believe he decided to apply for the assistant coach position. Now, if he could only make it through the interview.

An African-American woman came out of the office marked Principal. He looked at her, trying to keep his face neutral, but inside his thoughts were whirring. Wasn't she the same principal that had run the school when he attended?

He walked forward then stopped to hold out his hand. "Afternoon, Principal Parker."

"Mr. Carter, my have you grown. I'm sure you don't remember me, considering you never came into my office."

He chuckled. "I thought it was you, but you looked young, so I didn't want to say anything."

Principal Parker laughed. "Flattery will get you everywhere. Step inside my office, Mr. Carter."

Evan sat down and said a quick prayer. He couldn't believe how nervous he was.

"I see you were a coach in Chicago. What made you move back to Freedom Lake?"

"I moved back home after the accident. It seemed to be the best move for me. I've bought a home, so I intend to remain in Freedom Lake. After all, it's where I was born and raised." He swallowed, wishing he could loosen his tie. Did he sound fake? Was it believable? Granted he hadn't wanted to return home, but he knew now this is where he was supposed to be.

Freedom Lake was home.

"That's understandable. And you're willing to coach at Freedom High? We don't have the prestige as some of the private schools in Chicago. Our boys pray and hope that they'll get a scholarship to Purdue or U of I, but it's not guaranteed. There'll be no fame or glory."

"But there'll be family." He shifted in his seat and wiped his palms against his slacks. "One of the things I remember most about high school was the family atmosphere. Our coach pushed us hard, but he also treated us like family. I'm okay with not being famous, Principal Parker."

She sat back and looked at him.

He met her gaze, praying he didn't blink or fidget. He didn't know what she was thinking but he prayed it was only good thoughts. "Well, I can't say this officially, but welcome back to Freedom High...Coach Carter."

Evan grinned. "Thank you so much." He grabbed his crutches then stopped. "Um, my disability…"

"Is not a problem. If you need any modifications, simply let us know."

"Will do."

～

Jo carried the tray into her grandmother's room. "Breakfast." She smiled, thankful Nana was back home. She had been ordered to rest for a few days and had been placed on a strict diet. Jo looked down at the egg white omelet, wheat toast, and bowl of grapes. *Lord, please help her stick to this diet.* After all, the woman did love her soul food.

"Thank you so much, JoJo."

"Of course, Nana. Happy to help." She sat the tray over Nana's legs. "Let me get my breakfast and I'll join you."

She came back with her plate. Jo figured she'd eat the same meals to show support. Besides, if the heart problems were hereditary, it would make sense to eat better.

"I appreciate you sleeping over these past few days."

"Of course." She took another bite of the omelet. *Not bad.*

"How are you and Evan doing?"

"Better. We've been on a few dates and, of course, I see him for Bible studies."

"I just love that you young people are studying the Word. Have you finally come to the place where you feel you understand God?"

Jo paused. *Had she?* "I don't know if I would say I understand Him. There's so much that goes on in the world that, to say yes I understand Him, kind of simplifies it all. But, I do understand He loves me and wants the best for me.

The rest will come when it's supposed to."

"Very true. Have you finished Evan's house?"

"Yep. Furniture arrives tomorrow and then I'll do the reveal. Kind of cheesy I know, but I'm so excited to show him how it all turned out. He agreed to wait another day."

"When are you two going to get serious and tie the knot? Or did you just take my recipes to fool an old woman?"

Laughter burst out of her. "Nana, you aren't that old and certainly nobody's fool. I would never try to trick you. For right now, we're dating and enjoying each other's company."

"Well, don't drag it out forever. Time is short. Trust me. I know."

౿

Evan waited as Jo unlocked his home. He couldn't wait to see how it looked finished and furnished. "JoJo, it's cold."

"Hold your horses." She twisted the knob and stopped as it open. "Close your eyes so that I can open it all the way."

He chuckled. "Fine." He closed them.

"Okay, open."

His jaw dropped as he rolled his way into his new home. He couldn't believe it. She had completely transformed the place. "Wow, JoJo, this is awesome."

"You've seen almost all of this, but you haven't seen your bedroom yet. Let me show you."

He followed her, wondering if one day she would share this home with him. She opened the door. The walls were painted a light gray, matching the gray-and-black bedspread. The black wooden sleigh bed took center stage. He stopped, speechless. To think this was all his.

Jo led them back into the living room. The whole house had been styled to perfection. "I love it."

And I love you. Evan stared at her, wishing he could relay his emotions, but he couldn't. Not until he knew she could handle it if he never walked again. He hadn't told her his good news about the prosthetic or new job. He needed to know she could handle him at his worst. It was the reason he sat in his wheelchair now.

"I'm so glad." She smiled at him.

He took a deep breath and plunged forward. "Does it bother you that I'm in this chair?"

"Of course not." She looked at him like he asked did she want to take a trip to the moon. "The chair doesn't define you, Evan. It's merely an accessory."

He wheeled closer to her. "If I never get out of this chair..." his voice trailed off. He didn't want to finish his question, but he had to know.

She sat down softly in his lap. "If you never walk again, I wouldn't care." She licked her lips nervously. "I love you, Evan Carter. If, God forbid, you lose another leg, I will still love you. I love you, the boy who used to make me laugh. The man who treats me with dignity. The one who sees me behind the overalls and tool-belt-wearing self. That won't change because of your height, weight, or age."

He touched his forehead to hers. "I love you so much, Jo."

"Really?"

"Without a doubt." He ran a finger down her face and grinned at the rosy hue her complexion took on.

Evan looked into her eyes then made his way down to her lips. Slowly, as if asking for permission, he leaned forward, steadily watching her expression for acceptance. When she closed her eyes and kissed, he knew returning home to Freedom Lake had been God designed.

ACKNOWLEDGMENTS

To my husband: thank you for walking this life journey with me. Thank you for giving me time to write and sharing me with the laptop.

To my kids: I love you. Never forget to love everyone and to follow God.

To my critique friends: This book has been through many drafts and reviews. It was the second book I ever wrote, so it has seen many eyes on its journey. Many thanks to Jessica Berg, Peri Bever, Andrea Boyd for your wonderful critiques.

To my early readers: many thanks to Kara Esslebach, Carrie Schmidt, and Melissa Henderson. Thank you so much for offering me feedback on how to make this story better. Your encouragement and willingness to find those nuances I would have missed was a huge help. I appreciate the time you took to read Returning Home and offer me feedback. Sending prayers and blessings your way.

To Kathleen: Thank you Kathleen Zuniga for the suggestion of Guy Pierre's twin girls. I appreciate you!

To my mom: Thank you so much for the help with the research.

ABOUT THE AUTHOR

Toni Shiloh is a wife, mom, and Christian fiction writer. Once she understood the powerful saving grace thanks to the love of Christ, she was moved to honor her Savior. She writes to bring Him glory and to learn more about His goodness.

She spends her days hanging out with her husband and their two boys. She is a member of the American Christian Fiction Writers (ACFW) and president of the Virginia Chapter.

You can find her on her website at http://tonishiloh.weebly.com and signup for her Book News newsletter at http://eepurl.com/cmNFKD.

Made in the USA
Columbia, SC
02 November 2017